B. Hrabal's grave
forest
Main road
from Sadská to Chlumec
Chlumec →
n.Cidlinou 51km

BOHUMIL HRABAL
RAMBLING ON: AN APPRENTICE'S GUIDE
TO THE GIFT OF THE GAB

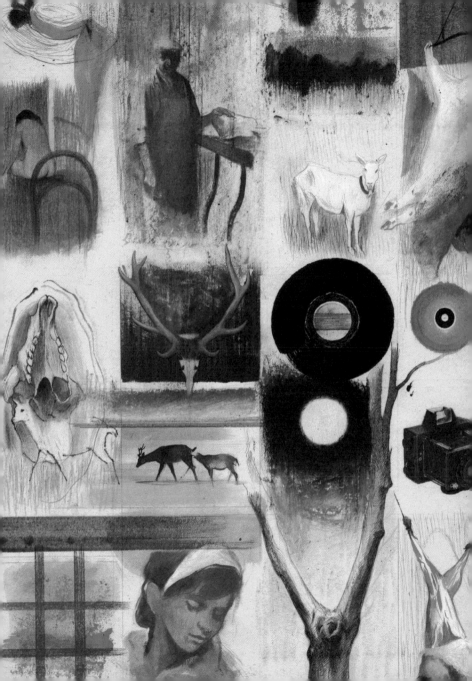

Bohumil Hrabal

Rambling on:
an Apprentice's Guide
to the Gift of the Gab
Short stories

Charles University Prague
Karolinum Press 2014

I dedicate this translation first and foremost to the memory of my good friend and fellow-translator of B. Hrabal James Naughton, who sadly died just weeks before this volume saw the light of day, and also to the memory another of our colleagues, Michael Henry Heim.

ds

ISBN 978-80-246-2316-0

*In a lightweight play one may find
some most serious truth.*
Gottfried Wilhelm Leibniz,
philosopher of the Late Baroque

Essential to playing is freedom.
Immanuel Kant,
philosopher of the Enlightenment

*When you're pissed, Kilimanjaro
might even be in Kersko.*
Josef Procházka,
roadmender and my friend

1 THE ST BERNARD INN

WHENEVER I PASS Keeper's Lodge, a restaurant in the forest, I always see, lying there on the apron, the patio outside the entrance, where in summertime patrons sit at red tables and on red chairs, a huge, wise St Bernard dog, and the patrons either stepping over it, or, if they've ever been bitten by a dog, preferring to look away and walk round it, their peace of mind restored only after they've sat down inside the restaurant, but if the St Bernard were to be lying inside the restaurant, these timorous patrons would rather sit outside on the red chairs, even on a cold day. No St Bernard ever did lie here, and probably never will, but my St Bernard will lie there for as long as I live, and so the St Bernard and I, outside the Keeper's Lodge restaurant in the forest, we two are coupled wheelsets... It was way back when my brother got married and had a haulage business, driving his truck and taking things wherever anyone needed, but the time came when a private individual wasn't allowed to drive on his own account any more, and so my brother, his private company having been shut down, was out of a job. And because he was jealous, so madly jealous that his wife wasn't allowed to have a job lest anyone else look at her, he suddenly got this weird idea that my sister-in-law's gorgeous figure couldn't be exploited anywhere better than in catering. And if catering, then it had to be the Keeper's Lodge forest restaurant. And if the Keeper's Lodge, then the place should be made into a real pub for lorry-drivers and foresters, locals and summer visitors. About that time, the manager's job at the Keeper's Lodge fell vacant and my brother did his utmost to make the restaurant his. And in the evening, he and Marta would sit for hours, and later on even lie in bed, weaving an image of an actual Keeper's Lodge, a fantasy restaurant whose décor they carried on planning even in their dreams or when half-asleep. When my cousin Heinrich Kocian heard about it, he's the one who'd risen highest in our family because he thought he was the illegitimate scion of Count Lánský von der Rose, wore a huntsman's buckskin jacket and a Tyrolean hat with a chamois brush and green ribbon, he turned up at once, drew a plan of the Keeper's Lodge restaurant and made a start on the décor with some rustic tables of lime wood, tables that he would scrub with sand once a week and with glass-paper once a year, around the tables he drew what the heavy rustic chairs would be like, and on the walls, which were decked with the antlers of roebuck and sika deer shot long before by Prince Hohenlohe, the feudal lord of the line that had owned these forests for several centuries, he added a couple of wild boar trophies. And cousin Heinrich decided there and then that specialities of Czech cuisine would be served, classy dishes that would bring the punters in because out on the main road there'd be signboards with the legend: Three hundred metres from the junction, at the Keeper's Lodge, you can enjoy a mushroom and potato soup fit for a king, Oumyslovice goulash or pot-roast beef with stout gravy. My brother and sister-in-law were over the moon and the Keeper's Lodge was like a padlock hanging from the sky on a golden chain. But even that was not enough for cousin Heinrich. He insisted that any decent restaurant should have a corner in the kitchen set aside specially for regulars and any other patrons worthy of the distinction. So he consented to purchase six baroque or rococo chairs and an art nouveau table, which would always have a clean cloth, and that was where the regulars and any guests of honour would sit. This rococo corner so excited my brother and sister-in-law that thereafter they wore blissful smiles and they would drive out every day to check on the painters' progress in the kitchen and dining area of the Keeper's Lodge, the painting jobs seeming to them to be taking an unconscionably long time and they wanted the painting completed overnight, as fast as their own dream of the Keeper's Lodge had been. And when they saw all the outdoor seats lined up in the garden of the Keeper's Lodge under the band-stand, nothing could stop them having all those night-time visions and dreams of the garden restaurant by night, all the tables painted red, all the red chairs in place round the tables on the lawn, with wires strung between the oak trees and Chinese lanterns hanging from them, and a quartet playing discreetly and people dancing on the dance-floor, my brother pulling pints and the trainee waiter hired for Sundays serving the drinks in full French evening dress, and my sister-in-law would be making the Oumyslovice goulash and the pot-roast beef with stout gravy, and the patrons would be enjoying not just tripe soup but also the regal mushroom and potato soup. One day, cousin Heinrich Kocian turned up, joyfully waving the bill for the six chairs which he'd bought for a song, and when he and my brother went to have a look how the painting of the walls and ceilings of the Keeper's Lodge was progressing and when my brother confided that he'd further enhanced the woodland restaurant with a garden and dance floor, our cousin said that in this corner here there'd also be a barbecue smoker, where spiral salamis and sausages would be heated up and uncurl over hot coals and he himself would take charge of it at the weekends, despite being the illegitimate son of Count Lánský von der Rose. And my brother and sister-in-law were happy, spending the happiest years of their marriage forever moving chairs around and manically seeking ways to make the restaurant even more beautiful and agreeable. And so it came to pass that when I heard about it and when I saw the Keeper's Lodge forest restaurant for myself, I said, or rather casually let drop, that what the kind of beautiful restaurant that my brother and his wife wanted to create out of this lonely building in the forest needed was a nice, big, well-behaved dog, a St Bernard, lying outside the entrance. And at that moment nobody spoke because cousin Heinrich was coming to the end of his story of how the Prince von Thurn und Taxis had taken him in his carriage, which had been waiting to collect him off the evening express, to his palace at Loučeň, and when the coachman jumped down from his box to open the door, the prince exclaimed: 'Johan, you're barefoot! You've drunk your boots away!' And the coachman explained tearfully that he'd had to wait so long for the later express that while he had indeed drunk away his boots at the pub by the station, he had salvaged the Prince's reputation by blackening his feet with boot polish... and as our cousin finished this story about his friend, the Prince von Thurn und Taxis, and having made it plain that when such important personages as the Prince von Thurn und Taxis are spoken of a respectful silence is called for, he asked, though he'd heard full well, what I'd said. And I repeated that such a beautiful restaurant in the woods should have a well-behaved St Bernard lying outside the door. And my brother watched our cousin, as did my sister-in-law, almost fearful, but quite soon our cousin's face broadened into the smile he would smile as he envisioned the future, looking far ahead, and at the end of this vision lay St Bernard's very own St Bernard with its kindly furrowed brow, which thus became the final full-stop, indeed keystone of the entire conception of what the Keeper's Lodge restaurant in the woods was going to be like. At the admin headquarters of the Co-op, which the restaurant in the woods nominally belonged to, they had nothing against the young couple's interest in the place, saying they were even pleased because managers as well-versed in book-keeping as Marta were far to seek. And so our cousin fetched the six rococo chairs, my brother cleared a corner in their existing flat, cupboards pushed together, settee out into the corridor, and there and then, under the watchful gaze of cousin Heinrich Kocian, they set the chairs out as they were going to be in the Keeper's Lodge forest restaurant. And they put a cloth on the table and my brother opened a bottle of wine, and the glasses clinked in toasts to such a fine beginning, since there was no putting it off. And as Heinrich sat there in his Tyrolean hat,

one leg across the knee of the other, sprawled out, he started on about the time when, following Prince Hohenlohe, Baron Hiross became the owner of the forest range within which the Keeper's Lodge lay, and how one day he'd been staying with him and had personally bagged a moufflon at the upper end of Kersko, at a spot called Deer's Ears. "But that gamekeeper Klohna!" cousin Heinrich started to shout, "the tricks he played on the baron! I'm sure you know that aristocrats, when their gun dog gets too old, they just do away with it! And so the baron gave the word for his setter to be disposed of and Klohna duly shot it. But the dog was a handsome beast and the gamekeeper fancied it and duly skinned it. And after he'd cut off its head and buried it along with the skin, the landlord of the restaurant on the Eichelburg estate, close to where there's that sawmill, near where the Kersko range ends, where there used to be that spa where Mozart once took a bathe, the landlord asks, 'What's that hanging there?' And the gamekeeper said it was a moufflon. So having given him two thousand for it – it was early on during the Protectorate – the landlord marinated the moufflon and because I was visiting Baron Hiross along with a number of aristocrats, he, the Baron, booked a sumptuous dinner at that restaurant on his estate, which specialised in game dishes, and sumptuous it was; for starters: salpicón, turtle soup, and I've never ever tasted such fantastic sirloin as on that occasion," cousin Heinrich said, sipping his wine and smoothing the tablecloth... and my brother and sister-in-law envisaged this corner in the Keeper's Lodge and looked forward to having cousin Heinrich there to hold forth and divert the regulars and the better class of patrons... "...but when the Baron came to pay, and he paid sixty thousand, because afterwards we drank only champagne and cognac, we all asked what kind of sirloin it had been, and the landlord said it was moufflon. And then they conveyed us to our various homes near-dead, because in aristocratic circles it is the done thing to render oneself unconscious with the aid of champagne and cognac, and Baron Hiross at once leapt into his britschka and careered off back to his gamekeeper's cottage, where he started bellowing at the gamekeeper, the latter in his long johns, having already gone to bed: 'Klohna, you've got poachers, d'you know what we've just feasted on? Moufflon! I'll see you sacked!' Baron Hiross ranted... and so Klohna had to get down on his knees, swearing that he was a faithful guardian of the forest, and that what they'd just feasted on wasn't moufflon, but his lately shot gun dog... And Baron Hiross, just as the Prince von Thurn and Taxis had forgiven his coachman after the coachman had drunk away his working boots, the baron said: 'So I've actually gorged myself on my own dog masquerading as moufflon and paid for it twice over...'" Then my cousin turned to the newspaper and my brother and sister-in-law buffed the arms of the chairs with polish to bring them up to such a fine shine that their image of the corner for regulars in the Keeper's Lodge became one with reality. And suddenly cousin Heinrich whooped: "Right, mes enfants, here it is: *For sale: a St Bernard dog, to a good home only. Price negotiable. Gel.*" He stood up, pulled on his buckskin gloves with a small shot-hole in the top side and said: "I'm off to get that St Bernard. If the corner with its baroque chairs is ready and waiting, let's have the St Bernard ready and waiting as well." Next day, my brother and sister-in-law not having slept that night, cousin Heinrich Kocian arrived, and that he was a very small cousin we knew – whenever he was about to eat a frankfurter, it would hang down to his knees before he'd taken the first bite – and so from a distance it looked as if he was leading a small cow. When he reached the house, my brother thought he was leading a big calf, a young bullock. But it was the St Bernard. "Six hundred crowns he cost, the owner's a writer!" he shouted excitedly, "and he's called Nels! The author's name's Gel!" Nels was a handsome beast with a washing-line round his neck, secured with the writer's dressing-gown cord, and the dog instantly made himself at home, lying down on the cement floor to cool off, and the way he lay there was exactly as if he were practising for how he was going to lie outside the entrance to the Keeper's Lodge restaurant. And cousin Heinrich sat down on a rococo chair, legs crossed, in his Tyrolean hat, and with one sleeve rolled slightly back he reported how the writer had made him welcome and explained that the main reason he was selling the dog was because he loved him, but Nels loved his young wife much more, so whenever he laid a hand on her, the dog would bowl him over and growl into his face, so he had grown into a disturber of conjugal bliss, and that was why he was selling him. And he had immediately handed over the dog's pedigree and here it all was: Nels was famous, a descendant of the short-haired St Bernards of the St Gothard Pass and his father was thrice best of breed at the Swiss national dog show, and his mother had come from the St Gothard hospice itself... And cousin Heinrich added the dressing-gown cord to the bill, because Nels had grown up indoors and so in lieu of a lead Mr Gel the writer had let him have the dressing-gown cord for the journey. And then Heinrich left and Nels remained in the house. And so the day came when my brother and sister-in-law went to the Co-op offices to pick up their deed of appointment to the Keeper's Lodge inn in the forest range of Kersko. But the manager told them that, regrettably, the licensee who had been at the inn before had had second thoughts and decided to stay on, but

that there was a pub that had come vacant at Chleby, so that was the deed they were getting. The beautiful lantern-lit garden, the bright lights of the restaurant with its limewood tables and heavy rustic chairs, its corner for regulars with its baroque chairs, all that was extinguished, as if some malevolent magician had hauled it away somewhere on a circus trailer, including the St Bernard, who, along with the chairs, remained the only living evidence that it hadn't been a daydream, but a snippet of reality, one sector of a beautiful circle, one degree on the basis of which, with a bit of imagination, a circle might have been described. Nels, the St Bernard, was a crumb of the Host in which was the whole Christ. The inn at Chleby was a sorry place where living on the premises was impossible, so my brother and sister-in-law had to commute to it, the St Bernard would lie at my mother's feet and look fondly up into her eyes, and she was often caught not just talking to him, but lying on the carpet with the dog for a pillow. At Chleby, business was good, but for all that just business, the beer – and the goulash – were so good that workers coming home from their workplaces in town no longer went straight home, but sat around in the inn by the cemetery, drinking and eating until their money ran out, but my brother and sister-in-law were delighted that they'd turned the inn into a real pub, to the extent that finally the wives of the drinkers of its Kolín beer joined forces and complained to the local authority that their menfolk were drinking all their money away and, even worse, had stopped coming home and taken up residence in the inn. So my brother had to get back behind the wheel and become a cab-driver, but he never stopped dreaming, what if the manager of the Keeper's Lodge restaurant in the Kersko forest range had a sudden heart attack, or if he got slightly run over by a car? But the manager enjoyed rude good health and although he would have gladly left, the knowledge that my brother was so keen on the restaurant, and on no other, gave him added strength and stamina. Cousin Heinrich Kocian came back just once. That was the time when my brother entered Nels in the national dog show in Prague, at the Velká Chuchle race-course. And Heinrich insisted that *he* would parade Nels. And so that day, in his Tyrolean hat and buckskin gloves, and his leather hunting jacket, he stood there holding Nels tight on a leather lead twisted round his wrist, because the writer, Mr Gel, had written ex post that Nels was not only extremely strong, but also vicious. However, the children had so humanised him that they would lead him at the muzzle, like a horse, put a bathing costume across his back and take him swimming, but he insisted on dragging them out of the water by their trunks, persisting in the belief that the children were drowning and he had to save them.

He was only vicious to tramps and postmen, and one time he dragged a postman delivering telegrams, along with his mailbag, into his kennel, where he munched up all the registered letters and three telegrams, though he left the postman unharmed except for tearing his uniform and covering him in saliva, it being his breed's fate to slaver a lot, and whenever he shook his head, he spattered everyone and everything around with great gobbets of spit. In short he was a purveyor of showers. When our cousin saw that he and Nels were being filmed, he was on cloud nine. And he started spinning yarns to my brother, because such a glorious environment called for it, with so many dogs and so many people about, so many foreigners who'd brought their dogs along to compete for some award, like Nels himself, some certificate in whatever category their dog was entered in. Once again, Heinrich Kocian was loud on the subject of the Prince von Thurn and Taxis, his friend, and his friend the Baron Hiross, and because the turn of the St Bernards was a long time coming, he went on with particular zest about how his friend, Prince Kinský, loved riding around in his carriage drawn by four black horses, who had to have white socks, and how one broker and horse-trader had supplied his friend Kinský with a pair of black horses with white socks and the prince had hitched them up right away and they'd careered off together from Chlumec to

Bydžov over flooded meadows, so the white socks got left behind in the flood water. And Count Kinský had told him, Heinrich, that he'd had the trader come over so he could give him a present, and he, damn fool that he was, came, and the Count's grooms grabbed him and shoved him up to his chest in a barrel filled with manure, "…and then, my friend," Count Kinský had said, "I took my sword and swung it at the horse-trader's neck and he ducked down into the manure, so I did it several times more and finally told the grooms to tip the manure out onto the compost heap along with the trader…" and the band was playing at the Chuchle race-course and dogs were barking and finally it was the turn of the St Bernards, and suddenly – Nels puckered his brow, the way he would so as to peer after objects a great distance away, as was ever the wont of his forebears, sitting up in the snow-covered mountains and peering after anything that might stir amid those august heights, and there at the end of the race-course was Mr Gel, the author, alighting from a bus with his young wife, and Nels spotted her and peered towards her and the young woman called out, from a half a mile away: "Nels!" And Nels saw that it was his mistress who he had been so fond of and he broke into a run, haring off to get to her as fast as he could, but my cousin Heinrich had the leather lead wrapped so firmly round his wrist that he had to run too, initially, but then Nels pulled out all the stops and my cousin went flying through the air like a banner being pulled behind the dog, who was pelting along and getting his rear legs tangled in his ears, and Nels ran past the twelve tables where the judges were sitting in the sun, a hundred or more sworn experts on dog breeds and pedigrees, and experts on all a dog's pluses and minuses... and as cousin Heinrich flew over the tables, hauled along by the wrist of one hand, he just had time to raise his Tyrolean hat with his free hand and salute the dog show committee, though they were horrified at this strange apparition, and as cousin Heinrich shot through the air in the wake of Nels the St Bernard past the chairman of all the chairmen the latter gave vent to his disgust: "Outrageous! Not even lunchtime and some competitors are already drunk..." Nels meanwhile had reached his mistress, lain down on his back and presented her his underbelly so that she could kill him, the weakest spot on his body... Cousin Heinrich doffed his Tyrolean hat and introduced himself: "Heinrich Kocian, illegitimate son of Count Lánský von der Rose...," and he set about flicking off the grass and dust from his coat, then, grabbing himself by the elbow, he found that a hole had been worn right through the leather to his very skin. The young woman knelt down and lay her head on the head of the St Bernard and the two friends, the woman and the St Bernard, merged in a mystical union, and the writer, Mr Gel, said: "Nels must weigh at least ninety kilos now and the strength of him, eh? He must have dragged you through the air a good hundred metres...," and cousin Heinrich said: "What do you mean dragged? He was only obeying my command; once I did the same thing before the company at my friend the Prince von Thurn and Taxis' place, only that time it was a Great Dane..." And Nels purred with delight and, as he lay there on his back, he cast sheep's eyes up at his mistress and signalled to her with his paw that he wanted her to put her arms round him again, and again... But all that, including Nels, is now lost in the sands of time, though whenever I pass by the Keeper's Lodge, that restaurant in the Kersko woods, I see a huge St Bernard lying on the little patio, the apron, lying there and watching and greeting the patrons and puckering his brow, and dreaming of quiet music playing in the abandoned and jumbled restaurant garden, of cloth-covered tables scattered about the lawn with the customers sitting at them on red chairs, chatting quietly and sipping beer and ordering pot-roast beef with stout gravy and Oumyslovice goulash...

2 A MOONLIT NIGHT

ALL OVER THE WORLD, wherever there's a chapel or a church there's a parish priest, everywhere in the world the parish priest has a university degree, and wherever in the world the rectory is home to a man with a university degree, he will have a command of Latin and his native tongue, and in his native tongue he will seek to have some influence on the citizenry entrusted to him and in Latin he will report to Rome any news that reaches him from his parishioners, and so every year, gathered together in Rome from all over the world, summary reports state how many murders there have been throughout the Christian world, how many adulteries, how many burglaries and robberies, how many people have had doubts about the Church's teachings and how many are in a state of apostasy or are lukewarm in their faith, and so I, police commandant in the area entrusted to me, I note that I'm not university educated, that the members of the National Committee aren't either, and that for now I must just do what I do, keeping a close watch on anything criminal going on on my patch, but, more than that, I try

by my own diligence in office to keep myself, the district, the region and even the Interior Ministry informed of what people are thinking, how they live their lives, and what they commit in the way of petty misdemeanours, from which it is only ever but one little step to bigger ones. Most of all, I like performing my duties within the Kersko forest range, a place close to my heart since childhood, a place where I know everyone, where as a boy I played or did battle, as a youth I chased the girls and gave and received many a bop on the nose or punch in the ribs, so I don't feel on duty here, more on a kind of holiday, so pleasant is it to be working in the place where I grew up, which is why it's such a pity that time passes so quickly in the day, and because, come the evening, I still haven't had enough and going to bed, well, that would be a sin, I stroll along the one metalled avenue through the trees of the Kersko woods, having left my Volga parked down a side track, and in the darkness I keep my ears to the ground to check who's about, who's talking to who, sometimes revealing my presence, sometimes just leaning quietly against the wing of my police Volga, and I rejoice in the beauty of outdoors and at the adventures the main road brings at night in the form of cyclists with and without lights, and driving quietly past Keeper's Lodge, I work out from the cars parked outside who's in there, who, as a driver, is drinking black coffee, and who's having a beer or, horror of horrors, spirits. But when the moon rises over New Leas and the smells of the fields drift by on the breeze, that's when I'm truly happy to be on duty and I'm amazed that the State pays me for the privilege, that I have this uniform and that I am in command. Properly I ought to be paying for all these beautiful things out of my own pocket, so much is it like I'm on holiday, and so beautiful is night-time in the Kersko woods. But *I know*, vigilance, I have to be vigilant, because no one knows that crime never sleeps, and suddenly bang!, a shot, and there's a policeman lying in a pool of blood, several hundred of us have fallen, four hundred and thirty-six dead, and there's an end to gazing at the rising, beautiful red or yellow moon, and that is the mission I'm destined to pursue, watching and guarding the achievements of this young state of ours, this Party of ours. And so there are two conjoined centres in my brain, one that watches over and cherishes all that is beautiful in our society, and the other that enables me to enjoy the forest rides and clearings, the tracks that lead from one wood to the next across the fields that I love as if I were a farmer myself, because, even though on duty, I'll get out of my Volga and have this sudden urge to head for the fields, where in the spring I pick up a handful of soil and sniff it, and when the grain crops are ripening I take a stroll past the endless fields on the pretext of running a check and there

I stroke the ripening barley and wheat, sometimes plucking an ear and, like a farmer, rubbing the grains out into the palm of my hand, sniffing at them, smelling them and my nose, like an agronomist's, tells me that this very week the grain has come ripe and it's harvest time. Yet the most beautiful thing is still when you're in the forest and the moon is high, that moon gives me such a thrill, the rising moon, the moon rising? But a figure emerged from the light of the inn to be drenched in the shower of light cast from a street lamp, and it gathered up its bike and mounted it and rode quickly off, riding into the outline of itself as the moon pushed at its back, and I could tell at once that it was Joe, a childhood friend, but nowadays a prodigious consumer of beer and black coffee and rum, sometimes he has a certain charm, one day he got so drunk at lunchtime that he rode his bike onto some private land, he was still a roadmender back then, and my cousin had fallen asleep after lunch, it being so hot, and suddenly, in a daze, she thought she'd caught a whiff of beer and rum and coffee and there was Joe the roadmender, leaning over her and whispering "I nearly kissed you, my beauty", on another occasion, this time even before lunch, he careered onto some private land, into a half-dug trench where some weekend-cottage owners had been putting down a mains electricity cable, and he did a somersault and started shouting his mouth off: "Who gave you permission to dig the road up, this is going to cost you, digging up a public right of way, where's your permit, I'm in charge of the roads round here!" And so, with no lights, Joe rode on, not even needing to peddle with the moon pushing at his back, and then towards New Leas the metalled road goes on and on downhill, not many people know that the road is a hundred and eighty-five metres above sea level and at New Leas it's only a hundred and seventy-seven, so there's a clear downward slope, the Kersko woods really forming a kind of shallow saucer, because the other side of New Leas the track rises again to the main road from Hradišťko to Semice, to an elevation of a hundred and eighty-five metres above sea level, but Joe, he kept swerving to the ditch on the other side of the road and right back again – how come he still has the appetite for it? How come he's still quite with it? And I stepped out of the trees, but Joe was probably half-cut, he called out to me, that was ever his way, always, instead of a bell or a torch, calling out into the darkness: "Out of the way, folks, I'm going too fast to stop!" But I flashed my service torch twice and Joe hopped off his bike and says: "Good evening, me old pal!" And I says: "Where's your light?" and pointing to the Moon he says: "Up there!" I says: "Where is your headlight as required by the Highway Code?" "In me bag," said Joe and by the light of the moon he opened his bag and in it glinted a

carpenter's axe, and he took a nickel-plated torch out and switched it on, then put it back in his bag and says: "But I'm supposed to carry a light when there isn't enough light from elsewhere, and the Moon's shining, hell, a bright shining light, the Moon, damn' beautiful light, don't you think, Harry…" I says: "What's your name, sir, show me your papers…," and again he rifles about and offers his ID card to the light of my torch and I leafs through it and asks: "What is your name?" Joe looks at me, eyes full of reproach: "Don't tell me you don't recognise me, Harry!" I says: "What's your name?" He says, cleverly: "But you've got it right there." And that rattled me, because I could smell he reeked of beer and rum. I says: "Have you been drinking, sir?" And he bows to me and says: "I have, and I do and I will drink just as I've been drinking for as long as I can remember, d'you remember that time when a keg of beer fell off the back of a lorry at this 'ere bend and I 'id it under some branches and that night I shifted it into a cottage I 'ad the keys to? Then for a week the pair of us, we drank it together out of a litre glass and for a week we was pissed from daybreak on? And how my wife wanted to chuck me out, she said she was fed up of it an' it 'ad to stop?" I handed him his ID back and says: "That was then, but now I'm on duty, right? And what's the axe for?" Joe says: "You know I'm a carpenter, I do odd jobs, like." And I says: "And do you have a license and pay tax?" Joe says: "Of course, I do, I pay my taxes…," and he tottered and says: "Don't you reckon that's enough? Can I go now?" And I could tell he was going to fall into the ditch again, so I unscrewed one of his valves and tossed it over a hedge into an irrigation channel and the tyre let out a sigh and I decided: "Look here, Joe, you're not as young as you used to be, you'd be better off on foot…" And Joe stood there speechless, I could see he wanted to say – and inside he was saying – 'you filth, you bloody piece of filth, what a way to treat an old pal, you shitbag, what a way to treat a friend you've known since we were kids, what a way for one worker to treat another!' But he said nothing, just set off, wheeling his bike with the vein on his forehead swelling with rage. And I stood there and watched him go, the Moon lifting so as to push him along by the shoulders. Joe's shadow had shrunk, like when you look down on a cello or double base from above, and I wondered, had I done right by tossing his valve, or not? In the end, I decided I had been right to let his tyre down because, like a father, it was down to me to prevent an accident, so I wasn't even surprised when I heard Joe calling back to me from the spring: "You should be ashamed o' yourself, treatin' a fellow worker like that!" And then I ran after him, took him by the shoulder and said: "And because you were riding without lights, I'm going to fine you fifty crowns, and

let that be an end of it, all right?" And he looked at me, and I could just see him in the same situation as that time, long ago, when I was a warrant officer and riding along on my bike, and as I reached the point where there was a culvert under the road, I thought I heard someone shouting: 'Help! Help!', dully, like from inside a house... so I leapt off my bike and kept running into the woods and then the voice came again as if from the road, so I ran across to the far side of the road and beyond, and then it sounded as if it was on the road, so I kept running hither and thither and reducing the actual distance to the road, and all the time there was this terrible shouting: 'Help! Help! good folks, help...,' by which time I could tell the shouting was coming from the very middle of the road, so I went towards the culvert and there in among the wild raspberries and brambles lay a bicycle, and a pair of legs were poking out of the culvert, and I grabbed the legs and pulled and out came Joe, the roadmender, rumbling drunk. He sat up and rubbed his eyes: "I thought it were night-time! Thanks, pal, you saved my life, I owe you fifty pints an' an invite next time I kill a pig..." – this time I shone my torch and knew that as he handed me the fifty crowns he was thinking of the same thing as me, how for fifty pints I'd saved his life beneath the culvert, but I wanted to take him down a peg, teach him a lesson, that he had to have lights, because rules is rules... And then he took himself off with his bike, meek and barely able to walk, it wasn't just his tyre I'd let down, but his soul, too, and that's how it should be, when I'm on duty I don't know even my own brother, I once fined my son for parking in the wrong place, and though he hasn't spoken to me since, I'm quite happy talking to myself and the Moon, the Moon hanging up there in the sky, I talk to the pine trees when they let out their smell, these are my friends, and I can tell that ditches and streams and ponds are my friends, I don't care for others any more, I don't want to know them. I'm a loner. So I sat down, the Moon sat on my lap like some girl or other, I held out my arms and the moon-light licked my hands like a kitten, or a police dog. By now the lights in the inn were all out, some cyclists rode past me saying things that I didn't like very much, some folk, when they're on their bikes, they're so loud, it's not exactly anti-state jibes, nothing conspiratorial, but they can say such treasonous things that if I were the least bit inclined, I could have them up in court and into jail, but from their general tone and tenor I took it to be the beer talking, and when all's said and done, things come to my hearing like to a confessor, I hear what people are thinking, I hear them having a rant, and when I'm talking to myself, I also have the odd rant, but never out loud... So I got up and strode moon-wards back to the inn, the restaurant in the woods, inside they were all asleep, I took a chair, one of the red folding chairs, stood it by the edge of the road and thought awhile about myself, then with some effort dispelled the image of my wife, who had left me, and of my son, who had left me, and saw myself sitting there, abandoned, on a folding garden seat, powerful, but alone, and if I didn't have the Moon, and if I wasn't so fond of drainage ditches and didn't love pine trees and ripening fields and the sweet-smelling furrows of arable land, I'd actually have no grounds at all for feeling happy, more the reverse, but whenever I started getting a bit morbid, I'd place a hand on the medals I'd been given, the decorations, and that gave me strength, and I would tell myself that people who've received the highest honours, they're not all happy either, their wives and sons might have left them too, but when they look at their medals, they attain that happiness, that recognition that equates to happiness, so I began to smile and I was proud of myself and at peace with myself. And then a car came out of the trees down below, I could tell it was a white Trabant and could see it belonged to none other than Mr Kimla from the chemist's, so I switched my torch on and waved it up and down, and when the car slowed, I shone the torch on my medals so the driver could see it was the commandant himself waiting here for him, and he drove right up to me and stopped. He wound down the window and asked disconsolately: "Should I get out or not?" I said: "You can stay where you are, Mr Kimla, but how many glasses of wine have you had?" Mr Kimla brightened: "Two, two small ones." And I said: "Not more?" He replied anxiously: "Not more…" I paused, letting him suffer, I was tormenting him, all was quiet and the night came streaming through the leaves of the oak trees and moon-white blotches like coconut milk formed on the ground. I said: "And what kind of wine was it, white or red?" And the chemist agonised: "Red, and I had a lot to eat and I was also drinking mineral water." He had spoken and I could see that he'd had rather more to drink, but I could see what a beautiful night it was and how beautiful the Moon was and so, as with Joe, I was indulgent, magnanimous. I crossed one booted leg in front of the other and said: "We might suppose that's not very much, mightn't we?" And the chemist rejoiced: "Very little…" And I pulled myself up to my full height and said: "But it's enough to lose your license for. However! I'm in a good mood and so a fine of five hundred crowns will put matters right. And get out of the car!" And I could see that he couldn't get up out of the seat, not that he'd been drinking, just mortified at the image of a five hundred-crown fine, mortified to the extent that his rheumatism got him and he started staggering and I was wallowing in it – I couldn't stand people who broke down in the face of a fine… And I says: "Lock

the car, and have you got the money on you?" He picked up his bag and said: "No, I've only got a hundred...," which he offered to me, but I says: "And at home, have you got any money in the house?" He said: "Yes..." And I says: "My Volga's parked there in the ride behind those oaks, so we can pop along and get that fine...," and I strode off ahead, and the fact that the chemist followed me wearing only slippers rallied my spirits and my class awareness, and so we got in my car and the chemist squirmed and whimpered, he didn't have much money and would three hundred do, and I let him hope by saying wait till we got to his place... and so we reached his place, well, a cottage like that could only belong to a chemist of substance, all those valuable pictures and beaten copper jugs, and he wandered about explaining that the pieces came all the way from Italy and he went on and on, but I told him to get the money... the fine, and he pulled out the hundreds as if they were thorns jammed deep into his palm..., I picked them up, tore off a receipt and put it on the table... The chemist shoved his wallet in his breast pocket, smiled and said: "Shall I get some glasses?" I said: "No," and tore off another receipt for two hundred crowns, and the chemist blanched and came over queasy and his hands shook as he shelled out two hundred more in fifty-crown notes. I rose, jingled the keys of his Trabant and my mind was made up... "Now you can

walk back to your car, by the time you get there you'll
have sobered up enough from your two glasses of red
wine..." He moaned: "Take me back in your Volga,
Comrade Commandant..." But I was unrelenting, and
held the door handle. "I've told you. It's three kilometres, so walk slowly, treat your lungs to the fresh air
and sober up. And as you pass the St Joseph Spring,
have a sip of the water...," and I left, ran down the steps
and strolled over to my Volga, which shimmered and
shone in a bottle-green colour that was edged in silver
and covered the car in fantastical flashes. On the way,
I was thinking how wonderful it would be when every
national committee all over the world would be chaired
by someone with a university education, when that
chairman would speak both his own language and then
Russian, and he would send reports to the district authority, and the district to the regional authority, and
the region to the Central Committee, and the Central
Committee would send reports to Moscow and there
all the reports from all over the world would be assem-
bled, showing how many thefts and robberies there'd
been all over the world, how many murders and adulteries there'd been and how many crimes against the
state, and there the Comrades would know, just as for
a thousand years the Catholic Church has known, how
to set about reducing crime and elevating mankind, to
which I myself, though with no university degree, have

already been applying myself, like today, in the Kersko forest, when I let Joe Procházka's tyre down and then opted to return a drink-driver's car keys to him, but leaving him to walk three kilometres, sober up and then return home with the car... *Governor of Kersko, Governor of Kersko...* I whispered to myself, but that Soviet-style nickname was invented for me by my enemies and enemies of the state... but there's something to it, I have no degree and yet they call me *Governor*... that's nice, it's quite pleasing, I thought, reaching for my breast, for the orders that covered the beating of my Communist heart... so tomorrow I'll give my friend Joe his fine back and buy him a valve for the tyre I let down today...

3 MR METHIE

IN SECLUDED SPOTS IN THE FOREST, in autumn or wintertime, when the sun doesn't even peep out to show its face, not even as a sample with no commercial value, or to show that it still is, but is no more, when at seven-thirty in the morning it's still dark and at quarter past four it's already getting dark, spleen and melancholy descend and the damp soil is leafless and without hope. I sat at my window in the dark and looked out into the dark, not knowing what to do, whether to jump under the train which can be heard on such evenings from somewhere far away beyond the river, or to hang myself, as foretold for me by the fortune-teller Mařenka, who did me a tarot reading in the ladies toilet of the Kingsway hotel. And as the wick of my lamp lowered its tired eyelids, a motorbike turned off the main road towards my gate, stopped, and the dark figure of a man came in through the gate, and when I put some lights on, in the boxroom and outside in the yard, I saw, in his leathers, Mr Methie, and Mr Methie was radiant and laughing and two eyes blazed out from his thick eyebrows and long side whiskers,

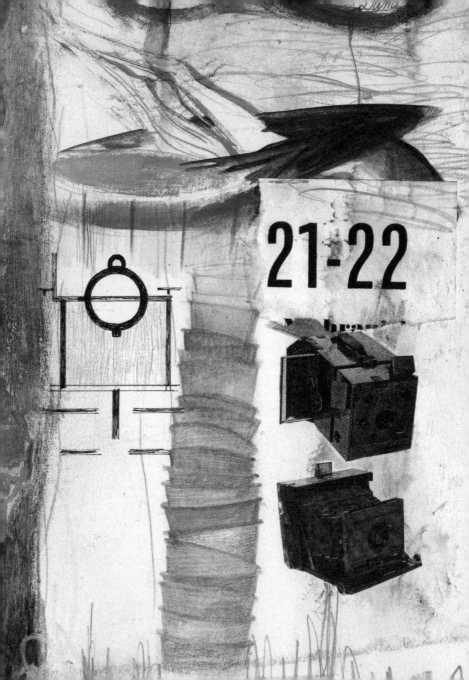

eyes that couldn't restrain their joy and pride in themselves, their huge satisfaction that so contrasted with the landscape, rid of the leaves that were plastered down over every track and footpath, flower-bed and forest clearing, and all the ditches and glades and fences and oak nurseries. And Mr Methie signalled for me to follow him so that some of the happiness, the fascination out there beyond the gate, might rub off on me, and when, in the slanting light of the lantern dangling from the corner of the cottage, I saw the source of his elation, my first thought was that it was a rocking-horse lying upside down in his sidecar. It wasn't a horse though, but a dead, stiff sheep, skinned, and with its lungs and liver poking out of a slit in its belly, like a handkerchief in a dandy's top pocket. "What's that?" I asked, recoiling. "Magnificent, eh?" Mr Methie jubilated, "a real bargain, only cost me a small electric motor and fifty crowns." He was over the moon. "But what," says I, "what am I supposed to do with it?" "Obvious," says Mr Methie, "you're going to help me butcher it, they tell me your spicey offal hash is the best, then we'll marinate the meat and have escalopes and leg of mutton, and we can leave the rest in the marinade and turn it into sausages...," Mr Methie enthused, and despite it being winter and his face being as purple as the sheep's liver, this noble objective shone in triumph from his features and precluded any sense of cold, because the very image gave warmth, he having bought it for such a good price. "Right, Mr Methie," I said, "let me get my fur coat and I'll come with you, have you got a wooden washtub or a large bucket or vat at home?" So many options, but Mr Methie shook his head, he possessed none of the above. "So," I said, "I've got a tub, we can take that and it'll have to do, all right?" And Mr Methie grinned, baring all his teeth into the bargain, and the teeth enhanced the bargain-fired joy that flooded over him, joy in which he was literally basking, nay, wallowing. "Look," he said after a moment, "Listen, don't call me Mr Methie, call me Mike instead, would you?" I said: "But here in the forest everybody calls you Mr Methie," I gibbered and ran back to the kitchen to get my fur coat and pick up a torch. When I came back into the cold of evening, Mr Methie said: "But that's only a nickname, Methie, short for Methodius where I come from, so do call me Mike." I said: "So Mr Mike, you've never been to my place before?" And Mr Methie said he hadn't. And I set off through the pine trees, the lamp on the front of the house, now we were behind the house, it cast a sharp shadow outlining the edges of the cottage skywards and heightening the depth of the shadows through which we were walking towards the stream to fetch the tub, and as we walked I shone my torch on the ancient pines, which exuded the turquoise scent of their needles. "Mr Methie," I said, "have you

got any thyme? Allspice and pepper and bay leaves?"
"No, I haven't," said Mr Methie, gazing thoughtfully
upwards at the slender tree trunks, over ten metres tall,
and their rhythmically outcast branches in the canopy.
"Hell!" he vented his appreciation, "Great timber!
Brilliant for planks and boards, nice healthy, mature
wood, why don't you cut them down?" I said: "You
should know, Mr Mike, that each of these pines has its
own name, this one's Elegant Antonia, this one, as a
tribute to her sister from the Chobot range, is Jaunty
Josephine, this is Comely Caroline, the most beautiful
one of all, see how exactly her crown is branched. This
one's fit for a window in Chartres cathedral, which is
why she's called Our Lady, Notre Dame, and this one,
from her physiognomy, see? – she's St Cecilia with both
breasts knocked off... the thing is, Mr Methie, when
I come out here to get away from Prague, it's a habit I
got from the lady teachers I bought the land from, they
also had names for the pine trees, and whenever they
came out here they would first bow to the trees, a deep
Slav bow from the waist, passing from one pine to the
next, and as they left, the same again...," I said, and we
came out onto the grass that sloped down to the brook,
which you couldn't see, but it was babbling away as if
it had just cleaned its teeth and was gargling in different
keys and agglomerations of sounds according to the
inclination of its throat. "Hell," said Mr Methie in

amazement, "and what's this here?" He took my torch and shone it on a tall, cloven-trunked willow… "Now that's something," he gushed and carefully shone the torch on the entire tree, already completely coated in new yellow bark over all its twigs and branches. "Mařenka told me my fortune…," I said. And Mr Methie pointed the torch and made the shadows of all the branches dance, "What fortune might that have been?" Again he looked about him with the torch and then, having gone down close to the brook and taken a long look at the crystal clear water rolling the tiny pebbles and bits of flint over and over and clattering into the green waterweed and grasses hidden in the water, he gave his considered opinion: "Hell, you're going to find it hard to die…," and I understood that Mr Methie had said something really nice on my account and I understood that if you have a beautiful girlfriend or a beautiful pine forest and an even more beautiful stream with living water, you, or anyone, would be loath to die, and all for that very beauty. "Right," said Mr Methie, "here's the tub, shall we take it?" And we tried to yank the tub out of the earth, but the wood of the base was still frozen solid. Finally we put everything we'd got into it, our legs giving at the knees, and we yanked the tub out, complete with soil and dead leaves. We carried it to the sidecar and I asked: "Do you have a set of butcher's knives?" Mr Methie said he didn't. "So I'll get my own knives and cutters, come from old army bayonets and combat knives, they do." Then I turned the lights out and the motorbike started up, I sat at the head of the dead sheep and held on to the tub, the edge of which, with all its soil and frozen leaves, dug into the dead sheep, and I held the tub in such a way as to keep its hoops from touching the liver and lights. Mr Methie drove, and to judge by the motorbike's sound it was a Jawa 250 Perak, he left the main drag down a side avenue, which was unsurfaced, skirting round puddles of ground water, because it's low-lying here, the lowest spot in Bohemia, the lowest spot in the area, which is why water gathers here and at just one spade's depth there's a gush of mineral water, so every cottage and every building is standing on water, which seeps through walls and piling like when the wick drags the paraffin up in an oil lamp. "Do you know," said Mr Methie, slowing down and putting one hand on his waist, "do you know what my tree is?" I said: "Pine." "Noooo," Mr Methie lowed. "Sallow or willow then," I hazarded. "Nooo," he said, adding quickly with a sense of satisfaction, "Aspen, because it's flowering right now, now at the start of January, because it's the first, and rather a nice harbinger of Spring. And he turned the handlebars sideways, put the foot-brake on and jumped off, went round into the light of the headlamp, took a key from his pocket, kissed it, then unlocked the gate, then he bent down, lifted the catch and proudly swung the gate open. Jumping back on the bike, he said proudly: "Made the gate myself, took me only a hundred and sixty-five standard working hours. Good, eh?" He turned to me and his white teeth and smile shone in the dark like the numbers on a phosphoresecnt alarm clock that has just started to jangle. I said: "Aspen, aspen, but that's the tree Judas hanged himself on, after he'd betrayed Jesus, and so did Durynk, having murdered the prince's page, thinking to please... But listen, Mr Methie, do you like mutton?" And Mr Methie spat and said: "Can't stand the sight of it..." I said: "So why on earth did you buy it, barter for it?" And Mr Methie jumped off the bike, switched on the lights that had gone out and said with such rapture that his voice faltered: "You have to understand. Not buy a thing when it's a real bargain? That's me, buying beautiful things cheap, maybe flawed, but not to buy a thing, when it's so cheap..." And he went and pressed the switch set into the wall of the house, which connected, downwards, to his workshop, which connected, downwards, to the outhouse, which connected, downwards, to the woodshed, the roof of which ended in the damp earth and which connected, downwards and last in line, to a lean-to, which had some pipes poking ominously out of it like the barrels of a katyusha rocket launcher or an array of little mountain artillery pieces. And over all this was

the fascination

the symphonic hum of the pinewood, which couldn't grow tall because of the ground water, all their lives the trees had stood up to their ankles in the acidic solution, which trickled slowly down to this point from all the more elevated black soils and pools and rust-coloured waters of mineral springs. And that whole stretch about the house, which is hidden in summer beneath a merciful growth of rampant raspberry bushes and baby aspens and birches, the whole stretch, which bore no trace of any cottage, was now illuminated like a circus at night, like a merry-go-round with all the lights on, or a freak show half an hour before the evening performance. On an open space stood an awesome machine, a two-ton monstrosity, something like a lathe. And Mr Methie watched my amazement: "Quite something, eh? All it's missing is the flywheel and engine, but not buy it when it was going for a song...?" and he took out a notebook and looked in it and raised his head jingling with joy: "If I put in a hundred and thirty standard working hours on this machine, I'll be able to cut planks, but not just planks, whole rafters! And the outlay will come back not once, but ten times over..." And I hauled the tub down and began to regret ever getting involved in this adventure with a sheep, though remembering that otherwise I'd have been sitting indoors moping over time that had stood still, I commanded: "Mr Mike, get me a scrubbing brush!" And

Mr Methie went into the house and triumphantly brought out to the pump a plastic wash-tub containing not ten, but fifty scrubbing brushes, I picked one and started scrubbing away at the tub in the stream of acidic water and saw the bristles of the scrubbing brush crumbling away, but when I took up another brush, Mr Methie jubilated: "Not buy 'em? One brush cost fifty hellers... Have you any idea what a bargain that was?" I said: "That's all very well, but fetch a table out here, so we can get on with butchering the carcass, the sheep!" And Mr Methie went into the house, I carried on scrubbing by the light of some lamps and spotlights that shone up into the black of the pine trees, I scrubbed away and was already onto my fourth brush... And Mr Methie dragged a table outside, stood it right up against the wall, which was bare brick, not a hint of plaster, and that whole summer seat was starting to look like the ghastly, crummy yard of some poor plumber or mechanic who, dismayed at all that he saw about him, had gone and hanged himself. Then we took hold of the sheep, lay it on the table, I got a knife and, revolted, removed the dry leaves and commanded: "Mr Mike, bring me an axe, will you?" And Mr Methie went to look for an axe and his voice remained jubilant and kept calculating numbers of standard working hours, which he multiplied up then exulted at the gleefully double-underlined total of standard working hours represented by some joyous objective unknown to me as the highlight of the strivings that gave meaning to his life, probably keeping him awake at night, and I worried at the surprises that the house, the workshops and sheds might yet yield up... And from the little shed Mr Methie rejoiced: "Haha! They think they can advise me what to do, when I'm a professional planner! Me! Advise me!" He laughed until he started to choke and he waved his arm around and drove away all that outrageous advice as he handed me an axe. "I've got thirty axes in all, but not buy them when they cost three crowns apiece? And you reckon they've been overfired? Well I'll just have to go easy with them... but what a bargain, eh?" And I sliced open the belly and like taking the innards out of a pendulum clock I removed the wonderful fleshy workings of the sheep's entrails and laid the pluck out on the table, the throat frill glittered like rings of chalcedony, the liver lay limp in the magnificent colour of a cardinal's hat and in the fluorescent lighting the lungs had the delicate pink of the fluffy clouds and sky after sundown that foretell rain, the lightly frozen caul fat formed beautiful white clouds floating across the sky of the table, clouds against a winter sky, clouds full of sleet and snow, and the flare fat like molehills on a meadow, like a human brain full of folds and incisions... "We'll make a spicy goulash with it tomorrow and add the tongue...," I said, and I cut off the head with its blue eyes and jelly oozing out of the nostrils, jelly as beautiful as royal jelly... and I split the head open, pulled out and cut off the tongue, dispelling the ghastly thought of how they'd cut out Jesenius' living tongue in the market place, a thought that went away, yet didn't, hanging on disguised in a nebulous haze... And so as to be rid of the haze too, lock, stock and barrel, I said as an incantation: "Fetch me a little bucket to put the offal in, Mr Mike, we can make a nice paprika goulash and use the brains for thickening!" and I tapped one half, then the other and out fell its thoughts, its last thoughts, its last image of a man with a knife, the man who'd cut the sheep's throat and swapped it for a little electric motor and fifty crowns, although the sheep had wanted to live, most surely she had wanted to live... And Mr Methie brought – it's a wonder he didn't topple over – a whole armful of nested pots, set them down, all in a ring, the pots, and there were twenty or more of them. "Quite something, eh? Not buy 'em? Three crowns apiece, when a pot like these can cost thirty! Who cares if the bottom's a bit chipped! What a bargain, eh? And they think they can advise me, when I'm a professional planner!" I gently tossed the entrails into a pot with a slightly chipped bottom and then Mr Methie held the sheep by its legs and I cut my way through to the hip joints, dislocated them, broke the hams off like a door from its hinges, then carefully cut the shoulders away, then probed about with the knife to find the last cervical vertebra and with one stroke of the chopper the neck fell away. "That's the greatest delicacy of all," I said, shaking the blood-stained scruff, but Mr Methie just made a face like the devil. Then I extricated and broke out the ribs and placed the superb fillet and saddle next to each other on the table. "There we are," I said, "now I'll just remove the fat – this sheep was awfully plump – you can render it down, or will you hang it up in chunks for the blue tits?" "For the tits," said Mr Methie and I listened to the lovely sound made by fat as it's pulled away using just a finger, a dry sound like when you walk through an oak grove, or oak wood, covered in freshly fallen snow, when your footsteps give a dry squeak and your boots make contact with the snow-covered oak leaves. "Take a break," Mr Methie said, "we can finish it off later," and once more he wore that smile of certainty, complacency, about all the things he knew and of which he could never have his full fill, about some grand beauty, some state of dangerous beauty that he wanted to share with me... And he opened the door and my hands glistened with fat, I held my fingers apart, and Mr Methie led me from one heap of things to the next, like a guide in a haunted castle and told me all about everything, his voice jangling with a fervour that had me thinking that Mr Methie had to be a paragon not only to himself, but to the entire world, because Mr Methie had never met such a wonderful, exemplary individual as himself, the professional planner. "So here we've got thirty bicycles, never mind the missing handlebars or brakes, but not buy 'em when they cost me a hundred and eighty crowns apiece?... And look at these, hanging here, and I'll let you have one in a minute, thirty-six waistcoats with little bees all over them, out of fashion now, but they'll come back in... they've got no buttons, or button-holes, because the tailor who was making them got terribly drunk, but not buy 'em when all each one cost me was six crowns fifty?... or here? What's in these boxes, these cases? It's theodolites... three of them, they might be old, but not buy 'em when one cost eighty crowns?... but if you were to set out to buy one, they cost eight hundred and more, not everyone's prepared to let me have things cheap, you know, but I can talk them round! One lens might be missing, but I've got a whole box of lenses right here, cost me a hundred and twenty crowns the lot, lenses for every purpose, I've got a lifetime's supply here... but now let me show you the shed, my main storehouse," said Mr Methie, as I hinted by pointing that it might be a good thing if we finished off that bargain-basement sheep... and he opened up the shed and switched on no less than six bulbs, and inside there were things hanging from the ceiling like in a salami shop, boots, tall padded work boots, and Mr Methie walked round, patting their shins and exulting: "With these I surpassed even myself, one boot cost me five crowns, I talked them round, I drowned out their protestations by the imperative torrent of my will until the manager of the seconds shop himself gave in..." "But I can't help noticing," I said, "that all your boots are for the left foot..." "Well obviously," Mr Methie threw up his hands, "they have to be left-footed, otherwise you couldn't get them so cheap, right? But look!" And to make his point he took his shoes off and pulled two left boots on, those stout boots, and started walking about in them as if he were sort of limping, or as if he'd got badly adjusted headlights, but he made a good fist of walking in them and revelled: "They're really nice and warm, like you're standing in warm water! That's because they're felted, see, no good for cross-country running, but ideal for standing while you work, in the workshop, and if you're just standing, it doesn't matter whether your feet are left or right, if you're standing, all you've got is feet, and the main thing's what? That they're warm... here you are, have a pair as a present from me." And now he was walking past something that looked like hats for water, but at once he explained: "These here are canvas water buckets! They do leak a bit, but I got a load of patches from the military at a knock-down price, so here you have one army canvas bucket and a sticking plaster... Each bucket cost me ninety hellers, that's nothing...," and he led me across to four wind-up gramophones and crowed: "They've got no spring, but, not buy 'em when one cost a mere sixty crowns? I'll get hold of some springs and in a few standard working hours... how much will I make? Thousands, many thou! I've already mended one. And Mr Methie brought the needle across and started a record, it was a well-known violin piece played by a symphony orchestra, beautiful and so haunting that I marvelled and looked with my mind's eye in the direction of the violinist's bow and arm movements, which bewitched both me and even more Mr Methie, whose eyes misted over, stirred perhaps less with emotion and more with the bargain purchase he'd made, and I too was touched... When the record stopped playing... half-way through, I said: "What's that piece called, Mr Mike, isn't it a quite typical intermezzo? Could it be *Die Mühle im Schwarzwald*? Or *Silver Fern*?" But Mr Methie happily shook his head and picked up the record, which one of his tears dropped on, and passed it to me, I added my own brace of teardrops, and, having blinked away the rest of my tears, I read: *Fascination*... Which I repeated aloud: "*Fascination*...?" And Mr Methie said: "*Fascination*..." And I said: "And the record playing only half-way through like that?" And Mr Methie beamed: "It's defective, but, given the chance, not buy thirty of

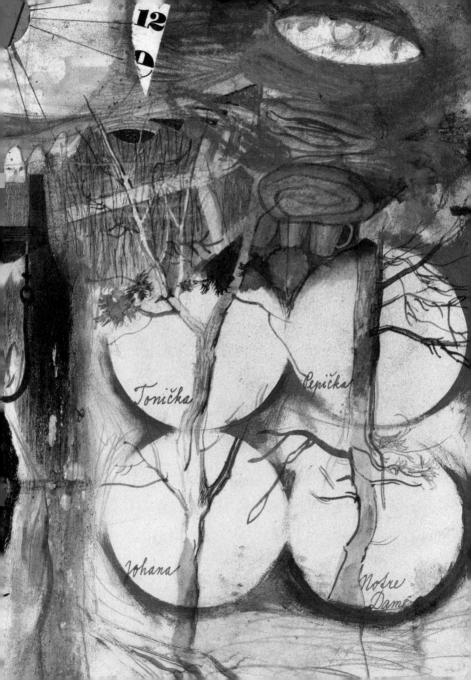

'em at only two crowns apiece? But then I also bought thirty others, equally defective, though that set play from the middle to the end. So rejoice! They're all of *Fascination*, so I've got a lifetime's supply of *Fascination* because now I won't listen to any other song, nor do I want to know any, this is my song, my life's song, my life-story... *Fascination*, so, what are they going to be playing over my coffin before they lower it into the ground?" And I said: "*Fascination*..." I took the plunge to enter the last structure, but before we could, we had, because of the slope, to lower our heads with our chins on our chests and at the nether end shuffle around on our knees, I saw Mr Methie's even more and most glorious purchases... so, when we came back out to salt the sheep in the tub to make sure there'd be a two months' supply of sausages from it, provided there was an extra five kilos of pork shoulder and two kilos of young beef to bind them and give them body... as I bent over the tub, overwhelmed by all the information, I stood up straight and said: "Do you know, Mr Mike, how hard you're also going to find it to die?"

All spring and early summer I avoided *Fascination* avenue, but one day I suddenly missed Mr Methie, it had taken six months for all those bargain buys and super purchases to evaporate from my brain, so I turned into the avenue, not that I actually meant to, but like when a bucket is hauled by winch or chain from a well I was all wound round with the sweet threads of the violin playing into the whispering foliage that mercifully shrouded all the workshops and woodsheds and lean-tos, so I followed the melody that was neither *Die Mühle im Schwarzwald*, nor that typical intermezzo *Silver Fern*, but *Fascination* as it trickled through the leaves like water through one's fingers or a drop net. And I stood at the gate and was struck once more by Mr Methie, who was standing, legs apart, in front of some instrument on three legs, and the instrument had its legs apart at exactly the same angle as Mr Methie and Mr Methie had one eye stuck in the instrument, watching a red-and-white stick, now, smiling, he took a few steps, moved the stick a bit further away and once more gazed with enormous delight through the theodolite, that instrument that he'd bought for a song along with a box of lenses, lenses to last to the end of time, and so to the end of the life, or the beginning of the death, of Mr Methie, who so desired to be called Mike. And again the strains of *Fascination* wafted from the gramophone and I heard a groan from the plot next door, the groan of a man injured not physically, but in his soul, an honest-to-goodness Slav cry of pain of one tormented by fate, though Mr Methie misinterpreted the lament of his neighbour, who was doubtless hearing *Fascination* for the thousandth time... Mr Methie pottered through the undergrowth to the overgrown fence and called into the leafage: "What is it? It's *Fascination*! Played by Helmuth Zacharias himself!" And as he made his way back, I quickly pretended to be tying my shoelace so that Mr Methie wouldn't see me, but he came affably towards me, and a little dog trotted up as well, and Mr Methie handed me his red pole and I carried it hither and thither because Mr Methie had taken it into his head to survey his entire plot in the forest, and as he did so, he explained enthusiastically about the slaughterhouse gun he'd just invented for killing twenty-four pigs at once, and the endless fishpond as a perpetuum mobile that meant that all the families on nearby plots could keep carp in the same water that kept circulating round and round, and as he told me all this, Mr Methie started to sing as well, cleared his throat and started singing, and then he explained the one thing I was afraid of: "I've borrowed a tape recorder and so as not to be idle of an evening, I sing, anything that enters my head, you can hear me, the very things I'm saying now I'm singing, what do you reckon, isn't it a glorious thing?" And he sang and walked about the wood, fingering some flimsy little stems... "See, I've got a total of a hundred service trees planted here, in five years they'll give me a yield of five thousand crowns a year... And you're wondering what service trees these are – they're not, they're black currant, and they'll yield another five thousand in five years..."

I said: "But they shouldn't get dripped on from above, and you've got them all under a canopy of pine trees." And Mr Methie sang: "You want to offer advice to me, me, a professional planner? It's all going to be lit with ultraviolet light rays to replace the sun, the sun..." "All right," I said, "but what are you hoping to achieve with this theodolite? Mr Methie gave a wave of the hand and put on the second half of *Fascination*, the violin section played by Helmuth Zacharias himself, and again it was as if he'd jabbed the needle into the brain of someone hidden behind the dense hedge, because as soon as the gramophone began to play, someone somewhere in the dense foliage groaned and squawked as if the gramophone needle were gouging a deep groove in his brain. Mr Methie took me by the shoulder and his eyes spouted a golden spray of rapture. He pointed to the area of five by five metres that he'd marked out with the theodolite and sang: "This is a dance-floor in the making... lanterns... subdued music... evening... can you hear it? Helmuth Zacharias!" I said: "Do you like dancing, Mr Mike?" And Mr Methie shook his head: "I've never danced, thing is, I'm creating this dance floor so as to prove to myself that I *can* do something, I've got this constant urge to create something of beauty, and can't you just see it? And at the same time, watch, I send this ball through this pipe, teaching the dog to run this way and that along the pipe, I keep on training him because, if I keep myself in training, why shouldn't I train a little stray dog? But that Zacharias fellow, he breaks my heart...," he said with a little more gravity, then he crossed the few paces to the theodolite and looked into it theatrically, I could see the instrument had no lenses, but Mr Methie tightened the screws as if the lenses were in place, and I, as requested, went pointlessly through the trees with a beautiful red pole, which I placed wherever Mr Methie indicated with the palm of his hand, several times over I had to move it there and back, one step this way, one step that, before he was satisfied and jotted something down in his notebook with such enormous pride and beaming yet again like the sun appearing from behind some surprised clouds... And on his feet he had two left boots, the same kind he'd given me in the winter, but I couldn't wear them, not because I didn't want to, I did try, but because I look at the ground as I walk along and the boots made not only my left leg veer left but my right leg as well, and I began to find walking hard and I started falling over and crashing my legs into each other and tripping myself up. But Mr Methie wore them magnificently, as he did that bee-covered gold waistcoat with no buttons or button-holes, and for a belt he had a kind of gold cord, like the rope they pull in church before the start of mass. I went on holding the red pole, the ranging rod, and suddenly I realised that Mr Mike Methie was in reality a poor wretch who wished not to have to contemplate the pointlessness of not only his own life but of all life, and so like the summer leaves that mercifully conceal the little houses and sheds and confusion on the plot in the wood, Mr Methie used each and every bargain to conceal any view of himself, any glimpse of his own self, a sight that scares and horrifies each and every one of us. But that's probably as it should be... Mr Methie! Mr Mike, do you think I'm any better off?

4 A FERAL COW

THERE'S NO SHORTAGE of stray dogs hereabouts, dogs that have been chucked out of cars and now sit around by the filling station or at the lay-by in the forest, inspecting every driver who stops to see if it isn't the master of one of them. But the belovèd masters of belovèd doggies don't stop in the hope of being reunited with their loyal little mutts; more likely it's to chuck out another little dog and make a quick getaway, which is why there is no shortage of dogs in our forest. You can see it on the main road as well, because dogs know they must wait for their masters at the point where they were left, much like when one goes to buy milk or bread or the paper, hitches him loosely to the door-handle and is back out in no time. Doggies who wait like that are calm at first, but then they start trying to spy if their master is coming, looking into the shop through the window. And so even in town it can happen that there's an Alsatian tied to a railing, all morning and all afternoon he's there, watching the door of the grocer's shop for his master to come out. And any dog like that pads up and down and waits for his master to appear and for them to be both back home, where in quieter hours they can celebrate the latest instalment of the mystical fusion of master and dog. The main road runs live with dogs, and when lights are ablaze and headlights dazzle as the cars slow down, the dogs come running, each thinking they are the eyes of his master, but the tyres of lorries are merciless and can steamroller a dog out flat as a rug, a bed-side mat, so by the time you've travelled from here to Prague you'll have met, say, ten, sometimes twenty dogs squished into two-dimensional figures from which any driver can tell what breeds the faithful unfortunates had been. One such dog, probably he was used to sleeping on straw at home, bedded down in our cowshed, and whenever the dairymaids came in to feed the cows, he thought it was his master, his lord and master, but seeing that it was strangers, he would growl and stand guard over the straw he probably slept on. And so I, being the officer on duty, was informed that there was a suspicious dog on the straw in the cowshed, so I went along and I shot it with my service pistol. When I took aim, he got up on his hind legs and begged me with his front paws not to shoot him, to let him live, because he had to go and find his master, his lord and master. Two shots and he fell and then they took him away to be skinned, because in our village roast dog is a delicacy, and, when all's said and done, it's right: if a dog has no master, it's more humane to turn him into a roast dinner, just like a gang of men working on the motorway who'll adopt any stray dog, take a whole gaggle of them along to the shops or the pub, treating them nicely, giving them their lunchtime leftovers, or buying a whole crate of milk for them – not that they're particularly fond of dogs, but a dog that's well-nourished tastes better, and with plenty of lovely milk in its diet the meat is more tender. So every week, they kill one dog, painlessly, by pushing a piece of pipe up its muzzle, skin it and roast it. Sometimes it could be two a week, but no one can hold that against them, for who other should be despatched with a pipe up the muzzle and stripped of his skin but the dog's master who chucked him out of the car. But anyway. As I shot that dog in the straw, one of the cows, a heifer, took fright, she was a real beauty from as far away as Mecklenburg or somewhere, and she broke loose and flew right at me, because I was stood in the doorway with my pistol. I barely dodged her as she flew past me like a bull past a toreador, and I felt her hairs brush against my uniform and the medals I wear on my chest, and with her tail held high and terror in her eyes, the Mecklenburg cow jumped the fence round the cowshed and disappeared into the forest. I gave orders for the animal's keepers to go in search of her, but you'd never find a cow in Kersko forest, never in a month of Sundays! Like looking for a needle in a haystack! A month later she was spotted by some mushroom-pickers, but the minute she saw a human, such was the fear I'd put in her with my smoking service pistol, that she high-tailed it into a covert and kept running like crazy. So in our woods, besides all the stray dogs, we also had a roaming cow, a feral Mecklenburg heifer, a beast weighing in at half a ton. So I thinks to myself, we go on a hunt every autumn, so... I'll call the hunters together, because I'm one too, a fully paid-up member of the hunt, and we'll shoot the cow, having tracked it down first, because a feral cow might start attacking people and man is the measure of all things, not only notionally, but also for real, and doubly so in our own time, when all other comrades and I, we guard the substance of socialism against the foe, even if that foe turns out to be a feral cow. So that Saturday, we turned up on a collectivised tractor, from the collective farm the cow had escaped from, spread out in a long line and proceeded forward until we ran the feral Mecklenburg heifer to earth. This suited us very nicely, just the thing for true huntsmen, hunting a huge beast as heavy as two stags, a heavy heifer weighing as much as ten roebucks or seven moufflons, no meek barn cow, but an honest-to-goodness feral cow, like when on an earlier occasion we'd shot just as heavy an elk that had wandered across from Poland somewhere, it had attacked three different cars on the main road, lifting them up with those massive

antlers like the hopper of the kind of digger they use for making roadside ditches, levering up three cars and lifting them off the ground, he was only slightly injured and he tossed the three cars, while they were moving, into the ditch like they were just toys. So, the feral cow made to turn and was going to attack us likewise, but then she thought better of it and ran out of the trees into a grassy clearing, but striding out to face her went Kurel with his hunting rifle, an outstanding marksman, with a limp, but I could rely on him – if the heifer came within range, even if the cow went on the attack, he'd fell it. We were followed along by a tractor as our war wagon, so if anything happened we could leap onto it like Hussites in the Middle Ages, whose latter-day heirs and very embodiment we were, so we formed a circle round the cow, she snorted and stamped her hoof, almost kneeled down to select who to attack, then went for old Kurel, who must have hit her with a single shot, but she charged off, only stopping on the ploughland, where she stood, legs apart and head down ready to attack, and old Kurel hobbled after her while me and the other huntsmen thought it wiser to hop onto the flatbed trailer behind the tractor and rush to Kurel's aid with our war wagon, he took a shot at the feral cow from fifty metres, but she remained standing, and we of the tractor crew circled the cow at a distance, each of us firing off a death-dealing bullet at her bovine heart, but she remained standing, staring wide-eyed ahead of her, we were seized with terror as our ammunition almost ran out, and I even took a pot-shot with my service pistol, but the cow remained standing and staring ahead, and we didn't know who she was going to attack. Then I got out my walkie-talkie to summon the fire brigade and their beautiful red truck so they could despatch the feral cow with their water cannon, when out of the trees came this pretty girl, walking along so prettily on her beautiful legs, and she came towards us, heading right for the cow, and we shouted at her and I ordered her as police commandant to stop and turn back because the cow was feral and could trample anyone to death, yet the ingenuous girl kept getting ever closer and we roared ourselves hoarse and rode round on the tractor and trailer with our hunting rifles raised ready to fire if the cow did attack the girl so we could bring it finally to its knees with a concerted burst of fire. But the girl went right up to the cow, raised her hands and pushed it in the side and the cow rolled over like a statue, her legs stiff, she fell on her side but with her eyes still wide open, so we hopped off the tractor and the girl turned our way, and as we got closer she took the cow by its wrist, lay against its flank and said: "This cow's been dead for half an hour, terrified to death, this, gentlemen, is what they call rigor mortis, a muscular spasm after death, you needn't be afraid of her." I said:

"What do you mean, who's afraid? We knew that, didn't we, comrades…" Then we had ourselves photographed, each with one hunting boot on the feral cow, a group photo because I was minded to see news of the event in *Svoboda* or the *Nymburk Gazette*, with a photo. Then I said: "And what are *you* doing here, young lady? Where's your ID?" And she handed me her citizen's ID card, I read how young she was, then moved straight on to 'employment' to check she wasn't a social parasite, living as a vagrant or prostitute, but she was a teacher. She said: "It's so beautiful here, who'd have thought how lovely it is in such a flat area?" And I said: "Officially speaking, that's a different matter. But what are you, a teacher from Prague, doing here?" She said: "Do you mean to say you gentlemen don't know that Mozart played the organ in that little church over at Sadská?" I said: "We know that, and that he played the organ, but we prefer brass bands…" And she said: "And do you know that in that village over there, Hradišťko, two head teachers used to live who were friends of Mozart's? And that, at Mozart's request, one of those headmasters gave him several songs that he then used in *Don Giovanni*?" I said: "And did the teacher have an export license?" And the girl said: "You didn't need a license in those days, the export of art objects wasn't against the law back then, they didn't see it as ideological sabotage. Gentlemen, I'm glad you saved my life from this feral cow. I'm glad to have met you, gentlemen, and now I must head for the ferry, otherwise for one thing I might miss my train and for another, the ferryman told me he stopped ferrying at five, he was off to play cards, something I like too, not just canasta, but poker even, and it was poker, the game, that led me to believe that this feral cow, even from a distance, as I approached, had been dead for half an hour...," she said and set off, and we looked at her beautiful legs and her undulating walk, she walked the way young girls walk, and it delighted us no less than having felled that feral Mecklenburg cow and thus saved our forest and village from devastation just as, the year before, risking our own lives, we had overcome a sorry, massive elk that had wandered across from Poland, all the way to our forest. "Dammit, that's no human, she's not a living being, I reckon she's got no body, I bet she's a fairy," old Kurel, my good old marksman friend, started yelling. I said: "She couldn't have been a fairy, Kurel," I said, because fairies don't carry, and are not entitled to carry, a citizen's ID card. See!" And old Kurel hobbled off with his rifle after the girl as she receded into the distance, shouting as he ran: "If she's not a fairy, she must be a wood nymph!" And he took aim and fired, then again, the rifle making his shoulder jerk, we could see a target on the girl's receding back and old Kurel, not that he missed her, he hit her, because old Kurel was never off target, but I was afraid to write a report on it because that beautiful girl walked on and looked back and waved to us with her hankie... so, as you can see, in our neck of the woods all manner of things can cause people, driving along the tree-lined stretch of the main road, to dump dogs on it, all manner of things can happen when I, in a good cause, shoot a dog in a cowshed and a priceless Mecklenburg cow breaks loose and goes mad, like the one lying here with its legs in the air, with the result that the return on thirty thousand crowns is animal flesh for the rendering plant or the zoo. So: do not cast dogs from your cars!

5 A GRAND PIANO RABBIT HUTCH

"I HARBOUR NO ILLUSIONS as regards mankind," said the solicitor and walked on with a gait so bizarre that you couldn't but feel compassion. He looked as if he'd been run over by a tram years before and left to his fate, for his body to take charge of itself and make the best of having had nearly all his limbs smashed. Even his face was so crumpled that in order to see where he was going he had to look in a completely different direction. And as he went, he oscillated far over to the right and then again to the left, as if he were walking not on his own two feet but on short stilts, and his arms were like two bent withies, so if he happened to be carrying a pail of mineral water from the St Joseph Spring, the pail would swing about like a carter's lamp and by the time he got home he'd have spilled almost all the water he'd collected. They said he'd been a solicitor and that during the purchase of a small house next to the grocery store he'd contrived things so fiendishly that he didn't pay the owner a single penny, and so his infirmity was the just reward for what he'd done. He lived alone, and it was a miracle that he could put his

clothes on, it took him nearly two hours to dress his rheumatic, twisted frame, so he recognised it was better to get dressed on Monday and stay dressed, because as soon as he got dressed it would practically be time to get slowly undressed and ready for bed. When he went for a bucket of water, he had to make some complicated manoeuvres before he could turn off the road towards the spring, like trying to turn a car with all its wheels blocked. He would reverse a few times, then take a few steps forward, then keep on reversing until he got the direction right and then the main thing was to find the way to the spring, his eyes apparently only being able to see in one direction and as if he were looking through a tiny slit in a black mask, so he saw the trickle of water only after ten or a dozen goes at finding and fixing that thin shaft of light on the tinkling water. And he was fat and he perspired and his face was the very expression of torment, nay horror. And yet he lived on his own, he didn't want anyone, he was the house's sole occupant, and though he certainly had money, he didn't hire anyone in, so he struggled on his own, and he even relished the struggle, seeing it as a kind of triumph, and it was a great triumph when he managed to get to the co-op to buy bread and milk and other bits and pieces to sustain him, or to fetch water. It was quite a sporting achievement to hobble his way to wherever he desired or needed, a great moral victory, and he himself made no secret of the fact, full of admiration for himself and, you might say, wallowing in the preparations for each new excursion, even charting out improvements to his route, especially if the sun was shining. Anyone else was glad of the sun, but for the old solicitor sunlight might be the death of him, because the glare in his tiny cone of light was so strong that he could scarcely see at all, and he had constantly to shade his eyes so as to avoid stepping off the path into the ditch. So he would always stop, and the best thing was when he lifted his bag or pail up above his head, awful to see if you hadn't seen it before, the pail and beneath its shadow those dire features with their permanent expression of surprise, groping to find the only spot from which that fine laser, that sole line of light stemming from his eye would ring true, for what sight the old solicitor had was in one eye only. But the sheer joy when he finally saw that he could see, when suddenly, as in the depth of night, he'd shone the slender beam of his torch onto the path, got his bearings and could walk another dozen metres or so until once again, although the sun was shining, he found himself in total gloom. And never ever would the old solicitor let anyone help him, take him by the sleeve and offer themselves, he would stand there, panting his defiance and wearing such an expression that anyone would, however horrified, just leave him to it, preferring to walk on rather than look into that seemingly absent, almost moronic face that suggested both a bewildered horror and a great readiness to wallow in the dreadful fate dealt him, but he wasn't giving in, certainly not. Our solicitor proceeded in the same way when going to collect grass, lifting his basket into the sun, in the direction of the lights tumbling from the heavens so that, shading his eye with that large surface, he could see the grass. And he would kneel down a bit in the same way, not a real kneel, more a collapse as if he'd just been shot, as if he was collapsing under some moral reprimand, just like when Raskolnikov dropped to embrace the earth and accept its forgiveness. So the old solicitor fell to his knees to feel for the grass that he'd previously got a good feel for by eye, and he tugged at the grass, angrily plucking handfuls of grass, then he would twist his head around this way and that until the thread of his sight spotted the basket, then he would keep putting grass in his basket until he had picked as much as he deemed necessary. And again, as he rose, again it looked as if it was someone terribly drunk trying to rise, constantly falling back down, like someone who'd been run over by a car in the night, sent flying into the ditch and left to his fate. But the old solicitor adopted an angle that yielded the only position in and from which he was able to get onto one knee and then onto both feet. "You're the only man ever to win hands down," I once told him, having gazed my fill at his indomitable will and desire to stand up. He looked round for me, un-comprehending, following the direction of my voice, but then he had to keep turning his head for a while like some complicated scientific instrument until he got it aligned by tangents and cosines like a ship's compass or some complex piece of mountain-top meteorological kit... and I saw that his gaze was as straight as a length of wire and just as cold, but humanly cold, because it was human. "I harbour no illusions as regards man-kind," he said, then set off back home with his basket of grass, zigzag, this way and that, like a lunar module on legs. Yesterday, some electricians dug a trench and lay a cable in it, being rather casual about earthing it over. I saw the old solicitor coming along in his usual way, I saw him step, in all innocence, into a void instead of solid soil, and, before his foot reached the bottom and the rubble covering the black cable, his entire frame rolled down, sinking into the trench, falling with his face in his basket, like a piece of machinery, then scrab-bling back out of the trench and walking on, shuffling and jangling like a machine that was more or less work-ing but churning out rejects, except that the old solicitor knew what's what, knew that if ever he failed to get back on his feet, if ever he lost heart, that would be the end of him, that they'd haul him off, like some redundant piece of machinery, to the recycling centre, or some waste disposal site, or to the tip outside the village among the general waste, prunings and stinking tin cans. So he strode on, heading for home, hearing my footsteps beside him, and I could tell that what pleased him most was that I didn't try to help him. "Thank you," he said appreciatively. And he felt for the brick pillar, then the gate, and he entered the pathway lined with the branches of young spruces sweeping down to the ground, and as he went his zigzag way I saw the branches stroking him, brushing him down, scratching his face, but the old man, as if just for the pleasure of it, the pleasure of distress, fondled the trees, their fragrance, their new-grown pale-green tips, which were like the green fingers of recently ripped little gloves. "Can I come with you?" I asked uneasily. "Do, so you can see how it is I can harbour no illusions as regards mankind...," and so the old boy walked round to the back of the house and that's where I really got a shock. In the middle of the yard stood a grand piano, a black Petrof, slightly atilt, and from it issued a strange kind of concrete music, an odd plunking of the wires, then a long excruciating squeaking sound fit to freeze the blood, and it dawned on me that I used to hear the same sound as I made my way home at night, thinking it was the nocturnal moaning and vocalising of barn owls and pigmy owls and the wailing of little owls summoning death... but this time I could tell that the wailing came from inside the piano, the cries bolstered by clumping sounds and some quite noisy knocking. Leaning by an old pine tree there was an assemblage of rabbit hutches with a doe happily basking in each one, some with young, and these rabbits were so quiet, so calm, as if they were taking the sunlight and a bit of grass and spinning them into the serenity of a cloudless summer morning. "When I was in America," I told the solicitor, "I saw an amazing event, and it only cost a dollar. A helicopter carried a piano just like yours five hundred metres up into the air above a playground, then there was a roll of drums and the helicopter let go of the piano and you should have heard the bang and the music, which went on for the best part of ten minutes, and from the bowels of the piano the strings and pins roused themselves to action, the keys were flying everywhere, leaving not just me but all five thousand spectators terrified… but I'm even more terrified by this piano of yours. "I harbour no illusions as regards mankind," the old man squeaked, and once again the piano gave up a long, steadily rising squeaking sound, to which the old gentleman bent his ear with sheer delight, the very opposite of the horror with which my hat threatened to take its leave. "What *is* that?" I asked. And the old man raised the black back lid and I saw that this grand old piano was running live with full-grown rabbits, dozens of rabbits for slaughter, although the stronger ones, bucks, had been gnawing the nuts

off the weaker ones, I saw how bloodied and terror-stricken the weaker ones were and how proudly triumphant the big ones, and how the eyes of the tormentors gleamed with satisfaction at the power they'd brought to bear, while there among the strings in the corner huddled those whose turn – at this rabbit ritual – it had just been. "Just like people," said the old solicitor, adding that this lot who were in power today – their turn would come too, and the ones who hadn't had 'em chewed off yet, they'd finally gnaw each other's nuts off until not a one would be left uncastrated... "Hence all the squeaking, because once they've castrated each other, I'll be along to kill them, because the flesh of castrated rabbits is much more delicate, the torture leaves its mark and the meat is all the tenderer for it." "But tell me, how can these little guys have any fun, and what with?" "And how, sir, does mankind have its fun? Creaming off the best, all the time, time and again the best are castrated and deprived of great strength... inside this piano, sir," said the old solicitor, tossing the rabbits some grass in among the strings, "this is the Czech question, a question as old as the hills, and more, see?" He croaked and smiled a wonderful smile. "This piano cost me fifty crowns, they were taking it to the tip by St Adalbert's, and I thinks, a fine rabbit hutch, that, and for only fifty crowns..." I said: "Not bad, but even better, I reckon, is the man from near where I lived who would go to the park carrying a violin case, the children would all gather round, and beg: 'Play us a tune, please!' but he just opened the case and out popped a bunny and he said: 'Look, children, Joe is going for a graze...' and when the bunny had grazed its fill, it would hop back inside the violin case and the man would take it back home, because ever since he'd bought the rabbit meaning to kill it for meat, he hadn't been able to kill it, poor little thing, and so that it wouldn't get bored he would bring it out in a violin case and let it have a good graze; that means much more to me." "First sign of degeneracy," said the old solicitor, adding: "Goodbye, and close the gate behind you, will you? You know, I harbour no illusions as regards mankind," he said again, with greater emphasis and eyebrows raised. And he tapped the lid of the Petrof grand.

At the gate I turned, feeling a stab in the back from a shiny knitting-needle... and there by the black grand piano stood the old solicitor, shading his nightmarish features against the spray of sharp sunlight with his basket, his frame all twisted, and firing at me with the death-ray of his eye, which passed through me and cast such a bright light on the white brickwork of the gatepost like if I'd focussed a lens so as to burn a hole in the back of my hand or was waiting for my cotton sleeve to catch fire. Such was the power of this human stare, this fine wire of a strange aqueous humour emitted by the wretched, but triumphant old solicitor. I called out: "Who are you?" And the old man gibbered, bowing towards me: "I'm a corpse who's forgotten to die." And the sun shone on the rabbit house, which, divided into separate hutches, reared up behind him, with the does basking in it, their babies before them, fond does, perhaps impelled by their love to cherish the day when their offspring would grow up and have the good fortune to move into the body of the Petrof grand, where they would wage that age-old, terrible struggle, which goes on among men as much as among animals, for sexual supremacy, a struggle victorious until one even stronger comes along and bites off the vitals of the strongest rabbits, depriving them of their power, because this is the only way of progress, the only way for the strong to maintain their position, while all that awaits those who have lost out is the knife or a blow to the skull, though the meat of the emasculated, the castrated, is always more tender and free of the obnoxious odour of sex, that odour that makes the world go round.

6 JUMBO

WE'VE BEEN UNLUCKY with our pub landlords, or have we? For one, Mr Sborník was such a chilly mortal that the enamelled cast-iron stove was red-hot even in summer, and as he conveyed mugs of beer from tap to table, mine host Mr Sborník wore a long fur coat and shivered with cold, while we dripped with sweat in proportion to our vast intake of beer. Those endless beers! Another licensee was, for his part, so fired up the whole time, so jealous was he of his wife, that he didn't have any heating on even in winter. It was enough to look or smile at his wife and he would threaten to cash up and close the pub for the day. And sometimes he did. This publican was called Zákon, which means 'law', which is why he had a complex about bringing the patrons' behaviour into line. So when he brought a customer his beer and the customer wasn't sitting like kids in school, he would hold the beer back and even start yelling at him: "Is that the way to sit in a pub, all sprawled out and cross-legged like that? You're getting no beer until you sit nicely." And even as he taught his patrons how to behave, Mr Zákon still managed to keep

an eye out in case anyone was looking knowingly at his wife, exchanging signs with her, or making sheep's eyes at her. Finally our best landlord was the landlady called Romana, who had a gall bladder problem that she treated by drinking diabetic brandy or whisky, and she had with her a gorgeous little daughter, who she bathed every night in the bar sink, because our Keeper's Lodge was devoid of sanitary facilities. If at that moment a patron ordered tea or coffee, with the little girl sitting in the sink among the cups and saucers, Romana would wash a cup in the soap suds and then serve them a really nice coffee with lovely bubbles and the flavour of an honest cognac. She was nice to all the patrons, she'd come and sit with them, and they would help treat her gall bladder with brandy or whisky. The only one she didn't like was Mr Bělohlávek, an aircraft mechanic who didn't come often, but when he did, it was worth it. As he took his seat he'd be down in the dumps, but after four beers and black rum coffees he was fine and then one time he asked me what I was doing on the sixth of January. And when I said I was free, Mr Bělohlávek invited me for tea in Voronezh, enthusing about how we'd take off with Chief Pilot Mazura and spend the evening in Poprad, where he had a gipsy band ready and waiting, then in the morning we'd set off for Voronezh, where he would repair a broken-down TU134, in the afternoon we'd have a bite to eat, caviar and champagne, and land back in Prague in the early evening. But that wasn't what drove a wedge between Romana and Mr Bělohlávek, the aircraft mechanic. Once, after five beers, he unwound and told the whole pub, with passion: "So, being a pilot, that's no mean thing! In essence it's a world of mathematics and geometry, and in this entire district, that world has been entrusted to me and Mr Hubka the engineer alone!" Mr Bělohlávek exulted, full of sparkle and on brilliant form. And Romana took a sip of brandy and said: "And what about geometry and me? Could it be entrusted to me too?" Mr Bělohlávek pulled himself up to his full height and exulted even more: "No, lady, it is entrusted only to men, certainly not you!" And Romana said: "Why on earth not?" And Mr Bělohlávek banged his fist on the table as proof of his zeal and bellowed: "No, because, lady, it can be taken for granted that you're dumb." Romana reddened and said: "Thank you very much!" And Mr Bělohlávek had been on form ever since the time he'd taken a tractor-load of open sandwiches and the police were waiting for the tractor by the main gate of the collective farm, and Mr Bělohlávek, clutching fifty open sandwiches, commanded: "Head for the fence, ram the fence and enter the farm from the rear!" And the tractor-driver drove through the fence and then they'd carried on drinking and feasting in the cow-shed while the policemen vainly rubbed their hands as they waited by the main gate with a breathalyser. When Mr Bělohlávek finished this story, I asked him the fundamental question: "How come you did that, what gave you the idea, Mr Bělohlávek?" And he shouted triumphantly: "Why? I'd had six beers and six rums and I was on form!" And so from that time on he was on form, not often, but sometimes he was, because otherwise, when sober, he was shy, reticent, diffident and given to blushing. However, like I say, Romana had been the licensee before Mr Zákon and I want to tell you the sort of things that happened during the time he was landlord. Back then, winters were harsh, but Zákon kept a coal fire in the kitchen and in the little room where has wife and child must have been. Any patron who entered the pub would be shivering with cold and Mr Zákon let anyone who wanted, and it was but a moment before everyone wanted, drape a white tablecloth round their shoulders. So they all sat there in their white tablecloths, the tables had white cloths, and outside there was the covering of white snow that had fallen. So we the patrons could get warm, Mr Bělohlávek suggested putting three ashtrays together and warming our hands over some burning cigarette papers and dog-ends. Then mine host Mr Zákon brought in an enamel crock pot, a huge great pot, brown, with handles, which he stood on the three ashtrays in which bits of paper and newspaper and finally some wooden toothpicks were burning, then he brought his tiny tot in and slipped it into the pot, and it was freezing cold in the pub, but the baby was warm and cosy inside the enamel pot and having our hands warm brightened the rest of us a bit too. And at that moment the door swung open and in among the white figures of the patrons and the white of the tablecloths came a chimney sweep, the village sweep with his brush, and he was so miserable that he didn't even help himself to a tablecloth, but just as he was, still covered in soot, he sat down at a table, placed his head in his hands and ordered a strong grog, and then he stared absently at the ceiling and said: "Well this year's been awful and the one that's coming's going to be ghastly... It says here I'm charged with raping my wife, yes, wife!" And the other patrons were startled: "You what??" And Mr Zákon pronounced: "That can't be right." And the sweep took out his wallet and he rose, leaving the imprint of his elbows and hands on the white tablecloth, and then he went and placed his hands on a clean tablecloth and showed us the writ from the district court charging him with raping his wife. And the patrons scrambled over one another to read the writ and the sweep walked round and round, leaving hand-prints like dirty footprints all over the tablecloth, and the landlord shouted: "Wait!" And he spread a newspaper out and told the chimney sweep to sit in one spot and keep his filthy mawlers off the cloth and on the

newspaper, or he wouldn't make him the grog he'd ordered... And the sweep rambled on about his wife having found another bloke, that she loved him and that she'd already got herself a solicitor and wanted a divorce, and so one time the sweep had forced her, under threat of violence, like the ancient Romans did when they carried off the Sabine women, and she'd had to bow to his will. The patrons were amazed, re-read it, and the landlord, Mr Zákon, shook his fist towards the kitchen at his wife beyond the wall, a rare and timid beauty who may have weighed seventy-eight kilos, but her hair was the colour of straw or limewood shavings, and her blue eyes were such a surprise out here in the woods that none of the patrons could tear themselves away from her hair and eyes, and that drove Mr Zákon mad. Mr Zákon said menacingly: "Huh, if my one tried pulling a trick like that! A true Slav household's not supposed to have an axe in sight, and I've got one!" And the sweep rose, and, probably so drunk by now with grief, he kept grabbing the table with his hands, and so his palm-prints promenaded from tablecloth to tablecloth following the publican, and the sweep went on, "Good man, don't do it, you mustn't kill her, she's a human being..." "What!" Mr Zákon roared, "And what am I then? Her spouse or what? Let her be obedient unto her husband!" And the chimney sweep leant on the bar counter and the door opened and in came the beauty who was the landlord's wife, her hair, radiant as the sun, warming the eyes of all the patrons, and she set down the double-strength grog, and everyone was watching her, Mr Zákon searchingly, wondering whether she might have a lover and, through her solicitor, go and sue him for rape… And suddenly he saw her as so beautiful and desirable and so capable of and predisposed to being loved by a third party that he let out a whinnying sound. And he bellowed: "As of today you're going to wear a headscarf! Or I'll shave your head bare, I'll swear you've got lice and that hair will come off!" And he plumped himself down and started shivering so much that he took a tablecloth and put it round his shoulders, one from the pile of tablecloths as a white drape across his shoulders, and he pulled his chair up as the sweep greedily drank his grog and called towards the kitchen: "Another one! And, my friends, that's not all! The court charges me with obstructing an impending happy marriage…" And there was silence, the tiny head of the baby slumbered sweetly inside the crock pot, which radiated its warmth like a cast-iron stove, a pleasant warmth, we all had our hands on the pot and watched the sleeping baby, which let out a sweet sobbing sound, and there was silence and suddenly Mr Bělohlávek ordered a whole bottle of old engine oil, meaning Fernet-Branca, the landlord staggered off to get the bottle and some glasses and we all got to figuring out and trying to imagine what sort of law it was, what prescription, that sided with a lover and protected him, and so protected an impending happy marriage against the husband. Having poured out the glasses of engine oil, Mr Zákon got up again and satisfied himself that his axe was still propped against the doorpost, then sprawled out on his chair he gazed absently through the wall into the very heart of what had befallen the chimney sweep, who was back on his feet, running his hands over the white, already multiply crisscrossed tablecloths, and dripping tears onto the grime- and soot-stained cloths. "How did you put it?" Mr Zákon enquired. And the chimney sweep got his bulging bag, took a document out with his black hands, it was the wrong one, so along with some soot he shoved it back and then found the right one. He handed it over and the landlord read out: "Re: – obstruction of an impending marriage..." and having read it, he passed the paper round and pronounced: "I'm going to buy two more axes, then let someone come and say I'm obstructing someone's impending bliss!" And the door opened and out of the kitchen came a straw-yellow radiance of wavy hair, and the landlady was beautiful, as if she had been born of the waters of the sea, a sea of beer and foam, bearing a steaming double-strength grog, and everyone rose, and the tablecloths rose as they also covered their heads, and the eyes of all were fixed on the awesome sight. The landlady had the unfortunate habit of smiling with a slight squint, and her squint was more beautiful than everything else, a squint that left all men with a sense that mine hostess had glimpsed infinity, that she wrote poems, that her heart held some secret. The landlord said: "And I'm going to apply for a gun licence, I'm going to join the hunt!" And the chimney sweep picked up his cup of double-strength grog and his hands shook, and the little spoon chattered even more than his teeth. Then he sat back down and his hands were so large that they completely enfolded the little cup with its inscription 'Greetings from Hlinsko' and he cooled his drink with his cold hands. "Gentlemen," cried Mr Bělohlávek, cheery and relaxed, having downed his sixth beer, "gentlemen, let's turn the page! Do you know where I went yesterday? Africa, and I flew over Mount Kilimanjaro." And the men seized on Kilimanjaro and started arguing about where it was. "It's somewhere near the source of the White Nile," said Mr Kuzmík. "No way, it's in South Africa," said the gamekeeper, Mr Gromus. "Come off it, it's up near Kuwait, there's all of thirty trees there and twenty of them belong to the sheikh," said Mr Franc. And I said: "It's somewhere where the Germans used to have a colony..." And the last to raise his head was the roadmender, Mr Procházka, who'd been sound asleep, but, as always, heard everything, and he came to and said: "Listen carefully to what I'm about to say: if you're pissed, Kilimanjaro can be right here in Kersko... All right?" He'd had his say and started drifting off again, then his head dropped to his chest and he was sound asleep. And again silence reigned, and so as to drive away any thought of raping his own wife and attempting to thwart marital bliss, Mr Kuzmík said: "The finest tool in old Russia, my friends, was the broad axe..." The landlord cheered up: "That's what I like to hear!" And Mr Kuzmík went on with his story: "All your Russians of olden times had an axe slung from their shoulder on a kind of suspender attached to a strap under their coat... you'd never believe the things the old Russians could do with it, they could even carve themselves a rustic wall clock with it." And Mr Bělohlávek banged his fist on the table and neighed with delight: "Another bottle of engine oil... Gentlemen!" And the landlord rose, brought a bottle and, having broached it, poured out the glasses, and he brought some beer as well, so soon everyone felt warm, hot even, they sat back away from the smouldering papers, ashtrays and the warm enamel pot, the landlord extricated the gurgling baby and carried it off to their little back room. When he came back, the chimney sweep was wandering about again and trampling his hands all over the cloths in the corner as well; the landlord cast an eye towards the stockwhip hanging on the doorframe, but then dis-

missed it with a wave of his hand, and Mr Bělohlávek shouted: "Gentlemen, what are you doing on the twenty-sixth of July this year?" And all the men, having fortified themselves by turns, said they were off work that day, or would take time off. And Mr Bělohlávek blared: "Good, you're all invited to the airport! A Jumbo is due in Prague, on my taxiway, my tarmac, for the first time ever!" And the ones who didn't know what a Jumbo was voiced their surprise: "What? A jumbo?" And Mr Bělohlávek rose and the figure of the man in a white tablecloth was a figure of progress: "Yes, a Jumbo! A Boeing 727 Jumbo, gentlemen, a giant that can seat three hundred and sixty passengers! This giant carries twenty-five thousand litres of fuel in each wing! But me, I'm in charge of the landing, so what if the concrete doesn't go sixty centimetres down? What if the Jumbo lands and starts shunting the concrete slabs ahead of it and hurling them like icefloes far and wide, way out towards Kladno somewhere, and the Jumbo goes and crashes on me!" Mr Bělohlávek exulted, tearing at his hair. "How'll I answer for that at a court martial? I'm in the service of the army, and I am in the service of Pan American, an American airline, so I get paid in dollars! Yes, dollars! In the spring I'm buying myself a Simca at the hard-currency shop, how about that, eh? Though I know I've gone and let out something I was supposed to keep as a professional secret!" Mine host Mr Zákon

said: "So how big's that piece of junk then?" Mr Bělohlávek took a sip, then tossed the engine oil right back, followed by a long swig of beer from the bottle, and yelled gleefully: "It's seventy-seven metres long, it's twenty-eight metres high, wingspan nearly thirty metres, our cabin alone, meaning for the crew and the captain, is as big as this place," he roared and made a sweeping gesture with his hand to describe the Keeper's Cottage restaurant. Mr Franc said: "That big! That's hard to imagine, but say, a jumbo, if a jumbo was standing here and me here, and the landlord and me were holding onto its wings, it couldn't take off then, could it, your jumbo?" And Mr Bělohlávek clapped a hand to his forehead: "What? You'd get swept away! One time they left a truck on the taxiway and a jumbo jet just swept it aside like a toy, like a kitten, a pussycat," he miaowed. And Mr Franc, he wouldn't give up: "If we all held on to a wing and dug our heels in, then it couldn't take off!" And Mr Bělohlávek said: "A jumbo jet's got a thrust coefficient of fifty-eight tons...," he gave another sweep of his hand, "it's an awesome plane, see, it's got two-storey restaurants, it's like ten super-sized barns, ten massive trucks, trailers an' all... have you all got torches?" And because it was evening and the depth of a winter's night, they all got their torches out of their coats on the coat-rack... Mr Jumbo Man said: "Who's good at pacing out metres?" Mr Franc said: "Me." And the patrons, merry and sweating, so as not to have to think about forced fornication with their own wives or attempts at thwarting someone else's marital bliss, went out into the raw night air; only Mr Procházka was sound asleep and he just flung an arm out in his sleep, said: "You bag of wind from Zeleneč...," and slept on. And the night was bright and cold, snow outlined the edges of the inn and the white birch trees glinted as if emitting neon light and the trunks of the oaks appeared black as the chimney sweep. Mr Jumbo Man was reeling, they were all lurching about in the fresh air, but Mr Jumbo Man was on form, he tapered the beam of his Hungarian torch and shone it up into a birch that was so tall that its outer twigs covered the entire inn. "Right," Mr Jumbo Man yelled, "how many metres tall is this birch?" Mr Franc said: "Twenty," and Mr Jumbo Man blustered: "So imagine it extended upwards by another half-birch and that's how tall a Jumbo jet is! There, and this is the cabin for me, like for the captain and his team, of which there are thirteen! Like a football side plus linesmen! And now pace out eighty metres along the concrete ride..." And Mr Franc set his pace and strode off and counted metre after metre, eleven, twelve... and fifty-three and fifty-four... and his torch receded into the distance and then stopped, rose and Mr Franc announced: "Eighty metres!" And Jumbo Man commanded: "Now two of you go off to the side and measure fifteen metres from the lodge." And off went two of the drinkers, tottering, so strong is the air hereabouts, especially when washed down with spent engine oil. Mr Kuzmík fell down twice before completing those fifteen metre-length strides, but finally, in the distance, a torch glimmered at the end of the Jumbo's tail, more torches at its wingtips, and so we had a reasonable idea of how big a Jumbo must be, and Mr Jumbo Man treated us enthusiastically to all the other details and particulars of a Boeing 727, then hollered: "So, Mr Franc, could you hold it back by its wing? You wouldn't even be able to reach up to it, given that you board one like from two floors up, that's how high its wings are!" And suddenly, on the apron outside the inn, there on the patio, some little lights lit up, as if on the flight deck and like the instrument panel was all lit up with its little red and gold and green lights, and so we were disconcerted and had to rub our eyes, because we thought it was the fresh air playing tricks. But a voice put us at our ease. "What are you up to here, my bonny kittens?" called the local police commandant, stepping forward and shining his torch, as was his custom, onto his chest, lighting up the medals and decorations he been awarded by the government and the Party, and he called us all over, so we tottered across to him and he shone his light in our faces and we were afraid that the chimney sweep had not only left his prints all over the tablecloths, but had left his sooty pawmarks all over our faces too, hence the commandant's exclamation about what we 'kittens' were doing there and why we were wearing masks. And Mr Jumbo Man said: "Officer, sir, we're trying to get some idea of how big a Jumbo jet is, the Boeing 727 passenger plane that's going to be landing in Prague this summer!" But the policeman was in a good mood and exclaimed: "Pull the other one! I reckon you were working out how to get the Jumbo to land right here..." "Officer, sir," Mr Jumbo Man wet his fingers and raised them to swear on his oath, "I'm having kittens over whether the airport at Ruzyně can take the strain of a Jumbo landing." "All right, all right," the commandant made to go, broody and absorbed, "play your silly games, kittens. If I wasn't on duty, I'd join in, but woe betide if that Jumbo does land here!" he said, once more shining his torch on his medals and decorations, and went off into the sixth avenue somewhere, to return to wherever he'd left his Volga, and leaving behind him confusion and surprise, as ever. We watched and watched, then we went back to the pub doorsteps, which some of us now had to mount on all fours, such a gale seeming to blow, even though there was a flat calm. So we went back in the warm, refreshed by the outside air, but the worse for wear owing to the Fernet engine oil. Our Landlord Mr Zákon, seeing all the tablecloths so, but so, smudged with the chimney sweep's palmprints, cast an eye towards his bullwhip, then thought better of it. Mr Procházka woke up and said: "It happens everywhere, landlord, at the Novák tavern he made such a filthy mess of the tablecloths that the landlord, a butcher, who's also suing over a meadow and a pear-tree, took his bullwhip and gave him a right lashing, so these days the sweep doesn't go near Nováks', how about that then?" Out of interest the landlord asked: "Exactly how many lashes did the sweep get?" And Mr Procházka said as he dropped off again: "How many ma-...," and slept on. The landlord pulled another round of beers, but the police commandant with his glinting medals was still floating before their eyes, so he brought another bottle of Fernet Branca, that old engine oil, and when we'd drunk a shot of it we could see the commandant before us all the more clearly, shining his torch on his medals, nodding and wagging a finger at us with his 'Play your silly games, my kittens!'. Mr Jumbo Man said: "So we're agreed then, twenty-sixth of July at the airport, just ask the chief for me, they'll go and fetch me, the grade 7 mechanics, you know, they drink at the Carioca, but me, on grade 8, it's my responsibility and I go last, so it's all down to me!" He had spoken and we all knocked back another shot of the liquor followed quickly and enjoyably by more beer, and Mr Procházka the roadmender woke up as usual, also knocked one back and dozed back off and slept, though his spirit was awake, nodding agreement with what was being said, or shaking its head in dissent, and whenever it spotted a need to intervene, he said his piece and slept on. Mr Franc, to help take the chimney sweep's mind off his lawsuits and the court, said: "After all your troubles, it's a good thing you can enjoy a spot of politics on the local council..." But the chimney sweep shook his head, took a newspaper, spread it over the soot-stained tablecloth, carefully sited his elbow so as not to get it dirty from the cloth, and said: "I can kiss goodbye to that too. I'd been really looking forward to the festival sub-committee meeting on the occasion of the presentation of the flag... and I'd prepared my speech, but I was hungry, and when it was my turn to speak, I got up, and was holding the microphone when they brought me a pair of frankfurters, and I could see Baštecký on my left and Horyna on my right taking one each and I hollered into the microphone: "Idiots!" That made everyone jump and only then did I register the mike, so I hollered an apology into it: "They've gone and eaten my frankfurters!" And the Chairman thanked me for my contribution and said that would do, that I'd made my position clear, since my mind was plainly on food instead of any solemn speech... And the bottle of Fernet Branca was empty and the men got up, by now the chimney sweep was walking straight and no longer

touching the tablecloths with his paws, fearing, as he put it, he'd get his clothes dirty from them.

When we came out of the pub, there was a frost, we all shot across the road, the engine oil casting us off the roadway against the far side of the ditch, into which we fell by turns. When we got to our feet, the Fernet ran us across to the other side into a wire fence. Mr Procházka the roadmender hopped on his bike and rode off, calling into the darkness: "Out of the way, folks, I'm going too fast to stop…," we saw his torch drive into the ditch, fall silent, then in a moment the light scrambled out and sat on the edge of the roadway, then it got up, gripped the shiny handlebars, wavered this way and that a few times – that was his shoelaces getting tied – and once more the light started hurtling along the road and we lay in the ditch and Mr Procházka shot past shouting: "Out of the way, folks, I'm…," and again he receded into the distance until he reached the main road and there the light rode into a snow-filled ditch. Only Mr Jumbo Man walked erect and in a straight line, and he hissed: "Shitbags!" and made off towards his cottage, his little house, to feed his dog before bed, and then in the morning, at four o'clock, he set off through the forest on his bike, taking the forest footpaths to Lysá station and then onwards to the airport, which he loved and loves as his own, more than his life. I was lying on my back in the ditch as Mr Jumbo Man pedalled past in his lightweight, blue nylon coat, gripping its tails on the handlebars to keep them out of the wheel-spokes, and with his beret perched jauntily on his head, heading off into the distance, while Mr Procházka the roadmender was again riding hither and thither on the main road and when he realised he wasn't back home, that he was going well but a hundred and eighty degrees in the wrong direction, he came hurtling back and shouted from a distance, because his bell was broken: "Out of the way, folks!" Mr Kuzmík was still lying beyond the fence and the Alsatian barking on the other side woke his master, who took his bullwhip and set off to give the innkeeper a thrashing because his patrons were making a racket, his dog was barking and he couldn't sleep, and so he found Mr Kuzmík and called to him: "Can I help you, sir?" And Mr Kuzmík, lying there, called back: "I didn't ask you for anything, you old brute, so you can leave me alone." So he lay there till morning, then he dragged himself as far as the electricity substation where he was found by the milkman, who drove him home with a broken leg. And Mr Procházka did finally make it home, but not before falling off his bike, grazing his face and ramming the bell on his handlebar into his cheek, five hours it took him to get home, just like me, though it's only half an hour on foot without engine oil. Mr Franc took only four hours on his bike and he went quietly to bed, but in the morning he was startled out of it by his wife screaming. "What's up?" he said. "Did you get drunk again yesterday?" And Mr Franc said: "Me, drunk?" And his wife grabbed him by the ear and hauled him out of bed to the window and said: "Look at that, you sodden sod!" And Mr Franc looked and there on the little snow-covered grass patch he saw his footprints like the handprints of the chimney sweep on the pub tablecloths, as if twenty people had been waiting for a bus, keeping warm by tramping up and down, and then there were a dozen or so bike-prints like spectacles wherever he'd tipped over into the snow, like turning the pages of a comic strip involving a cyclist. And while Mr Jumbo Man had long been tightening lock nuts and seals at the airport and sobering up in the cold air, Mr Procházka the roadmender was lying in bed, his face chafed from the hardened snow, and with the sunken imprint of his bell lever in his cheek, which led his granddaughter to come in and tinkle the bell-print on his face and ask: "Were you a bit sloshed last night, Grandpa?" And the roadmender, devotee of the truth that he was, made a Slav bow, prostrate, to his granddaughter and said: "Yes, I was, and I've counted a total of twenty-eight bruises, which I believe is quite a success, given that I've broken nothing, nor do I have concussion despite falling on my back several times and banging my head on the cold, frozen concrete of the road." The chimney sweep topped off the horrors of his year of tribulation by waking up in the morning in his clothes and with his brush in bed with him, he felt thirsty and popped out to his cellar to get a drink from a pot of sour milk, and as he was savouring the drink, he saw two eyes floating towards him; he thought it must be an effect of the engine oil, but the eyes got bigger and bigger until they reached his eager thirsty lips and into his mouth sailed some horrid living thing and the chimney sweep, having pulled it out, twitching, by the leg, he saw it was a tiny toad that must have fallen into the milk. Mr Zákon the landlord got a shock in the morning when he saw the tablecloths, he tried to turn them over but the soot and the sweat- and grief-soaked palms of the chimney sweep had percolated through to the other side, so there was nothing for it but to gather them all up and put out new ones... In the afternoon he went for a lie-down and as he gazed out of the window he thought he could hear a growling noise, thought he was in the cabin of a Boeing 727 Jumbo Jet and that he'd just landed, or was the giant plane about to take off with him on board? The golden mane of his wife's curly hair came in and Mr Zákon smiled at her, stroked her and asked: "No fornication under duress? Rape?" And the golden-haired beauty tipped her head and her squinting eye filled her with mystery and a forgotten culture. And Mr Zákon asked anew: "And there's no one who might endanger our marital bliss, is there?"

And his good lady blushed and shook her head and dropped her eyelids. "And there's no one to sue me for obstructing their happy marriage?" And she hugged him and gave him a kiss, of her own volition, as hadn't happened for several years. And Mr Zákon lit the stove, which hadn't been lit for a year, and as he went outside with the ashes, Mr Bělohlávek came cycling past, numb with cold. The publican called out to him: "Good afternoon, Mr Jumbo Man, d'you fancy popping in for a chat? A dram? I've got the stove on now!"

And Mr Jumbo Man nodded, but he was back to his timid, shy, awkward self and, blushing, he rode on, to turn off down one of the avenues and go and feed his little dogs and dream about the Jumbo and his marriage, which had broken down, just like the chimney sweep's.

7 MAZÁNEK'S WONDER

MR FRANC WAS SITTING on a bench in the middle of his orchard in full bloom, revelling in the blooming apple trees, and when he saw me watching him through the wire fence, he stretched and gave voice to his satisfaction: "Wonderful, eh? See how the little pink flowers above me keep falling on my head, that one's Mazánek's Wonder... and here," he got up and went under the apple petals showering down in the gentle breeze, "this is Kronzel Green, the best thing when you're shredding cabbage is to toss a few of these in...," he chatted away, and his huge figure in dungarees, with his legs shoved into rubber boots, bobbed along from one spreading apple-tree sunshade to the next, and as he went he stroked the trunks, as as if caressing the living bodies of girls, the way a workman strokes your bathroom when he's finished tiling it, he also appreciates his work with a nice stroke, just like a carpenter stroking a chair and table or anything else that has issued from his hands and tools. "It could be so nice here," said Mr Franc, coming over to the fence and sinking his fingers into the wires, following me hand over hand as I walked

slowly by, like King David of yore plucking his harp to accompany his beautiful psalm. "It would be so much nicer if I wasn't forever inundated with sheep. For three years running I've been disposing of sheep, but every spring I've got six more. My ram Bombo and my oldest ewe Vojanda only have to look at each other and she's tupped... And do you see this? These petals are from Summer Astrachan, a beautiful shade of pink, like a baby's ears, but I can't sleep because of the sheep. Last year I got some great advice, so to tame the ram, I tied a chunk of railway line to his forehead with wire, fifty or seventy kilogram/metre rail it was, so he couldn't mount Vojanda and tup her... but that's to ignore what rams are like! He spent the entire night in his shed banging the rail against his iron-clad trough, all that night and the next we got no sleep, or kept waking up, there was this constant, like, bell chiming, ding dong, dong ding, him ringing his rail, and I said: "Stay calm, kids, stay calm, dearly beloved wife of mine, his strength's got to give, Bombo's got to drop, weaken..." But this one here's a Holovousy Raspberry-Pink, takes your breath away when it's in bloom, it does...," so the giant Mr Franc rambled on, pitching his mouth so that, as he walked by, the delicate flowers would touch his fleshy lips, and he scented their scent, and as he touched the flower-heads he wallowed in the sun-warmed sprigs and blossoms... "And wouldn't you know it," he wailed woefully, again plucking a tune out on the wire fence, "even with that chunk of rail he did mount Vojanda and tup her, and that little ewe there as well, and I was mad enough to think the time when he was sexed up was over, but two months later, the ewes had got great drums for bellies, I'd culled two gimmers, but six more were born, so instead of me decimating the flock, it just grew. So old Vorlíček suggested –, but isn't this one gorgeous, just look at it!" Like a German spaniel, like a gun dog, he stopped, still with his paws in the wires, and with his legs slightly flexed as he was overcome with sheer delight. "This is another Mazánek's Wonder, grafted this one myself, I did, but just see how lovely Nature is, how things that bloom are so full of love-liness!... Going back to rams, old man Vorlíček suggested I stick a small tyre over Bombo's, that's my ram's, head and one front leg, claiming that such a contrivance would dampen his ardour, it would make it technically impossible for him to mount Vojanda, and so I could put a stop to the flood of ram lambs and gimmers... it was awful to watch, the poor ram having to go about on three legs, always falling on his face, so I ended up feeling quite sorry for him, but what do you know, three months later I'd got six more sheep, Bom-bo, supposedly incapacitated with the tyre, still went and tupped all the ewes, and it's driving me mad, I still want to enjoy life a bit, I want to cut them down to twelve, and I'm back to twenty-one again, and there's no end to it, no end...," Mr Franc moaned, tucking the fingers of each hand in turn through the wires of the wire fence and plucking them like a harp, and petals came pouring down onto his massive frame, his chubby cheeks showered alternately by a dense confetti of petals... and Mr Franc comforted them: "Now, now, little petals, dear petals, what's the matter...," so worried was he for them, and he shook the blossomy bounty from his face... and I looked towards his cottage in the forest, nothing but pine trees all around, but in the middle of the clearing his blossoming orchard stood proud, you could tell how well manured the grass was, how well filled out the apple trees' trunks were, but Mr Franc suffered endlessly... "How wonderful it would be if it weren't for those blasted hornets and wasps, see?" he pointed and only then did I notice that each trunk was adorned, like the handlebars of racing cyclists, with two milk bottles, and Mr Franc explained: "I can't abide wasps, there's a few drops of beer in each bottle... now you suffer, suffer in your turn... you torment me, wasps, now it's your turn to be tormented!" he was shouting, and I could see lots of dead wasps and hornets at the bottom of the bottles, and others struggling hard, but falling into the beer, getting up again and so it went on until they weakened and died, because there was no escaping from such a bottle. Mr Franc suddenly stopped, looking bedazzled, staring out beyond the orchard, beyond the milk-bottles and the drowning wasps, but, like a prophet, gazing up into the very sky, where I was certain he could see, if not the Holy Trinity, then surely a circle of blaring organs, or maybe a saint was looking down on him from Heaven and extending a hand to him, meaning to pull him straight up to join him, among Heaven's fluffy white and dark black clouds... he lay a finger on his fleshy lips and spoke in ecstasy... "I've got it, I've got it, I've figured it out! No rails, no tyres on the ram, I've got to start from the ewes... I'll make them some little panties, the kind they sell for rich dogs, bitches... I'll make the ewes some whatnots... panties!, out of a sack, an extra thick sack, little trews... contraceptive bikini bottoms... whatyamacallits," he said in a daze, and with the next puff of the breeze Mr Franc was standing in a glorious blizzard of petals from a Glassy Gold, as if he'd just tugged on a shower chain, and as he stood there in the dense shower of petals, in his dungarees and muddy rubber boots, the sound of a woman shouting came from the house... "You stupid boy, you've gone an' shat yerself again!" And a young, heavily-built woman came running out, shaking a little boy at arm's length, she ripped his trousers off and set about rinsing them in a wooden tub, picking out the little turds with evident distaste... and Mr Franc let out a low groan: "How nice it would

be here if my little grandson wouldn't keep filling his breeks, if he wouldn't keep pooping in his pants, how nice it would be here if my rams wouldn't go around tupping one ewe after another, if there weren't all these perishing wasps...," and the young woman called across to Mr Franc: "Grandpa, what are you gawpin' at? Go an' see to the sheep at pasture, and make sure you're back afore dark this time... d'you hear?" Like a flag flapping, her voice flayed the forest air, and it was as beautiful as the young woman herself, Mr Franc's daughter, powerfully built and curly-haired, full of figure and rosy of complexion, with her hair in ringlets that danced circles above her large eyes, and her voice that was as nothing compared to the voice that now rang out from the porch and thundered through the Scots and other pines like a tempest until their branches groaned audibly, and that voice so stirred the air, in the absence of any wind, that in the orchard petals came pouring down like flakes in a snowstorm: "Jerry!" the voice hacked into the air, and Mrs Franc appeared on the porch, a giant of a woman, the voice's owner: "Where are you?" the voice thundered on, "Here," wheezed Mr Franc. "You haven't got time for jawin', you should be out at the pasture...!" The voice sounded jangly and angry, and yet not unkind, I expect that in such a secluded spot in the forest people have to shout at each other, because by shouting they afford proof of their existence, of the love they have for one another... "Don't worry, I've only been here a short while, I'm enjoying the view...," said Mr Franc, resting his forehead against the trunk of Mazánek's Wonder. "Come off it," Mrs Franc shouted from the porch, "you've been away half an hour!" Mr Franc held his ground: "Quarter of an hour..." But Mr Franc's daughter and wife roared with great gusto: "Half an hour you've been gone!" And Mr Franc banged his forehead gently against the trunk of the apple tree and whispered: "But I've only been here a short while... it would be beautiful here if it weren't for the rams, if it weren't for the wasps, if it weren't for the shouting...," and he ambled off, waving back, and the two women on the porch hollered until the pine trunks bent and their branches cracked in the canopy: "Half an hour you've been gone!" And the woman disappeared, she reappeared on the porch with an alarm clock, and she pointed at the dial of the ancient Austrian alarm clock, which now started to jangle, giving out such a ghastly two-tone jangle that Mrs Franc had to wrestle with it as if it were an animal, as if it were some recalcitrant, silver bird of prey caught in her fingers. And the two women shrieked with glee and stood round Mr Franc: "So, is the alarm clock telling a lie? Go on, say something!" And Mr Franc rested his head against the cement and mica rendering of his cottage and gently knocked his forehead at the plaster, which came off and stuck to his damp forehead, and he gave in: "I confess, I confess... I was –, I disappeared for half an hour, but I was feasting my eyes in the garden of delight on Mazánek's Wonder... Summer Astrachan...," and the women jangled with laughter, and Mrs Franc descended one step, she was magnificent with a magnificent bosom and as she bent slightly forward, the centre of gravity of her breasts slid down to level with the step and she was lucky to grab hold of a window box full of dead petunias...

Then came summer, Mr Franc would lead his sheep to pasture on a fresh clearing in the pinewood, with a sack and a transistor radio, he would lie back on his sack, turn on the transistor and wallow in satisfaction at having put one over on Bombo the ram, his ewes being all wrapped in sacking, the sacks neatly stitched round their pelvic region, but Bombo the ram went for Mr Franc several times with such violence that once he had to sit on top of the bowser in the middle of the field, but the ram didn't give up, he'd have killed him, and Mr Franc knew as much, so he kept calling for help until the ewes came and guided the by then starving Mr Franc back home themselves. There was another time when the ram Bombo attacked Mr Franc because of the chastity bikinis, and there was pine bark flying all over the place, and Mr Franc, although the pasture was only half an hour away, took three and a half hours to get back home, ducking and diving from one pine tree to the next... but Mr Franc laughed it off, because he believed it was the ram's righteous reprisal for the contraceptive panties having served their purpose... though in three months' time the sacks starting swelling suspiciously, splitting at the seams, and Mr Franc realised that the ram Bombo was doing better than ever even despite the ewes' contraceptive bikinis...

I continued on alongside the fence and Mr Franc fingered the strings of the fence like the wretched King David, singing to me his lamentations and psalms... "It would be so beautiful here, such a good crop, look, there'll be a good two tubfuls of Summerglaze, not to mention the Summer Astrachan, I even feed them to the sheep, but out of the twenty-one, there's bound to be another six of them tupped... and three years back I wanted to cut them down to twelve and now there'll be getting on for thirty... at home no one except me eats them... but whenever there's lots of apples," he wailed, "there's also lots of wasps, just look at them! The bottles are forever full, I top the beer up every single day, and you can't keep the little gits' numbers down, any more than the sheep..." he wailed and strummed and slowly his rubber boots fell into step with the psalm and his fingers plucked at the strings.... "Jerry, Jerry," he wailed like the old King... "it's all piling up against you, everything you don't want to, the flock and the wasps... and here, look, remember this one...," Mr Franc brightened, "it's a Mazánek's Wonder! One of them's going to have five tubfuls of apples... but this one, which I grafted onto an old rootstock, it must have caught cold and here it's got just this one beautiful apple, see how it's smiling at me, like my little grandson, like the cheeks of a pretty young lass... see, my pride and joy... but what the − ?" he yelped in horror and dug all his fingers hard into the harpstrings of the wire fence. "What am I seeing, or maybe dreaming?" And he fetched a ladder and set it up against the old trunk and clambered up into the leaves, branches and twigs and called back down: "There's a wasp in Mazánek's Wonder! A wasp!" Mr Franc was aghast and his rubber boots slid back down the ladder... And Mr Franc fell silent and after a moment he popped and got some huge clippers, the size of a scythe, like two scythe blades turning on a stud bolt, and he smiled quietly, then, exasperated and resentful, he climbed up into the young twigs, opened the clippers and watched for the wasp to crawl back out of the apple in which it had already gnawed a hole as big as itself, bigger even..., and as the wasp reversed out of the sweet flesh, Mr Franc squeezed the clippers and nipped the wasp in half, and he looked at me triumphantly and gave vent to his feelings: "Little sod, that's for tormenting me, now she's in for her own torment...," he revelled, but another infuriated wasp emerged from the apple, as if coupled to an axle-tree of vespine vengeance, and went straight for Mr Franc's face, he just raised the shears, like two scythes they gleamed in the glittering summer sun, and Mr Franc threw his arms out as in religious ecstasy, raised them to the heavens, the shears hesitated for a second then crashed with the force of gravity into the grass, sinking up to the hilt in the soft earth... and Mr Franc slid down the ladder onto the grass and lay on his back, then he propped himself up on one arm and fingered the bruise growing beneath his eye and the swelling left by the wasp's poison dart... and he rolled over and lay there lifeless... And a tyrannical female voice came from the porch: "Jerry!" and the voice was peevish and nourished by a fine anger, which was at the same time sheer glee at shouting, joy at possession of such a beautiful voice, such a vocal resource... and again even louder, until the apples shook on their stalks and the one that had been munched at proved too weak and fell to earth with the power of the voice... "Where are you? Just you wait!" the voice shouted and disappeared, and a moment later, there on the porch, glinting in the sun was the Austrian alarm clock, and the lady with the stupendous voice and frontage ran out into the garden of delight with the alarm clock jangling away in her hand, and she knelt down in the shade and the green of the grass and the scintillating colour-washes of the sun and yelled: "What are doing here asleep? Get up...," but Mr Franc lay there, then he came to, propped himself up on the wet grass with one arm, the alarm clock jangled, Mr Franc was saying something, but the alarm clock out-jangled him... and when it finished jangling, Mrs Franc bent down and said: "Oh, no! A wasp sting... ambulance, ambulance!" She kept calling out and clapping her hands to her chubby cheeks and Mr Franc lay there as if felled, terribly pale... and then someone or other came along in a car, ran across and knelt down beneath Mazánek's Wonder and set down on the ground a dazzlingly white first-aid kit with a dazzlingly red cross on the top, even its little brass key was unbelievably shiny... And her daughter ran out, and this gorgeous creature with curls falling into her gorgeous eyes screamed: "What have you done, Grandpa?" And she shook Mr Franc, set him back on his feet, with incredible strength for a kid she lifted her sixteen-stone father, but as soon as she got him upright in his rubber boots, he slid down again, as if he had no bones, just flesh – just overalls, pants and anorak on chopsticks... but he did come to and as they were about to pile him into the car, he raised himself on the ground, commanded silence with an expiring gesture of an expiring hand and said in an expiring voice: "Farewell, my darlings, farewell, my rams, farewell, my ewes, farewell my Sudeten Reinette, farewell my Mazánek's Wonder, farewell, my faithful little dog…" And Mrs Franc raised the Austrian alarm clock ready to strike and was about to smash it on Mr Franc's head, screaming, if in a low voice: "You ought to be ashamed! What's to become of me…? Me?" And his daughter: "Grandpa, what's to become of us, us?" And she pushed her little son forward for Mr Franc to bless him… And Mr Franc added: "And farewell, darlings, farewell, my Wonder, farewell, my faithful wife…," and his daughter said: "Grandpa can't tolerate wasp venom, that's the trouble, you see," she shouted, and Mr Franc fainted.

Ivarna
Tonka

8 THE SNOWDROP FESTIVAL

KERSKO FOREST IS SO DEEP that, as the legendary Czech wrestler Gustav Frištenský tells us, a black member of his professional Graeco-Roman group got lost in it and Frištenský never saw him again, as he says in his Memoirs. I was looking for Mr Liman, and I was so long looking for him that I nearly got lost in the forest, because I was facing a tumbledown cottage, a number of byres and an outhouse, in front of which, on a chair, sat an old man in dungarees, his white hair sticking out like horns, such strange strands his hair was in, like long coils of steel swarf, like wood shavings all intertwined and interlocking. He sat there and chickens were pecking all round him and he was scattering grain for them. I said: "Nice spot this, isn't it?" And he nodded and said: "It is too, but you're not from these parts, are you?" As I explained I'd only recently bought a second home, a cottage really, on Avenue Twenty-four the old boy interrupted and said in a sonorous voice that he knew the spot, that that part was called Nouzov, that the plots were bordered by a babbling brook called the Velenka, and that the meadow had belonged to the

Králs from Hradišťko, the meadow known as Alder Lea. I said how pleased I was that, if nothing else, the air here was wonderful. "True," he said, "the air hereabouts is raw, but wholesome, and then Kersko, a forest-city, is divided up and numbered on the model of New York, the metalled concrete road is like Fifth Avenue, and the avenues off to the side, they're like streets, if you leave the main thoroughfare, then on the right-hand side they're even-numbered, and on the left odd, so if you were to look down on this forest-city from above, the layout's like a fern frond," he said and stood up, and his hair stuck out awesomely, and it struck me that the tips of the curls could poke an eye out if they were made of bronze. He stood legs apart and asked: "Can I be of service? Are you looking for someone?" I said: "I am, but I'll not find him now, but tell me, how long is the metalled road, the concrete one?" Pleased at the chance to show off his knowledge, he said: "From the bus-stop to the Semice–Hradišťko road, it's two thousand three hundred and forty-eight metres, as measured by Mr Procházka the roadmender," he said, and he fetched a red folding chair, wiped the chicken poo off it and invited me to sit down. I thanked him, getting a whiff of the byre and an indeterminate, rank stench, but the old man was so behorned with that hair, and such was the power emanating from the tips of his curls that my impression was, as I gazed in amazement at his chrome-coloured hair, that in the event of a storm it must start discharging St Elmo's fire. I said: "I've heard there's an ancient pine tree somewhere round here and I'd like to see it." He glanced at the little pendulum clock hanging from a pine branch, and its striker struck the hour in a frenzy and with great gusto and a noise like a woodpecker... "I'm still all right for time... so, you mean Showy Toni? You're dead right, she's a beauty, magnificent, if you look up into her canopy and the sun's shining, the canopy's like that window in St Vitus' Cathedral, the spokes and fellies of her branches are absolutely precise, and she swings steadily in a circle with such precision... She was planted in 1620, and not far off there's her little sister, the rangers call her Slinky Tonietta, I think she's even more beautiful, with a little topknot, and her branches close kempt, like a pixie cut... and she's also a giant, except that her trunk got so gouged by lightning that her growth rate slowed...," said the old gentleman and a gentle breeze blew back the silken branches of a little birch grove, and the old boy extended a hand as if to caress them, and he did caress them, fingering the little leaves and restoring emotion to them. I could tell he was a sensitive old man and that he lived at the expense of the elements, and in harmony with nature, as befitted his age. He carried on, constantly putting out his hand, now as if he were warming himself at the flickering flames of the leaves wafting on the birch twigs: "We've got another classy number here as well if you go along Avenue Six, known as Nymburk Way, you go as far as the tract we call The Crest, right, and there by the brook you'll see a spruce, half its height jutting over the other spruces around it, it must be two hundred years old and more, and its nine lower branches are twisted upwards in such a way that their ends are like roots with more spruces shooting up from them, nine spruces, ten metres tall, and the tree holds them aloft like a juggler juggling plates on nine sticks, though plates spin round, it actually resembles a massive candlestick, that giant spruce..." He had spoken, and he lit a cigarette and sat on a chair next to me and his overalls, dribbled with gravy and something that smelled pretty awful, gave off such a terrible stink that I turned to leeward... For something to say, I suggested there might be a lot of woodcock in the area and pointed towards the birch grove that began beyond his plot and was twinkling over his fence. He took a long drag on his cigarette and it was almost like a light coming on next to his mouth, as if he'd bitten the cigarette off, so short it had become, and then the smoke came scudding out of his mouth, resembling the long, solid curls jutting out like little sabres jammed into his head. "This isn't their time, and there aren't many anyway, the days are long gone when assistant foresters would bet a bottle of wine that they could bag twenty or thirty in an evening. Woodcock do their celebratory mating dance around the end of March or beginning of April, after the sun's gone down and the first star's come out... the males fly about making a glorious love call and the females sit around in the cold grass listening..." He had spoken, he cleared his throat, a prolonged rasping cough rasped forth from him and the cuckoo flew out of the clock and rasped in exactly the same way, marking five o'clock. "I know," the old man told the clock, and he took another colossal drag and again it was as if he'd bitten off part of the cigarette, so far down had it burned, lighting up the stub... As he spoke, he pointed with his cigarette: "No more woodcock, a pair here and a pair there, but, come July, you do get nightingales warbling away in the night, magnificent, if you keep a lookout, nightingales also warble in your avenue, in the oaks at the forest edge... it's a violin performance, it's like when an artist starts cutting a beautiful image in a plate of pure crystal with a diamond stylus. I can't sleep a-nights, I prowl around, following the voices of the nightingales, and here...," he patted his chest, "...here I have this sensation of sweetness and I'm happy that there's still something beautiful so close by... but there's most nightingales by the ruins of Mydlovary Castle, across the river, like if you were to go from Přívlaky towards Kámen, or – you're a young fellow – if you go dancing at Kocáneks' in Hradišťko during the parish fête... after midnight, if you take a stroll with a pretty girl past the King of Clubs into the fields, across the football pitch at Ruždiny... then with the stream of cold air coming up off the water along the track the song gets louder and louder, and not one, but three, a quartet, sometimes I've heard as many as six nightingales, for an hour, an hour and a half, giving out a thin silvery thread and embroidering with their voices a violin concerto with no recapitulations, and when it falls silent you can spot one sitting, exhausted, on a branch, you can see the little chap must have lost at least twenty grams... and even if he were to shed half a kilo, tell me, why do they sing like that, and who for?" He'd spoken and was grave and so deeply affected that he bent a little and wiped away a tear with the back of his hand... and the spikes of his hair stood there right before my eyes and nose and I caught the dreadful smell emanating from that cornucopia of odours and it made me see stars and I leaned away so far that I lost my balance and fell flat on my back and as my legs flew up I caught him on the forehead with one knee. I rolled quickly over into the fallen leaves and as I dusted myself down, I saw I was covered in chicken poo, and I blushed, but as the old man stood over me I realised he was taller than me by a head and his gigantic arms were raised to form like a little shrine above me and he tried to be reassuring: "Don't do that now, you'd just rub it

in, once it dries it'll flake off... but let me draw you a map, since you're new round here, you don't have to mind about the people, but do mind about nature, to start with, avenues six and four, between them there's a clearing, and there you'll see hundreds of Siberian irises in bloom, and if ever you go to Mydlovary, across the river, I'm off there myself in a moment, you'll find some centuries-old oak trees, and one of them is so hollow that twenty or thirty people have sheltered from a storm inside it! But I've always liked going there and dancing in the spring, and sometimes even now: did you know, there was this lovely old custom last century when the young folk would meet under those old oaks and the girls would deck themselves with snowdrops and dance to the music of the band, right there beneath those ancient giants of the forest? Incidentally, why did you stop at my gate, why? Were you looking for some-one, not me, surely?" He pointed at the top of his dungarees, from which chicken droppings were hang-ing adrift, like ancient medals... "No," I lied, "I was just passing, but I'm glad you told me all about the forest." He gestured with his hand and, to the cuckoo, which had just popped out of the Black Forest clock, cuck-ooed and clattered back inside its coop, he said: "I know, give me half an hour and I'm off, but do you know what else is worth seeing hereabouts? Come the autumn, that little knoll over there, it's called Semická, is covered in hundreds, thousands of blue fringed gentians and yellow hawkweeds! They get scrunched by tractor tyres day after day, yet there's always more and more of them... and if you go a bit further west to the hill called Bílá, above Přerov, there you'll find, you won't believe this, wild asparagus, I mean, asparagus!" And he placed his hands on my shoulders and only then did I notice that his entire arms were dappled with chicken poo, and that his hair was full of bits of straw and chaff and scraps of hay and several flaky chicken droppings, all like bits of leaves fallen from birches that were old before their time, but now the old boy seemed in a bit of a hurry, he looked straight at me, beating time with one hand as he quickened his delivery: "Do you know that planks cut from the pines in this forest are a lovely copper colour and that they turn red with age? And do you know that in olden times pines from Kersko were floated all the way to Hamburg? And do you know that in olden times the drive shafts in Dutch windmills were made from Kersko oaks? That the fortress at Theresienstadt used up five hundred Kersko oaks in beams and planking? And do you know that you enter the council offices and three different cottages in Hradišťko through Gothic windows, which peasants made into doorways having taken them from the ruins of the little church at Kersko that got destroyed during the Hussite wars? And do you know that they used to make ships' masts out of Kersko larches? And do you know that what we call Lablets are oxbow lakes detached from the Labe, as the great River Elbe is known hereabouts, and that they're home to white and yellow water-lilies and greater spearwort, and spiked loosestrife? And do you know that the St Joseph Spring comes up from seventy-eight metres below ground and that its waters arrive along a fault all the way from the Jizera Mountains and that the water takes seventy years to get here? Do you also know which cottage in Kersko is the most beautiful? Right next to the concrete road, in Avenue Twenty-one, built by a ship's captain and made to look like a cabin cast up on the wave of a sand dune?" In a kind of fit, the old man hurled question after question and I wanted nothing more than for him to let go of me, the smell of his dungarees being in excess of a cowshed's, the quintessence of ripeness that threatened to wreak havoc – a faint or allergy, hives or maybe even death. And the old Black Forest clock began to strike, striking like mad, as if to upbraid the old boy, and swishing away with its pendulum like a nervous cow with its tail... And the old man came to and told the cuckoo, before it popped back in its coop: "I know..." And he kicked at the latch of the outhouse, the door of which swung open under its own weight and angle of suspension, and inside the shed, utterly filthy with chicken poo, stood an ivory-coloured luxury

car, the latest Ford with automatic transmission and sliding doors, studded with chicken poo, and with some chickens dozing away inside… And the old boy laughed and watched me, having let on he was the very man I'd been looking for and I hadn't recognised him, and he'd hidden from me so brilliantly in this retreat of his that never in my wildest dreams would I have expected what I was seeing now. And the old man swept the chickens away with an elbow, walked round the car and stood there amid a flurry of wing-flapping chickens who made hastily for the outside over his head and arms… and the old man, as he was, pressed a button and the door slid up into the Ford's roof, the very Ford that I'd heard was at Mr Liman's, and so there I was now, at Mr Liman's, and I'd wanted to ask where Mr Liman lived, though what I'd been told was right, it was just that the old man and his dungarees had confused me, but he knew I'd come to ask if he'd sell the car, he knew I was looking for Mr Liman, but he knew that the best thing is to cover one's tracks, like a fox, and then pop up at the far end when you're least expected… And the Ford rolled out of the shed and was a sight to behold, and I saw – how could I not see? – that Mr Liman was that one-time millionaire, the one whose sons in America sent him a car every year, and that it quite suited him, like some bank president, for all he was covered in chicken poo… and Mr Liman hopped lightly out of the car, leaving chicken poo-prints on the leather seat and the whole car full of feathers, but it all suited Mr Liman nicely, chickens and all. "I know," I said, "You're Mr Liman." He bowed and said: "That I am...," and, to complete my surprise, he opened the door of the other shed with its window onto the little garden, and out shot two billy-goats, almost knocking me over and followed by that awful stench, which now gave explanation of its source, and the billies were overtaken by a nanny-goat, and Mr Liman stood there like some god and bellowed: "Bobby, Lucky, Janey! Time to graze! Let's be having you!" And as the nanny-goat and one of the billies tried to scramble into the car, they got their horns tangled in the door, but the nanny-goat was quicker and she went and sat by a window and watched impatiently for the car to start, the reeking billy-goats went and sat with her and Mr Liman got into the driving seat, pressed a button and the doors slid back down from the roof, Mr Liman wound the window down and behind him there was a crunching sound and a fearsome, dry crackling of leather, and I saw all three goats' hooves digging into the leather, tearing it, and I felt a sensation of their hooves digging away inside my brain, I could feel my meninx cracking, ripping as the goats' feet sank into it, but Mr Liman laughed and said: "It tickles me pink to watch Bobby and Janey fighting over the window seat on the right..." "But what's with the left window?" I asked. "Lucky has that one, but you get a nice view of the river from the right one, see? Now, young man, we're going down to the river, then we'll row across to the other side to the Mydlovary meads, and there the goats will graze and I'll play my transistor and, under the ancient oaks and in remembrance of the snowdrop festival, I'll maybe do a little dance, with all the goats, like an old faun, an afternoon *of a faun, don't you know...*" And he beeped the horn and the Ford, six metres long, ivory-white, set off down the avenue of birches, whose tiny leaves were all a-flutter in the blazing sunlight, in the wafting perfume of blooming oleasters, oleasters blossoming somewhere beyond New Meads, which Mr Liman was now entering with his animals, taking them to pasture.

9 FRIENDS

WHENEVER LOTHAR COMES, things always get jolly in Kersko, because Lothar is the jolliest person in central Europe. When he arrives from Würzburg in his posh car, we're already waiting for him, and there's all the hugging and the laughter and smiling, Lothar shakes everyone's hands with his powerful arms, and there's all the planning where to take him, where to broach a keg of beer with him at night and barbecue some chickens and drink Jim Beam, the Kentucky whiskey that he always brings several bottles of, and we only ever smoke Pall Mall. We always get out a crate of Popovice Billy-goat beer, because Lothar loves nothing so much as beer and he can drink it with relish from first thing in the morning to bedtime, and even then he puts a few bottles in buckets beside his bed in case he wakes up in the night, in case he gets woken up by thirst. He always stays in the white cottage in the woods that belongs to Pavel, who keeps coming out in his wheelchair, impatient to see his friend arriving, banging away at the wheelchair's tyres with the palms of his hands, going round and round in circles and listening,

then going back inside disappointed and riding his wheelchair straight into the hallway, since his little white house has only one, low-pitched step, a step that looks like a diving board, and Pavel rides on into the kitchen, bends over a pot of goulash, stokes the fire, then comes riding impatiently back out into the woods, round to the back of the house, there to stoke the smokehouse, opening the little door to check by hand that the sausages and gammon are smoking nicely, all the time until Lothar's car tootles a view halloo at the crossroads and his Opel approaches down the forest track and Lothar's jolly face beams from the open window, his hand waves a greeting, but then goes straight back to the steering-wheel, because Pavel and Lothar alike have got both brake and clutch and accelerator on the steering wheel, just as if they were driving using their feet. And Lothar, having come to a halt, opens the door, and after he's shaken hands with all those waiting to greet him, his nephew, or if he's arrived alone, then Olina, the beautiful rehabilitation nurse, so beautiful that it might be Audrey Hepburn herself who has strayed into the Kersko Forest, Olina, who is Pavel's fiancée and is mind-bogglingly good at everything she does, Olina parks the wheelchair she's extracted from the boot beside Lothar and he, with the aid of his strong arms, moves over: taking his lifeless legs in his hands he keeps shifting them across until he can place them on the wheelchair and with a rolling motion he heaves his powerful frame into the chair and then he rides up and down, limbering up after the long drive, and as he rides about he whoops and laughs merrily, and Pavel, who adores Lothar, rides about with him, and it's a kind of dance of incapacitated nymphs, a dance in which, as they ride about, they shriek and shout to one another, calling out in their sheer joy all the things they're going to do today and tomorrow, and Lothar, because he knows, rides round to the back of the cottage and sniffs the smoky scent of the meat coming from the smoke-house and he and Pavel keep up the shouting until Olina comes out with a chopping board and Lothar, impatient, though warned by Pavel that it's not ready yet, can't resist, and he takes a piece out, burning his fingers, then puts the first piece to the test with great relish and Pavel rides off to fetch some beer, riding back into the hallway and there, at the foot of a wall hung with dozens of certificates and awards from regional motorcycle races, there, beneath the faded flowers and blanched ribbons, awards that Pavel had once won as a motorcycle racer, Pavel places some bottles of cold beer on his lap and rides back out into the light, pounding away at his tyres so as to be back with his friend as quickly as possible, and with the bottle-opener that hangs permanently from a string on his wheelchair, he opens a fine lager and offers it to his friend. Meanwhile,

Olina gets Lothar's luggage from the car, takes it up-
stairs to the little attic room where Lothar will be
sleeping, she smiles in silence and she, whatever she
does, from whatever side and angle you look at her, is
always photogenic and doesn't need to say anything,
just like Audrey Hepburn. And even after Lothar has
more or less drunk his fill, he keeps downing beers with
such zest as if Lothar plus beer were a bold advertise-
ment for the very beer he happened to be drinking, so
that anyone who isn't thirsty and sees him drinking,
develops a thirst, and anyone who doesn't drink beer
rues his abstinence, because no one round here has ever
met such a jolly and witty character except for Leli, who
is, like Lothar, not only jolly, but also well-read and a
mine of information. And Lothar wasted no time in
reporting the news from the wider world, whether he'd
won or lost playing the stock market, because from the
moment Lothar wakes, he listens to the radio all morning and reads all the papers, then he has lunch and goes
off to his little workshop, where he tunes in to Saarlän-
discher Rundfunk, which plays music and offers traffic
information to drivers and anyone else who's listening,
and meanwhile Lothar makes beautiful things out of
metal, repairs things for his neighbours, anything they
bring him, he's got his own welding machine and oxy-
acetylene torch, every conceivable set of drill bits and
a little lathe. On one occasion, Pavel, having come back

from Lothar's, said that not even the company he worked for, which developed racing bikes, had a workshop to compare with his. Lothar rides around his workshop and he sings and slowly drinks his lager, these days his preference is for beverages from the Pschorr brewery, he rides around and works away, because, as in his car, everything in his workshop is within reach, he just raises a hand and whatever tool he wants is there, he looks out of the window into the garden, where his mother's working, and Lothar never complains, he would, but he never affords himself the time to complain or start cursing, what happened happened and he's come to terms with it, he's had to come to terms with what happened to him, and having decided not to kill himself, he has staked everything on a perfectly ordinary life, and wherever he puts in an appearance, jollity breaks out, and Lothar hands out information left, right and centre, everything he's learned from all the channels that flow his way – books, radio, television and talking to people, and to everything he tacks on his own optimistic view that all that is good must be good, even his wheelchair and broken back, even that's good, because it's happened and there's nothing to be done but come to terms with it. And Lothar also speaks Czech, no surprise there, given that as recently as five years ago he was in the Chomutov weightlifting and wrestling teams, and he used to work as a welder, a Czechoslovak citizen, but of German nationality, he had a family, a son, but one day, as he was down a mine welding something with a friend at a height of six metres, the assembly they were working on crumpled and his friend fell into a pile of soot and Lothar fell on his back on a large lump of coal and cracked his spine so badly that six months later he was transferred as permanently immobilised to an old people's home, where he just wept and thought of ways to get out of this broken life, the more so after his wife divorced him and he was left all alone. And at that point he remembered his sister, who was a confectioner in Spessart, and his mother, who'd been removed from Czechoslovakia many years before during the postwar expulsions of Germans, then he left for Germany himself to be near his mother and sister, and so having got a pension of two thousand marks he started to live, he healed and steeled himself, and so now he comes to Kersko to see Pavel, who he'd got to know at the Heidelberg Olympic Games, during the paralympic javelin competition. All we know about Pavel is that his dream was to make as big a mark as František Šťastný, he'd raced motorbikes, won one district or regional race after another, as testified by the certificates on the wall in his hallway, but one day after he'd won a race, a friend came along and dragged him out of bed to go hunting for girls out Sázava way, and as they were riding along on the winning bike, Pavel went into a skid and landed so badly in the dark that he was left unconscious, and his friend, the one who'd dragged him out of bed, and that's probably where things went wrong, hauled him from the middle of the road towards the verge, and that's probably where things went wrong again, because Pavel says that when Professor Jirásek was operating on him he suddenly felt his legs leaving him, his body was lying there, but the legs were going and going and kept going and he saw his legs walking along as just trousers, he saw them going off beyond the far horizon, and when he shouted out, his legs disappeared beyond the horizon for good. And ever since he pulled himself together, he's had to trundle aound in his wheelchair, and he's got everything you work with your feet in the car adapted to his hands, and also, before he came to terms with it, he couldn't believe it, whenever he woke up in the morning and looked up at the ceiling, he thought it had all been a dream, but when he sat up and wanted to swing his legs out, he couldn't, so he'd quickly get into his wheelchair, go quickly down in the lift, roll himself quickly into his car and strain to haul the folded wheelchair in after him, and he would drive about, all over the place, all day long, for days on end, until after six months of driving around, with the movement denied to him entrusted to his tyres, he regained his composure, grew more relaxed and finally convinced

himself that he had to accept what he had, live as best he could, trust in those things that tallied with his lot, and for the first time he smiled, then he laughed, and laughed long, until he laughed himself into that quiet smile in which he found that a legless man can live in this world, enjoying perhaps a greater sensation of living than all those other folk who can run around. And the two friends each had their own truth, their moral fibre was so awesome that all who knew Lothar and Pavel, however slightly, if ever they were a bit despondent, if ever they began to wonder if life was worth living under such-and-such conditions, they'd all…, me too, when, at moments of such blasphemous thoughts, I think of Pavel and Lothar, I feel ashamed of myself compared to the moral compass that backs Pavel and Lothar's view of the world. And Olina, Pavel's fiancée, she's an angel you could follow about with dustpan and brush, sweeping up the feathers that fall from her wings, she came to know Pavel as a rehabilitation nurse and she fell in love with him, and he with her, and if you were to look for a pair of true lovers, forget Romeo and Juliet, forget Troilus and Cressida, forget even Radúz and Mahulena, just watch as Olina pushes Pavel along, as Olina hauls him up the steps, the six steps to steer him through the open door of the Keeper's Lodge restaurant, all you need do is watch these two lovers, these betrothed, who have already inherited the earth and are, by the power of their love and moral fibre, a living example to all who grow despondent or demand more of this world and life than is theirs to demand and so get the sulks and fret away in a corner somewhere.

One day, in the middle of April it was, Lothar came to Kersko, unannounced, but jubilant, and at once he told Pavel and Olina that he'd made a killing on the stock exchange and was going to buy a Mercedes, a diesel Mercedes, a white one, and Pavel said that if Lothar bought himself a white Mercedes, Olina would buy herself a white wedding dress, and the day that Lothar came home with a white Merc, he'd come home with a white bride. And with white April snow coming down, the two friends were so happy and in such a jolly mood that they drank all the beer in the house, and with their thirst rising to ever greater heights with all that joy, they decided to ride over to the Keeper's Lodge for some more beer and then bring more bottles home for the night, in case they got thirsty in the night, or, failing that, in the morning. So they rode out into the darkness, a darkness adorned with white flakes of snow the size of postage stamps, Pavel being pushed along by Olina and Lothar propelling his wheelchair into the blizzard with great blows from his gloved hands, each with a lighted torch between their teeth, and so over the bumps and through the spring mud they rode out of their side avenue onto the concrete road, and then they rode on with their heads down, forging through the blizzard in their fur hats, until they glimpsed a pink light issuing from the pub windows down the tunnel along which the spring snow was coming down, thick and wet. And as they grew near, the friends yelled with delight and thirst and the vision of the cosy pub, where the stove would radiate a great heat, and they revelled in the prospect and drove all the faster as if on the final straight at the Heidelberg Olympics. Then, in the pink light, they shook off the thick blanket of snow that covered them, wiped their faces and dashed away the topping of snow that had built up on their fur hats... and Olina pulled first Lothar, the heavy ninety-kilogram Lothar, up the six, snow-edged steps onto the patio, then Pavel, few others were any good at it – going up to the first step, turning 180°, then in reverse and with a mighty jerk at each step, dragging the man in his nickel-plated wheelchair up onto the patio, from where it was on the level through the doorway. I was sitting in the pub, the landlord, Mr Novák was in a lousy mood, again, treating us three drinkers as if he'd never seen us before, I sat there tight-lipped and sipped my beer, to which the ignominy had given an added bitterness, Franta Vorel was sitting by the stove and dreaming of the beautiful Hungarian girl who, years back, had combed his hair for him in the

Start inn in Starý Vestec, a Hungarian who'd never seen Franta before, nor he her, but out of the blue she'd started combing his hair and then told him she would kidnap him and take him back with her to Budapest in her car, since when he'd lived that dream, and now he was sitting there and dreaming about his glorious kidnapping to Budapest, Mr Procházka, sprawled out, was sleeping as soundly as in the dead of night, like on any other occasion, around nine he'd been overcome by the sweet sleep that granted him his health, which shone from his red face in the droplets under his nose. And suddenly the door flew open and the white snow flew in, that wet April snow, Mr Novák was holding on to the beer tap and was as astonished as I was, watching as Pavel came riding through the door, with Olina pushing along behind, steered towards a table and repeatedly wiped his wet, cold brow, then Olina went out and came back with Lothar, who was aglow with elation and hope, and the friends rubbed their hands and ordered some beers. But Mr Novák said in a strange voice: "I've just run out." And the friends stared ahead and their smiles froze, stuck to their ever-hopeful faces, and so Pavel said: "All right, we'll have some bottled, to take away...," but Mr Novák glanced towards a corner that the patrons couldn't see and said in a strange voice: "I'm out of bottled as well, delivery never made it...," so Pavel said, "We'll take a bottle of wine...," but Mr

Novák, heading for the doorway, said: "We're closing," and he took hold of the keys, a bunch of keys, and rattled them, jangling them like the last bell before closing time, closing, closing... and he opened the door, and Olina, red and rubicund, pushed first Lothar, then Pavel back out onto the patio, the white snow was falling even harder now than before, flakes the size of postage stamps came hurtling into the hallway, and a draught, a furious draught banged the pub door to, and Franta Vorel went on sighing sweetly beside the stove, dreaming on about the beautiful Hungarian girl combing his hair, and Mr Procházka went on sleeping the healthy sleep with which he restored the vigour needed for the bike ride that he would shortly undertake to return home through the forest to the village where his cottage stood. Mine host Mr Novák went back to his beer taps and drew me a pint, and mentally I rose to my feet and shouted: "Have you no shame? Have you no shame, you're a barbarian, turning customers away like that, and them in such a sorry state, I shan't be coming here again, I'll have you know, you monster, you'll never see me in here again, and if you do, it'll be while you're away, because who else but you could do anything so shameful, you, you, you...," in my mind I couldn't find the words, and when Mr Novák set the beer down in front of me, I said aloud: "How much do I owe you...," and quickly downed the beer, got up to go, pulled on my fur overcoat and rammed my cap on low over my forehead, and Mr Novák asked in parting: "Will you be in tomorrow?" And I said I would and dashed out into the blizzard and charged down the road until I caught up with the two wheelchairs by New Meads, still lighting their snow-covered way with the torches that Pavel and Lothar held in their mouths, and I offered to walk ahead of them and light the way, and I took a torch and strode ahead of the wheelchairs and lit the way, and I wanted to launch into a lament and a stream of abuse at the publican, but the bright and breezy voice of Lothar was yelling: "It's good you're planning a trip to Italy, Pavel, stop by my place on the way and we'll pop into Munich for a pint or two, the choice'll be yours, best if you leave it till the autumn when the beer tents go up, that's quite something, you'll see," Lothar jubilated, "tents for four thousand people, Löwenbräu tents and Mattheus Bräu tents and Pschorr Bräu tents and Augustiner Bräu tents, and brass bands everywhere and thousands of people and white puddings and roast ham hock, which they brush with beer to make the crackling nice and crunchy! I'll take you there, or if you come in the summer, we'll find a beer-garden, all the pubs in Munich have gardens big enough for thousands of people, the one at Augustiner Bräu alone can hold two thousand! Or suppose I took you for a Kreuzberg beer? It comes from a Dominican monastery that brews a mighty fine lager! Yes, that's where I'll take you, there's always singing in their garden and if the patrons start singing too loud, a monk in a white cowl comes along carrying a sign that says: 'The brothers are at prayer, please keep your voices down.' That's where I'll take you..." Pavel shook his little arms about in delight, quivering with excitement, "Yes, yes, yes, great idea, I can't wait, but tomorrow I'll take you to one of ours where they've got Pilsner Urquell – now which pubs have got few enough steps for us to get our wheelchairs up? *And* get to the toilets..." And Lothar interrupted Pavel, "We don't have to worry about the toilet any more, I've brought you the thing I use, you just fix it over your member the way you would a condom and down by your feet there's a flask with a tube that goes into it and you can carry on drinking for hours and only empty it down the toilet later, it's an English patent, I've got one in the car for you... so where to tomorrow then?" Pavel got to thinking amid the falling snow, I walked ahead with my eyes narrowed, but behind me I heard his ecstatic voice, as blithesome as a lark in spring... "Best thing would be to go to Sojkas', there's only one step there, three at the Pilsner place... we could manage that, or we could try the Two Cats, there's only one tiny step there, aw, to hell with it, I'll take you to Pinkas', there there's no steps at all, and the staff know me. There, that's that sorted out! You'll take care of Munich, and this week I'll see to the Staropramen... what did you say was the name of that Dominican monastery where they do such a good brew?" "It's in Bavaria, on a clifftop well beyond Munich, the Kreuzberg...," Lothar's gleeful voice roared "So you're off to Italy, and will you be seeing Bibi?" Lothar asked, and Pavel enthused: "Yes, I always look in on him, ever since we met at the rehabilitation centre in Kladruby, did you know he also married a nurse? That she helps him into his wheelchair? I'll be stopping there, in Milan, and his mother always makes me – you'd have to taste it to believe it, it's got to have all kinds of meat in it, like having the meat of six different fish to make a bouillabaisse, well this dish, it's called, and no one can make one as good as Bibi's mother, it's called Spaghetti alla Bolognese, that's what she makes for me, but listen, Lothar, you've had holidays in Italy, I've got a map at home, we'll make a cuppa and put some of your Kentucky whiskey in it and you can show me all the most wonderful places in Italy, in your own view like, and taking account of my wheelchair as well, okay?" And Lothar exclaimed: "Sure, my friend, we'll work out a honeymoon trip for you, we'll fix you a beautiful itinerary, a bit off the beaten track, little coun-try towns, and wine and food everywhere, a honeymoon away from those commercial packages..." And I strode on into the snow, and, happening to turn my face away from the direction of the buffeting blizzard, I spotted, in one of the side avenues, a Volga parked, with the police commandant leaning against it, lost in thought, just as he always popped up, so he popped up now, whenever he wasn't expected, up he popped, again he shone his torch, not on his medals, but on his forehead, his fur-trimmed cap with its glittering red star... and then he came up quietly and said quietly: "Your ID cards please, sirs...," and he signalled with his torch that we were to follow him to his Volga patrol car, then he took one ID card after another and handed them back, having inspected them in the shelter of the car, holding them through the open window to protect them from the snowflakes. "Thank you," he said, and as he returned Lothar's passport he asked: "How come you speak such good Czech?" And Lothar said: "How come? Obvious, I went to school here, I'm a former citizen of Czechoslovakia, I used to wrestle for Chomutov..." "That's all right then," said the commandant and went on: "But your Czech being so good?" And in his quiet voice, beyond which you could hear the snow rustling in the branches of the trees, landing quietly on the roadway onto the layer of snow that already lay there ankle-deep, Lothar spoke: "But I grew up among Czech boys, I went to school with Czech boys, see? Can we go now?" The commandant placed a hand on Lothar's shoulder and said quietly: "Yes, everything's in order... but I can't get my head round how good your Czech is, and the Opel parked over there, is that yours?" Lothar rode off, turned and said: "Yes, it's mine, I'm trying to sell it, it's for sale..." And I shone the torch to show the way, followed by the sound of the wheelchairs' tyres carving through the snow-covered road, no one had gone that way yet, we were advancing down a road pure and unsullied by boot or tyre, each of us relishing the mystique of first footfall and tyrefall on the lying snow, through which no one had walked or ridden before us... And from far behind came the voice of the commandant: "And what are you going to buy?" Lothar put his hands to his mouth and shouted: "A white Mercedes, white as this snow...," and we listened out, but the policeman just emitted a sigh... and then we were silent, thinking perhaps of the policeman, who, leaning against his Volga, was staring silently into the tumbling snow, maybe silently relishing the descent of the snow that added charm to his time on duty, just as, in the summer months, he would relish the scents wafting across New Meads in the night and watch as the late moon rose... We said good night at the parting of the ways and the two friends were shivering with cold and a longing to be back indoors, in the warmth of the stove, there to spread a big book of Italy out on the table and draw in and map out the white honeymoon route for Pavel and Olina, once Lothar had bought his white Mercedes. For some little while I stood and looked at the white house with its lights on and saw a light go on on the stairs that led up to the study in the loft, I saw Lothar disappear from his wheelchair and then I saw him, like when soldiers crawl through hostile territory, haul himself up with his powerful arms one step at a time, dragging his powerless legs behind him... and then Pavel the same, by his elbows... and I saw how they both had to pause half-way, how though the trip to the pub hadn't got the better of them, those twelve stairs had, and they had to summon all their strength, turn and turn about, to haul themselves up to the top. And, with all the lights on in the white house, the two friends were surely talking about the white honeymoon trip, about all the world's beautiful breweries and beautiful beerhalls, about a white Mercedes, while Olina went to bed and fell asleep at once, her fatigue permitting her to dream about a white dress and wedding flowers and her wedding breakfast.

10 FINING SALAMI

"YEAH, LIFE WERE GREAT 'ERE, when we was young, yeah, life were great when we'd got money, me even a million, I were a millionaire," said Mr Svoboda, lying on his front in his little garden, with a stream running past him, with young willows and rows of blackcurrant and gooseberry bushes, Mr Svoboda was lying on his front next to a bed of parsnips, or rather he was lying on his side with his great belly lying next to him like a barrel, one arm like a pillow under his head and the free one weeding the weeds from the parsnip bed, the sun shining down on his unbelievably huge paunch, his breasts like a huge wet-nurse's, with pendulous nipples, and Mr Svoboda, catching me looking at his frontage, said: "It's not lard, it's tallow, like what boars, wild boars have, but life were great 'ere, till it left through that gate," he pointed to the broken hedge, rank with hazel and elder, and contentedly, as if he'd been telling himself the same story for the hundredth time, he carried on plucking out the weeds with his fat fingers, and when he'd weeded as far as his reach would allow, he raised himself up like a monstrous walrus and shifted himself on a bit and his body contentedly settled back down and Mr Svoboda carried on weeding and talking: "We used to amuse ourselves different from young people today, like the time I put an advert in the paper: 'Wanted to buy: large guarddog, travel expenses will be reimbursed.' And my pal, he's got that cottage on Dyke Road, above the pond in the forest, I mean Kožíšek the chemist, when he opened the blinds in the morning, he nearly fell flat, outside his chemist's shop there was at least ten blokes with dogs, and Kožíšek asks: "What are you doin' here?" And they said: "We're here 'cos you advertised for a big guarddog, so we've come," and they showed him the ad, since he, my mate Kožíšek, didn't believe 'em yet. Meanwhile more men arrived with more dogs an' the dogs started fightin' and bitin' each other, so Kožíšek decided he *would* buy one, which he did, so as to be shot of the other dogs, but the dogs' owners started shoutin' about suin' if they didn't get their travel costs back as advertised, so Kožíšek had to pay not only their fares out here, and some came from as far away as Moravia and Vimperk, but also their travel back, but if you've got the money, you can afford to have fun, see?" And he added: "But Kožíšek repaid me twice over, he threw a big party and I had this stupid habit of always havin' my pockets full of false teeth from their makers an' I tossed one such mandible in Kožíšek's coffee, 'cept he slipped his coffee my way an' he drank mine, an' I've got such a delicate stomach!" said Mr Svoboda and he stopped weeding, made a mooing noise and retched and puked something up with the memory of those wonderful years of his youth, buried it in soil with his great big paw and continued: "I drank it an' the teeth got jammed in my mouth like some great fish bone an' I started to choke, an' I could easily have died, 'cos I weren't expectin' it, so I got my own back on Kožíšek when he were pukin' outside the front into his rose bushes an' I puked out of the window right down the back of his neck, so when he came in he were right surprised, an' his wife was too, like how could anyone puke down the back of their own neck... like I say, we was young and when you're young it's time for fun." And I nodded cheerily because I liked being with Mr Svoboda and his bare belly, and I liked listening to him talking, saying, artlessly and sincerely, all those things that one is more inclined to feel shame than pride at, and Mr Svoboda, seeing the admiration in my eyes, continued, slowly plucking out the weeds with his fat fingers, himself a very picture of endless contentment and ease: "But the biggest bastard's my midget friend Eliáš, there's no other candidate for the title... so one time, during the Protectorate, when cement was the Reich's life-blood, I like an idiot thought, no, I wasn't thinkin', but I did get fifty bags of cement on the cheap an' took it into my 'ead that 'ere, between the gate and the cottage door, there could be two strips, two cement walkways, just right for the wheels of a car or for people in the rain to walk up... an' suddenly I gets this telegram, which said, in German: 'Herr Svoboda, Kersko, Revision und Kontrolle ihrer Parzelle, Dienstag', signed by SS Sturmbahnführer Habrman. So first I shat myself, then my wife shat herself, then we had an argy-bargy over who on earth had had the bright idea of the cement pavin' for a car, then we shat ourselves again jointly, an' I, all miserable, drove to Kersko and begged the mayor of Semice to loan me a couple of carts for the weekend, for which I'd pay him regally, an' so all day Saturday an' all day Sunday, I 'ad farmers fetch me soil, an' I raked it out over the concrete tracks an' slowly they disappeared, all fifty metres, an' I was thinkin', why hadn't I built the cottage right next to the gate! An' when I'd finished, I scattered pine needles on top of the soil, fortunately this was in the autumn, so I went back and forth fetchin' and spreadin' leaves like children at Corpus Christi, until there wasn't a trace left, and come that Dienstag I waited, throwin' up now an' again, even though I'd had nothin' to eat, kept retchin' and pukin', reduced finally to whimperin' and bringin' up no more than spit, too scared even to shit myself, didn't have the wherewithal, just some green watery stuff... an' I waited an' that morning seemed like a

week, an' the afternoon another week, a fortnight's fear
I got through in a single day, but nothin' happened...
an' suddenly it dawned, it was my mates what had done
it to cheer me up, for a lark...," said Mr Svoboda, heav-
ing up his belly like a 200-litre barrel and pushing it
slightly aside and backing up after it and puffing
and smiling, though he'd paled at the recollection, and
he went on: "... but I got my own back, the chemist,
Kožíšek, 'e 'ad a garden like mine, back then we 'ad
apples an' we was amateur gardeners, an' I offered to
take 'is best apples to the flower an' produce show an'
set up his table for him, an' I ate all his apples and
collected some windfalls and set 'em out an' next to 'em
I put the sign that 'ad been beautifully written by
Kožíšek 'imself: James Grieve an' Jonathan an' Nonnet-
it... an' so on, an' at the corner of the table I puts a big,
fancy sign: 'From the garden of my friend Jan Kožíšek,
Kersko', an' although there was fifty growers of fine
fruit there, most people was clustered round my friend
Kožíšek's table, it were the sensation of the county
show, a blockbuster, an' when Kožíšek 'eard that most
of 'is friends an' other people was clustered round 'is
table, 'e grabbed the family and took a carriage, that
was a sight to see back then in Kersko, for a hundred
crowns farmers would hitch up a carriage, oh, the carriage journeys we 'ad, legless, at night, by the light of
the moon, by carriage all the way to Poříčany to catch

the last train, the sidelamps lit up the horses' back ends beautifully, young folk would stand, holdin' onto the box, with one foot on the step an' holdin' bottles or flowers in their free hand, we'd 'ave the seats... but where was I? Kožíšek arrived at that memorable flower an' produce show in the carriage with some flowers an' his wife an' he had to part the crowd clustered round his fruit, an' as he stood there beamin' over his windfalls with the whole place eruptin' in laughter, Kožíšek suddenly shrunk by fifteen or twenty centimetres an' his wife were burnin' wi' shame an' embarrassment, an' so they went back 'ome in utter misery, not by carriage this time, but by the back way, through gardens an' along cart-tracks, back to Kersko... But that was because we was young an' we'd got money, an' when you're young it's time for fun, an' to this day I get awful hungry, but back then, every time there were a pig-feast, I'd eat eighteen white puddin's an' three plates o' goulash, I never even counted the black puddin's 'cos I already weighed a hundred and thirty kilos. One time we was invited by Baroness Hiross to their huntin' lodge, an' while my friends was admirin' the huntin' trophies, I were sat at the dining table, then down the stairs comes the baroness wi' my friends behind 'er, affected by 'er showing them 'istoric portraits of 'er and 'er husband's ancestors, an' from the stairs she says: "And now let me invite you to partake of a small collation," but the table was empty an' I were just stuffin' myself with the last plate of fifty open sandwiches, one sandwich after another, but I were young an' I'd got money, an' the baroness took it in good part, 'cept there were no more food at the lodge, so she sliced some bread for my friends an' spread drippin' on it, Christ, I can feel the hunger even now, such wonderful hungry times they was, but I don't have so much money these days, an' even though I don't get so hungry any more, I can really enjoy a whole salami sausage, salami that I hang in my toilet ventilation shaft to fine it, but I never leave it to get fully fined 'cos I always eat it whole the very first night after buyin' one to fine, only once did I eat a fully fined salami, it was during the Protectorate and I'd got a whole Hungarian salami, anyway, I were comin' in and saw, down in the basement below our flat in Prague, the concierge with a great chunk of salami in a vice, cuttin' bits off it with an 'acksaw, an' I could tell from the colour of it that the swine was slicin' salami, so I 'eads straight down and says: "My mouth's fair waterin', 'ow much do you want for that salami?" an' 'e says: "Two thousand," so I gives him the money, but the salami really were that 'ard that you really did need an 'acksaw, so I gave 'im an extra two hundred an' 'e 'acked it into rounds for me, I completely lost control an' wolfed down each slice as he cut it off, until I wolfed down even the string at the end, 'cos there were this woman walkin' past an' I bent down to see up her skirt from down below in the basement an' grabbed the last piece an' that's 'ow I ate the string as well," said Mr Svoboda and he heaved up his mighty belly, plopped it back down and rolled over on his other side, his spine following his belly, then he switched hands and again put one massive paw – as thick as my leg – under his head, like a pillow against his ear, and with his free hand he weeded the bed of parsnips, slowly and totally engrossed in the task, as if he were extracting sharp needles, and he went on talking, quietly, dreamily and with a smile, revelling once again in his youth..., "an' a week later it dawned! an' there an' then I 'eaded for the larder, an' there an' then I throttled the wife and then the maid, an' in tears the maid said that, when they was 'avin' a clear-out, they'd found a salami of sorts 'angin' there, all mouldy and rotten, so she'd slung it in the bin in the yard, an' just like Baron Hiross, who paid twice over an' feasted on his own huntin' dog as a moufflon, I paid twice for an 'Ungarian salami... but you, my friend, what I'm tellin' you isn't true, every week, before leavin' for Kersko, I do fine a salami, salami fined off in the ventilation shaft 'as a special flavour, the draft takes warm air up from the central heatin', an' I really must fine a salami to perfection one day, an' that takes a lot o' will-power, but one day I *will* get the better o' myself, one day I really will fine one to perfection, one day I'll

Koupím také severské fotografi
časopisy a knihy. Zn. „Nabídněte"
270F

KOUPĚ
Koupím levně starý fotoaparát

129
130

bring one all the way out 'ere so you can 'ave a taste an'
see what a delicacy it is, salami fined for a fortnight, like
what I ate in Moravia... but I'll bring it when you're
not hungry exactly, but you'll still fancy somethin'...
just for you I'll buy a whole thirty-five crown salami,
just for you I'll hang it in the central heatin' ventilation
shaft, there's a little hatch, see, in the toilet, like the one
in a farm smokehouse, an' that's where I'll fine it, except
the moment I lie down, even on a full belly..., like when
I'm on the way 'ome from work, I spend an hour in the
shop, my bag's full, an' it's a hundred grams of this
salami an' a hundred of that, an' a hundred and fifty
grams of Silesian brawn an' two hundred of ordinary
brawn an' some mayonnaise an' little pots of pickled
fish, Russian sardines *an'* rollmops, that's 'ow I live,
whenever I see 'em in a shop window, I get such an
appetite an' I weaken, so straight into the shop, an' first
I order a plateful to eat in, then I buy all sorts of chees-
es, then it's 'ome, not walkin' but runnin', an' at 'ome
we eat it all in front of the telly, an' I keep reachin'
forward until there's nowt left on the table, 'So I've
eaten it all,' I says, then we go to bed, an' I wake up at
midnight an' it's like there's this golden salami hangin'
from the ceiling before my very eyes, the salami that's
hangin' in the draught in the ventilation shaft in the
toilet, the salami glitters an' gleams like crown jewels,
an' I shade my eyes, but the salami so seduces me with

its beauty that I tells myself: 'You're finin' it for your friends, you're finin' it for your friends,' but on an impulse I gets up an' 'Bollocks!' I says, an' I goes into the toilet, cuts 'alf of it off an' tucks into it there an' then, to finish it off in bed, an' the wife says, in 'er sleep: 'Don't get grease on the duvet...,' then she sleeps on, I drop off as well, but an hour later I sees that fined salami again, the salami that's only been being fined for less than a day, an' I can't 'old back an' I get up, then I lie back down an' I'm beginning to get the better of myself, a moment longer an' I'll overcome that cravin', that urge to eat the rest of the salami, until, just when I thought I'd won, I let out a deep sigh an' the wife half-rose an' said: 'Stop torturin' yourself, Karel, eat the damn' salami...,' an' havin' waited all day, all night, I wolf down the rest of the salami, then I sleep like a loach..." Mr Svoboda carried on meticulously weeding the parsnip bed where he lay, the sun bobbed up over the pine trees and flushed the garden with the pre-noon heat of a glorious July day, and like a machine he pulled up tiny weed after tiny weed and loosened the soil round the parsnips to give them room to swell, because weeds know no greater delight than to strangle anything more noble, destroy everything they enclose and convert it into humus for their own benefit... "You mustn't think...," said Mr Svoboda gently, "it's not unknown for me to buy an extra salami, so I've fined two at a time, I'd wolf one down in the night without finin' it properly, but the other one – twice now – hung there the full fortnight, it must have been fully fined by then, it was a salami for you an' my friends to taste what an ordinary long-life salami is like after it's been fined, tastes like 'Ungarian salami, an' twice I've set off with one in the car, but I got as far as Počernice an' I had this vision of it danglin' out of the sky on a string in front of the radiator, a gold salami fined by me, an' just past Počernice I had to brake an' shout 'Bollocks!' And the wife 'ad to say: 'Stop torturin' yourself, Karel, or you'll crash…,' an' I lifted the bonnet an' I took a knife an' went an' sat in the ditch, that disgustin' gully behind the Počernice abbatoir, in among the stinkin' vapours an' old pots an' a pile of shit here an' there, but I really enjoyed wolfin' down that salami an' afterwards I could drive easy, an' all the next week I was resolved to bring specially for you that other fined salami, and I did get further this time, I nearly won, but near Mochov I suddenly got so hungry that I weakened and the cravin' were so strong that I started seein' things, again the fined salami was danglin' out of the sky on a golden string in front of the radiator, an' again the wife says, me havin' started to weave across the road: 'Stop torturin' yourself, Karel!' An' I stopped an' hopped right into the ditch with the salami, that salami fined for a fortnight and meant specially for my friends... but next time I eat a salami, when I'll 'ave got as far as Semice with a fined salami an' eaten the whole thing there on the green, without bread, chopped into little cubes, after that, once I've slowly but surely got the better of myself, I *will* bring one all the way 'ere for you, 'cos from Semice to Kersko it's no distance, though even havin' got this far, I can't vouch for myself, havin' arrived with it, I'll start soundin' my horn at the edge of the forest, at Vicarage Lane, and you'll 'ave to drop what you're doin' and come runnin', because I can't vouch for myself, if I got the fortnight-old fined salami out, I might dive right into it, there and then; before you can take it from me it might be inside me, 'cos though I don't get so 'ungry as in the past, I do get cravin's, and they can be more dangerous than your actual hunger...," said Mr Svoboda and he raised himself up, knelt and set his belly on his knees, then quickly lifted his paunch and prised himself up from the knees with it, then stood upright, from behind Mr Svoboda looked slim, so erect and proud was he as he bore that vast, unbelievably huge belly before him, and his 130-kilo persona strode off in his glazed-cotton boxers – three metres of the fabric went on them – and as he strode over the stream, the footbridge sagged and Mr Svoboda turned and said gleefully: "Right, I'm off now, an' before I start weedin' the carrots I'm goin' to polish off a whole long-life sausage that I've got ready for finin' and bought yesterday in Semice..." I said: "Why torture yourself, Mr Svoboda..." And, contented, Mr Svoboda withdrew through the greenery beneath his fruit trees and on past the trunks of Goldilocks pines to enter his cottage with its green shutters, and I used to see him every Easter, doing the rounds on Easter Monday with his friends, who deliberately let him carry their baskets of eggs, and at every cottage and every chalet they'd get eggs a-plenty, because everyone looks forward to Mr Svoboda coming, and they're honoured to be able to treat the visitors to dozens of sandwiches, and Mr Svoboda rewards them with his wonderful account of fining salamis, stories that everyone knows already, but every Easter Monday the people in their cottages in the forest look forward to hearing them again. They love to see how, after the thirty or forty sandwiches he's eaten in the thirty cottages and chalets, he can still manage more, and his appetite is at its height when, at the back of the procession of carollers and brandishing his randy-pole decorated with red and blue ribbons, Mr Svoboda can down eggs whole, shell and all. And each time his carolling friends say: "Karel, didn't you just swallow a whole egg?" And Mr Svoboda, Easter caroller, gulps and says: "Me?" And his friends say: "Come on, open your gob!" And Mr Svoboda opens his huge mouth, and it's empty, the egg's already gone to join the dozens of other painted eggs down inside his stomach... Right now, though, with Mr Svoboda gone off in his glazed-cotton boxers that took three metres of cloth to make, it came to me that the man who'd gone off was a king. I'd noticed that Mr Svoboda had wonderful hair, as thick and curly as Africans', one little curly wire after another, clinging to his head like a helmet of curls. Mr Svoboda is actually quite a dazzler, and so a king.

11 LELI

LELI WAS A GREAT GUY, with so many pals he
never had time to get married, such a great pal he was.
No festivity in the Kersko forest range, and there's
some celebration or other almost every Sunday, because
anyone who's young, that's a cause for celebration in
itself, none could happen without Leli being there. Especially if someone had got a keg in. That was a major
kind of celebration, like when someone got married
or had a baby, then the litre glasses came out to be
drunk at whichever cottage or in whichever avenue
the wedding or christening was being held. And so
Leli would show up as MC and technical consultant.
Leli could cope with anything, because he was one
big technical encyclopaedia, he was so well read that
there wasn't really a book he hadn't read, and he could
give a lecture on anything whatsoever, wheresoever it
took place. One time there was a barrel to broach, but
the lads had brought it on a handcart, and when they
set it down in front of the fire under the old oak trees,
whose branches were bent low right over the barrel, no
one dared tap the barrel. Then suddenly Leli turned

up and at once: "What don't you understand? Where's the problem?" And when they said they were afraid to spile the barrel, Leli said: "Bring me an apron," and he donned the apron then gave a lecture on what a spile is and the principle it works on, then he set the spile, loosened the screw and with a mighty blow drove the spile in, but the lads who'd brought the barrel along on the handcart were right, the spile shot upwards like a spear, the beer spurted and fizzed in a mighty geysir up into the oak branches, and Leli stood there in that fountain of beer, handsome and soaked, and after the beer had shot up and was dripping back from the leaves onto the benches and us, Leli pronounced with an appropriate gesture: "Technical defect... bring me a bowl of water and a towel," and he untied the apron and blithely washed his hands of the technical fault, so we drank what was left in the barrel and then we went back and forth to the pub with jugs and ended up fetching crates of bottled Popovice lager, we sat on the benches and sang and played guitars till morning, beer never stopped dripping on us from the leaves, and we were all sticky and tacky with the beer and we smelled of beer, we were so fantastic because we were young. "Yep," says I, "Leli's a great guy." And again Leli would go around Kersko and wherever someone didn't understand something, he'd first give them a lecture, then his advice, or he'd get on and do what he'd advised himself. Mr Svoboda couldn't paint his kitchen, so Leli said: "What don't you understand? Where's the snag?" And Mr Svoboda said he was afraid to spray the kitchen, which he wanted blue, and Leli said how lucky Mr Svoboda was that he, Leli, was passing, and at once he prepared him a pail of blue wash, improving it with a few drops of oil from a special bottle he'd been and got, and Mr Svoboda painted the kitchen, but after he went to bed he was woken at midnight by a strange sound coming out of the darkness of the kitchen, like someone giving sloppy kisses, and when he put the light on and looked up at the ceiling, it had bubbles all over that were cracking open, crow's-feet cracks opening up everywhere and showering blue powder down to the floor. When Leli heard about it, he said "technical defect in the paint" and walked on unbowed, and he saw Mr Kuchař mending a windscreen-wiper on his car, so he went up, looked a while, then said: "Lucky I'm here, can I mend it?" And before Mr Kuchař knew it, Leli had given him a lecture on each of the components and on all the little screws, then asked Mr Kuchař to hand him a screwdriver, and with that and Leli having tightened the last screw, the wiper snapped and Leli pronounced knowledgeably: "There's a technical defect in the material...," and he handed Mr Kuchař the broken blade and departed, and the next day, Mr Kuchař was driving to Ústí on business and it was raining, and he steered with one hand and in lieu of the wiper wiped the rain away with the other through the open window, cursing all the way to Ústí: "Damn the man, that bastard Leli," adding some other salty Moravisms… Yep, Leli was a great guy.

At home in his cottage Leli had a wonderful workshop, and in the workshop Leli had some tall coat stands, on which hung various outfits and overalls to go with whatever Leli happened to be doing or where he was going. So if he was cutting something with a hacksaw, he'd put on dungarees and a cap like American workmen wear, the kind with a big peak, he would be so intent on the job in hand that woe betide anyone who came in, not even his dad dared, and when I once did persuade his dad, his dad went in and said: "Leli, there's a friend to see you," but Leli carried on filing the edge of a piece of sheet metal he'd got in the vice and confined himself to a lofty: "How many times do I have to tell you that when I'm working I do *not* want to be disturbed?" And he was right, Leli was a picture of dignity as he worked in his boiler suit, he always had such style. And when he went out on his bike, he'd put on some jodhpur-like cycling trousers, take a canful of milk and one of mineral water and set out as if he were going on the Peace Race, Leli, so stylish, so magnificent. When he went out animal-watching in the woods or fields, Leli would change into hunting green and a deerstalker and have a pair of binoculars on his chest so everyone would know that Leli was going stalking, that in the evening we'd be told everything he'd seen, always linked to a lecture, so we, his friends, knew everyting we knew from Leli, Leli was like our university. If anyone invited Leli to take a boat-trip on the river, Leli would turn up in a marine-blue suit like the captain of a corvette, with a cap to match, borrowed from his friend who worked, and still works, on ocean-going ships, sailing the world, and he's always at sea for sixth months and with us for six months, and we call him Sailor, so Leli in his First Engineer's cap would sit in an ordinary dinghy and keep a keen and close eye on who was coming the other way and who they were passing, giving erudite lectures on every kind of seagoing and commercial vessel, and warship, and warships were Leli's pet interest, he could go on for hours on end about them, drawing plans in the sand not only of the various types, but also of all the great sea battles from Trafalgar to Narvik. When there was a forest fire over where the game park begins, everyone hurried to help put it out, and we were on tenterhooks: When would Leli turn up? And whereas fire brigades had arrived from various quarters and even a water canon came into its own, as we made our way back from the extinguished blaze, along came Leli in an asbestos suit with a rake over his shoulder, striding along,

ramrod straight and head held high, relishing the wonderment he radiated from afar, and he promptly gathered us together and gave us a lecture to the effect that the best way to tackle a forest fire of burning moss isn't a water canon, isn't jets of water, but, at least for starters, rakes, with which you have to turn over the whole area that has burnt, because Leli's known this for years – and this fire now, Leli had survived four such – and he turned and spread everything with his rake, and he showed us, "See, it's still smouldering here, in three days' time it'll flare up again, 'cos smouldering moss and peat's a right bastard..." And so it came to pass, the fire wardens chased Leli from the site of the fire as if he'd been taking the piss and acting like a provocative yob, so Leli had shouldered his rake and set off home like Winnie the Pooh in an asbestos suit and was giving us this lecture on the proper way to put a forest fire out, turning back and pointing to the swirling smoke, insisting that on Thursday it would flare up again... and it did, in four days, just as Leli had foretold, the forest caught fire again, at the selfsame spot, from the smouldering moss and peat... Yep, Leli, he was a great guy, who thought not only about us and for us, but also through us, and he lived with us and we respected him. His great passion was motor racing, and he didn't just watch all the Formula 1 races, but he knew from foreign magazines every detail of the life of Fittipaldi and

Emerson, he even knew their family lives, and one time when we were chatting casually about something we'd read about Formula 1 in the papers, Leli took the floor and in a quiet voice spelled out all the details, he knew all there was to know not only about what this or that driver looked like, but also what a racing driver thought about. Leli also had a car, but a Trabant, and when he was at the wheel, he wasn't one to use a crash helmet and things, he invariably wore a sporty race suit, and having started the Trabant, he would slowly pull on his gloves, the very kind worn by Manfred von Brauchitsch, gloves with a strap at the wrist and huge almond- and tear-shaped cut-outs, and as he pulled away, it was only ever at full throttle, my, how he thrashed it, not that that mattered when all's said and done, because if Fittipaldi went flat out, Leli went flat out as well, except that Leli, because he was thinking more about his friends, often came seriously unstuck. Leli would often attend pig-killings, invited with his father by the farmers in the villages around, because they were also glad to have him come, because he would start by treating them to such a wonderful lecture on pig-killing, that the pig in question, if it had heard it, would have thought it an honour to be about to be killed, and so it once came to pass that Leli was holding the rope, just to show the right way to tug it so as to fell the pig at the critical moment, but the butcher who

was there to shoot the pig hit something soft, and suddenly Leli, pulling on the rope, flew backwards straight
into the manure heap, his white apron – Leli always
came in a white apron with his initials on the chest –
slithering into the slurry, everyone was horrified that
the butcher, instead of shooting the pig, had shot Leli,
though the butcher had actually shot right through the
rope Leli was pulling on, which Leli himself explained
as the cause of his fall as, covered in slurry, he was alert
enough to grab the rope and show that it had been shot
through and that he was unharmed, and they shot the
pig later in a corner of the yard. But by then Leli had
had a bath and a change of clothes, after which he en-
tertained them all, and how they all laughed, and how
happy everybody was, but Leli didn't laugh much, in
fact he hardly ever laughed, his face generally wore an
oddly amazed smirk…, and right above that grin were
his infantile, shining eyes, amazed at the latest thing
he'd discovered, or amazed at the amazement caused
by the information he had just dispensed so selflessly.
And when he came to a pig-killing, we always looked
forward to it and waited in the pub, because Leli always
brought a churn full of soup and white puddings, and
always just for his friends, for us. And so one time we
were waiting, but Leli didn't make it, then someone
came and said that Leli had driven into the ditch at the
very edge of the forest, so we took the short cut past

the spring and the tennis courts and past the pond in the woods, running to get to the spot as speedily as possible, and there we looked about us, but couldn't see anyone, and suddenly we did, Leli had gone straight into the ditch and overturned, and we when ran up we could see Leli still in the car, so we turned the Trabant back over and soup and groats came streaming out of it, and when we opened the door some white puddings fell out, and we said: "Leli, what on earth?" And Leli started combing the groats out of his hair with a little comb, along with clotted blood and marjoram, and he said in all seriousness that it was that buggering conditioned reflex you get on the way to see friends, at the bend the churn had started to tilt and was about to topple over, but remembering that his friends were waiting, he'd tried to steady the churn, but just then his racer ran into the ditch and he'd overturned not only the churn, but the car as well. So we got round the Trabant and with a "Heave-ho!" lifted it like some toy car and deposited it back on the road, Leli and all. Leli got out and said: "You might have pretended that a Trabant's heavier than it really is, you might!" and he started doling out the white puddings and black puddings, adding: "Sorry, but the soup's inside the body of the car." Then a week later Leli said: "Do you know, it was three days after and I still combed a groat out of my hair?" "Yep," I said, Leli was a great guy and only ever thought of his pals, and in the end *we* all thought of *him*, but Leli thought more of us than we of him, we can see that today, we all have to admit that today. When spring came, we could bet on it that Leli would bring us each a basket of fresh eggs, as usual from the farmers where he bought them, he himself couldn't stand the sight of eggs, but everything was for us, for his friends, especially for those with children. Then he'd bill us for the eggs and butter, but who else would be such a good pal as to turn his Trabant into a mobile shop? And another time we were waiting for Leli, he'd gone to get us two hundred and fifty eggs, fresh eggs for the children, but there was no sign of him, and suddenly a message came to go and extricate him from the same ditch as before, so we trotted off and it was exactly like with the churn of soup, that time round the pig-killing, Leli, before leaving the road, had braked slightly and rolled over several times before getting jammed in the ditch. We couldn't see Leli inside the car at all, the entire Trabant being caked in egg, like the cement caked round the inside of a cement mixer truck, the kind that keeps turning to keep the liquid cement fit for purpose, and when we opened the car door, Leli was still sitting there, holding the steering-wheel and all coated in egg, the eggs having been smashed to smithereens, like when you dip a wiener schnitzel in beaten egg before breadcrumbing it..., but all Leli did was ask us to wipe his eyes, because he couldn't see anything, which we did, and Leli said: "Remember, we learn by our mistakes, again, like that time at the pig-killing, the box with its neat stack of eggs started slipping off the other seat and instead of saying to hell with it, I meant to salvage ten or a dozen eggs for my friends, with the result that I smashed the lot...," after which we spent all that day and the next cleaning the Trabant, finally poking stringy bits of drying yolk out of all the cracks with bits of wire, and the spring sun beat down on us, and there was such a stench from the eggs that we got out the paraffin and carbon tetrachloride and cleaned and polished everything once again, but two months later Leli said the Trabant still smelled of sulphur dioxide, like Poděbrady mineral water, so he couldn't give anyone a lift except people in the know, 'cos strangers would automatically think he'd nearly shat himself... yep, a great guy was Leli, everything for his friends, we were always on his mind, while we were more attentive to our girlfriends, wives and children, his mind was on us. And another Leli thing: every time the fair came to Velenka or Hradišťko, he'd bring the children, from the fair, trumpets and pea-shooters and little drums, then he'd buy a whole slatted takeaway tray of cakes, and one time he was bringing them in his car and the tray threatened to shed a number of choux buns and creme rolls and make a mess of his carpet, but the main thing was that he wouldn't be arriving with them the way we usually got them, by the trayful that he used to bring onto the patio outside the pub like a confectioner, holding it cleverly aloft and carrying it the way waiters carry a whole tray of meals, but yet again he drove into the ditch and again he got out unscathed, except that the whole tray of cakes, as the car rammed sideways into the ditch, Leli fell, just like in an American slapstick film, face and gloved hands right into the creme rolls and creme slices and choux buns, fifty fancy pastries, all cream and meringue, he fell into them face first though he never ate cakes himself, he didn't even like them, if ever he was offered one he claimed it would make him throw up, even the sight of them made him puke... yep, a great guy Leli was, a great pal who only ever thought of his friends and their families, as if he were some kind of president..., and we never learned to appreciate it... Take this, on New Year's Eve, Leli would always organise a New Year's Party at the house of one or other of us, we'd have met a fortnight before at the Keeper's Lodge, Leli in the chair, first he secretly told the waiter: "Hey, mate, six Bechers for our table, on my tab...," and he broached every meeting in the same kind way: "Gentlemen, mates of mine, I declare this meeting of the Committee for a Dignified Farewell to the Old Year and Welcome to the New open..., right, I reckon the eats should be: pork, four kilos, for a special pork, potato, bacon and sausage bake, a large boiled ham…," and he went on to list all the dishes, and we all agreed or suggested amendments, and finally, and this was Leli's thing, eight litres of tripe soup, which he made himself, that was for the morning after… and in the pauses, Leli popped over to the waiter and in a whisper said: "Six double Bechers for our table, mate, on my tab…" Generous to a fault was Leli, and so once, as New Year's Eve approached, Leli was in his long white apron with its blue and red embroidered initials on his chest, since the afternoon he'd been preparing the pork, potato, bacon and sausage bake and the lads were already drinking, and there was still a keg of beer and some bottles and suchlike, but Leli, ever the true butcher, was sipping white coffee and nibbling marble cake, as soon as everything was ready he'd also have a Becher, a 'President in Exile', his favourite, but only afterwards, because, as he told us in a lecture, pork, potato, bacon and sausage bake is not as simple as it might seem, he'd known a chef at the Grand Hotel in Tatranská Lomnica, the very man the President had had helicoptered all the way to Prague Castle when he needed this dish to be spot-on, "and you can be sure," Leli concluded, "I kept a close watch on his hands, I'm very particular about making it like he did, most important's the preparation stage…" And when the pork, potato, bacon and sausage bake started cooking on the barbecue – Leli, just like Mr Čány, couldn't stand to have it roasted over hot coals, so we had to made a log fire outside and Leli, like Mr Čány, would take some tongs and bring hot pieces of charcoal in from the burning logs – as it was cooking, Leli undid his apron and said he was off to fetch his famous tripe soup, the one that would put anyone back on their feet the morning after and fortify them so as to be able to carry on drinking, so good was Leli's version of tripe soup, and no one else's was a patch on his, because Leli had his secret, just as the President had taken the secret of Becher liqueur with him into exile, and his secret was compounded by the fact that he got all his spices from the St Saviour pharmacy, hardly anyone else did, but Leli did because he was pals with the chemist and they'd talked a lot, and later Leli talked a lot to us, all about this spice we'd never even heard of. And Leli, having got in his car, suddenly remember the incidents with the churn of soup and the box of eggs and the tray of cakes, which he only ever brought specially for us, and got out again and took a moped, it would be safer by moped, and this we only learned later, he popped the short way home on the moped, donned his dinner jacket, put some bottles in his rucksack and the huge pot of tripe soup in a large bag, and to play safe he sat the bag in front of him, and so, all eager, he set off back to bring us the soup, which he would always stir, once it was ready, all the time until it went cold, because that's how it should be, as he disclosed to us, because if it was left to its own devices, the fat and the grease would congeal on the surface and you might as well pour the whole thing away in the morning and feed it to the pigs... and as Leli, our great pal, was on the way back, driving slowly, a deer suddenly ran across the road and Leli, not so as not to hit it, but so as not to spill the soup, swerved and went into a skid on the snow, and Leli, a man who for fun could execute every conceivable fall and do tricks that had us worrying that he'd get up with a broken arm or perhaps never rise again out of the sand, he would always hop off and shake the sand off him, this time, so as not to spill the tripe soup, Leli was afraid to kick free of the moped as it grated along the ground the way he normally would because he was thinking not of himself but of the soup, and as he held on to it with both hands so it wouldn't spill, he went spinning, and even as he caught the back of his head against a milestone he still managed to set the pot of soup down safely... With no sign of Leli, we set off to meet him halfway, and we found him, lying on his back and looking up at the stars as if he were dying, like when young Rosemayer crashed into that bridge near Darmstadt. When Bob lifted his head, his hand was all covered in blood, and Leli said: "Watch out, mind you don't knock the soup over...," and an hour later he died,

for his pals, died rescuing his tripe soup for them, like
I say, a great guy, a great pal was Leli, but who was
going to entertain us now?

12 BEATRICE

THE VILLA BERÁNEK is three storeys high, the summer seat of Beránek the Butcher, it also had its own game preserve, so whenever the chain butcher got the urge, he could shoot male and female roe deer and pheasants from his very own bedroom. A villa in the middle of a pine forest, a villa with a gardener and a caretaker and a telephone, so if ever Mr Beránek and his friends were to arrive for a banquet, a long weekend or the holidays, the rooms of the villa would be agreeably heated and decorated with flowers, and the drive from the main avenue, lined with a tunnel of pine branches and freshly resanded, afforded arriving cars an impressive sight, and not only his green, gamekeeper's short jacket and Tyrolean hat tipped down over his forehead, but also the hunting rifles and trophies displayed along the corridors gave the butcher, Mr Beránek, and his friends the glorious sensation of being God's elect. And since Mr Beránek also had shops and a restaurant in Prague and so there were pailfuls of leftovers from lunches and offal from the abbatoir, Mr Beránek recalled that his father had also been in the butchery business before him, but horse butchery, and he had also kept ten pigs, which grew before your very eyes thanks only to the whole horse entrails and all the horse poop that came from the knacker's yard and went straight to the pigs, who put on a kilo, or even more, daily. So Mr Beránek had a fifty-strong piggery created at the back of his villa and a lorry would arrive daily with pails of scraps from his restaurants and shops and the knacker's yard and nine months later, for next to nothing, Beránek's trucks would carry fifty pigs off and bring fifty piglets back to begin again, without Mr Beránek even noticing that, whenever the wind blew towards his villa and windows from the styes, despite their being concealed behind rhododendrons and co-nifers, the pig manure gave off a pungent, repellent stench. But to Mr Beránek the pig manure smelled sweet, he had no inkling of it, he merged as one with it, like a true feudal lord, he couldn't live without the fragrant smell of outbuildings and horse manure and animal urine. And so, in order to wash and cleanse his soul, Mr Beránek had a tiny chapel in one of his rooms, turned one room into a shrine, with stained-glass win-dows, scenes from the lives of the saints set in lead, and in front of the windows stood a little altar, above which shone an everlasting light, and a kneeler, and whenever Mr Beránek sensed that he was a bit forlorn among his abbatoirs and agencies and shops and restaurants, that he was surrounded by too much manure, he could kneel and cleanse himself through pious prayer so thoroughly that he glowed with good health and good humour, which anyway flowed from the fact that Mr Beránek was a millionaire, and all rich people were merry back then and crowed with contentment and were kind and generous, and generosity flattered his healthy pride and often helped him to shed a tear to himself, almost to burst into tears, at how kind and amiable he was to people... and his father had built almost an entire house in Prague, Hlahol House down by the river... But that was then, then came the time when Mr Beránek lost everything, when he lost his good temper and generosity as well, and now his villa is a home for unfortunate children who have been born with both physical and mental disorders and are a burden to society. There are forty children here, from five to fifteen, ten cannot walk and just lie there, some of the children are blind or deaf, five sit on special chairs with the seats removed, and they sit on them, belted in, and they eat and they defecate into prepared vessels. From time to time a child dies, and at its dying the other kids don't even register the tragedy, because their minds are in darkness and their only slightly human eyes seem now and again to recollect something, seem to look about them and briefly see all the horrors that enclose them before a mantle of mercy descends again and they retreat once more into the dark. And so the spirit of Beránek the chain butcher still enfolds the house in an odour of excreta, nowadays human, and three sisters in black dresses with white starched coifs and guimpes wrestle with the excreta, from morning till evening, and from evening through midnight to morning the house is full of moans and groans and whimpers, most of the children utter just squawks and snorts and whines, for a brief moment they may wear a beatific smile, but it's the smile of the blessed on the tympanon of a Romanesque cathedral, a beautiful smile, and Sister Beatrice does what she can to elicit this human smile, she is kind and beautiful, she is young and full of courage and fervour in the name of God, because, as they taught her in her convent, God is here, even in this house, here among these shit-filled nappies and pots, God is here where a feeble-minded youngster grasps his genitals – like a calf's foot – squawking and howling with puberty and adolescence, the two elderly sisters flee blushing and wringing their hands, and they go into Mr Beránek's old room where the altar still stands, surrounded by flowers and the everlasting light, and there they fall down to cleanse themselves with prayer and thrust aside the boy's blood-filled member, while Sister Beatrice offers comfort, sitting there and soothing the boy, stroking him quietly and turning his eyes towards her own, and because her God is right here now and not somewhere else, she establishes communication with the imbecile, she is briefly in a fusion with him, and for Sister Beatrice this fusion is the scale-pan in which she encounters her Lord, her God, who resides within her and lights up her beautiful face with an almost rococo impishness, and so she wipes the boy's member, washing it in cold water until it shrinks back to normal... she kisses him on the forehead and goes off into the next room, the playroom, as it's called, where, like other kids, these poor unfortunates play with the same toys as normal children, except that they don't know how to play, having been shrouded in a dark cloud since birth, since having scarlet fever, or some accident, a cloud that makes their play monstrous, they tear most dolls apart and start poking their fingers right inside them, they poke the eyes out of clowns and most of all they like to smear them with their own excrement, because with so many children the duty of care hasn't to be just to the one, but to all, and so it may happen that while the sisters are extracting soiled nappies from pants and skirts, other children who have soiled themselves may be picking out their excrement and throwing it gleefully up at the ceiling and then it falls back off the ceiling into their hair, making duties in this house, once that of chain butcher Mr Beránek, hard, quite a job for the three nuns and Sister Beatrice, who alone shines and smiles through any contingency the house may throw up. At night, during sultry summer nights, being on duty is even tougher, child patients as young as ten can show such powerful sexual instincts that they lie on top of each other with great, sweet pleasure, and, if the nuns don't intervene, a child might, by the morning, have one eye sucked raw, another its eyebrows, by the unrelenting and insatiable tongue and lips of those who seem to have some remembrance of the sweet maternal breast that was denied them, they suck away at anything that comes their way if it's warm, human, anything that projects, anything that carries an animal smell... and again, while the maids see to the children who aren't that big a problem, since they have some sense of order and rules, able to make their own way to the toilet, while the maids darn and mend the children's tights and trousers and skirts and blouses and pyjamas and nighties, and while ten children are in the back room, whether sighing gently in their sleep or troubled, in the three other rooms a state of heightened vigilance still reigns, dark Tertiary instincts struggle out through the children's flesh and manifest themselves in unpredictable situations that only Sister Beatrice can cope with, all smiles in her starched collar and surplice, aglow like little Saint Thérèse of Lisieux, constantly removing the hands the children poke in places they're not supposed to, calling to them soothingly, Beatrice clicks her tongue as you do with startled horses for as long as it takes for the children to settle, only for their freakish behaviour to break out again the instant she steps out for even a moment. I once went there to visit and it sent shivers down my spine because I had no idea... there was a girl lying on a bed, she was blind and mentally disturbed, her shift was pulled up, and because her periods had already started, she was absently wiping the blood with her finger and then licking it with a religious devotion, abstracted, enraptured, as if in ecstasy. Sister Beatrice caressed her, placed her arm across her ripening breasts and ran quietly out into the corridor and then into the sunlight outside the house, and there stood a line of children, fifteen of them, and they kept tottering, they were headed by the one who had least wrong with him, he was leading three blind children by the hand, they all held hands, and the procession set off for a walk, I'd never seen so much joy in children who were well as in these kids, who may have been grievously broken, as the way they walked showed, yet their eyes spouted a longing and a capacity to make contact with all the things around them that they alighted on, all that they scented, not only with their little noses but with some higher system of smelling with their whole bodies... and Sister Beatrice strode along behind them, turning to see if a car was coming, a seven-year-old boy walked along by my side, with me holding his drool-covered little hand, this was the boy

that Mr Krejčík took into his home for Christmas Eve, he had four children of his own, and the boy had kept whispering to me, in a muffled voice, but with enormous feeling: "I've got a home, I've got a home...," and most of all he had liked the little tree covered in lights, but he looked at the Christmas tree the way cats do, he could see it, but he couldn't explain everything, and most of all he enjoyed striking matches and that was how he set fire to Mr Krejčík's curtains and he was over the moon, but the curtains were put out, and as Mr Krejčík and I chatted about anything and everything, the boy went on striking matches and Mr Krejčík slapped him and said like he meant it: "Stop doing that, for God's sake!" And the boy smiled beatifically and told me: "I've got a home, I've got a home...," and this time too, he had snuggled up to my hand, tenderly drooling long strings of saliva all over it and whispering: "I've got a home, I'm at home, home, home!" I found this yearning for a home startling, the force and feeling with which he voiced his not wish, but the actual condition in which he really was, though outside the home, at home. And I felt like broaching, with Sister Beatrice, the subject of the irresponsibility of bringing children like this into the world, the suffering it brings them, living like this, and whether it might not be better for these children not to be, and she turned and said with a smile: "Homer was born blind," and I treated myself to a silent, pointless monologue on where all those beautiful and brave people were, all those people of sound stock with whom Homer had lived. All those nameless people had died, for all they were fully competent, while Homer, though by the laws of the earth he should have been cast on the rubbish heap, lives on forever in his writings. And I watched those blind kids, walking along in bliss and trust, one leading the other by the hand, walking along and inhaling the air and stepping up the pace the better to let the air in motion caress their cheeks. And Sister Beatrice told me how the priest came over from Sadská every day, how she went to confession every day, that she had hardly anything to confess, just her dreams, which were like the instalments of a soap opera, St Augustine would come to her, not the church father though, but the dark-skinned young man, the one who would chase pretty girls in Carthage on the coast of Africa, the swarthy playboy who took after his mother, whom she loved above all the other saints, St Monica, who was black, a black beauty... and the motley clothes of the children and their tottering gait, at that instant she seemed irradiated not by a higher something and a light from above, but by the way it was all framed in meadows and flowers and the shadows of pine trees, the clothes and faces suddenly told me how beautiful and complete any here-and-now is, only an actual moment in time in which all things and all creatures move as if illuminated by a sacred radiance that irradiates everything through a glittery, transparent sheet, and everything, anything, is not just beautiful, but breathtaking, including children who throw their excrement at the ceiling, and even that excrement glitters and is the start of a beautiful train of thought, and I had no other wish, if I could be someone other than I am, than to be Sister Beatrice, who reigns over everything like a sun, diminishing apparent ills and misfortunes thereby and receiving in exchange the pure and simple spirit in which she told me how, once a quarter, she had, however, to go to Mcely to super-confession, and with her rich feminine laugh and a healthy animal sensuality she told me that the priest at Mcely was a fine specimen of manhood, that, talking to him, she would even blush, because he was a little bit wicked, only wickedness put colour in her cheeks... was how she put it, and she nudged me and looked me in the eye and I could see it all, that is wasn't that as a nun she was cut off from sex as by some trauma, but, on the contrary, that there was in her eyes so much sensuality and pure womanhood that I quavered and dropped my gaze, while she kept showering me with an amorous tenderness and said something no one has ever told me before, that I had very fine legs, and I could see that she could see everything, that she could see, if she so wished, me walking along beside her naked, that she could see me tossing about in bed on a summer's night, and that I would toss and turn whenever I thought of her, just as she might think, in the quiet of the night, of the priest at Mcely, who, as she put it, was like the young Augustine before his sainthood, a man through and through, a male of the species, a sinner who only through sin had been converted and had become, like her, a friend and creature of God, much as the Villa Beránek had become a refuge for hapless children, a refuge in which Sister Beatrice, like a lamb of God, served her children and her God, the beautiful Sister Beatrice, whom I would drive the following week to her super-confession in Mcely, to the priest who so resembled a wise saint.

13 LUCY AND POLLY

RATHER LIKE ME, mine host Mr Novák was an odd individual. There were days when he would be welcoming to his patrons, smiling, shaking everyone's hands, his patrons would bring little somethings for his wife: flowers, a basketful of orange birch boletes, in winter white puddings and celebration soup after they'd slaughtered a pig, then a chunk of smoked pork, and all because he served a fine pint, and when he was in a good mood, he'd ask someone to bring a hare or deer and then put on a feast... all in all, on a good day, he was second to none as publicans go, when his missus was making dumplings, the kitchen windows had to be shut so the dumplings didn't catch cold, when they brought him his week's supply of meat direct from the abbatoir, he would lay each piece out on the vast kitchen table and inspect them all with great satisfaction, feasting his eyes on the meat and already speculating what each piece might go on, and when he was in an exceptionally good mood, he would immediately cut slices from a leg of pork and then he'd be round shortly with escalopes quick-fried in butter and drizzled with

lemon juice. And when he was having one of his wonderful days, which were getting increasingly rarer, he'd
bring round potato fritters, and his speciality was bull's
testicles egg-and-breadcrumbed like Wiener schnitzels
and served with tartar sauce. During such times he
would sit around with the customers, putting an arm
round their shoulders and looking straight at them and
taking bookings, and in the evenings his beautiful wife
would get her apron and also come and sit with the
customers, and we were all happy that at last we had a
decent licensee. They had two children, a boy, Vráťa,
aged five, who liked to sit on the customers' laps and
nuzzle up to them like a stray kitten, then he also had
a tubby ten-year-old daughter, Mílka, who, despite her
vast proportions, had the single ambition of becoming
a dancer, and so whether in the garden or inside the
pub she was always dancing, with a veil or without, and
as you approached the Keeper's Lodge pub-restaurant
down the drive, you could see from a distance the two
children, the tubby dancer, dancing just for her own
pleasure, completely immersed in an ungainly gymnas-
tics, a ballet of gawkiness. The first year, as Christmas
was approaching, well, it was absolutely wonderful in
our restaurant, ab-so-lute-ly! Franta Vorel brought a
spruce for the kitchen, then he cut down a pine for the
saloon, in the run-up to Christmas Eve the whole pub
helped decorate the tree and meanwhile Mr Novák

came round with the brandy and kirsch and that fabulous beer of his, his missus brought in the Christmas cookies, and nearly all the patrons reciprocated with a box of their own cookies from home, and so no one was in any mood to leave before closing time, or even then, and Mr Novák said that they were all his guests, so he locked up and then those wonderful days carried on behind locked doors. Following Christmas Eve, there was Christmas Day and Boxing Day, the guests had their set places, around and among the beer glasses Vráťa laid out his toy railway and the train ran clickety-clack over the tables that had been pushed together, the Christmas tree was a blaze of light and the children sat on everybody's lap, turn and turn about, snuggling up under the patrons' chins, and we were all in heaven, because it had been a long, long time since we'd had a publican like Mr Novák. But my reason for liking him was that he loved the cats Lucy and Polly, the two tabbies followed him everywhere, they did everything with him, when he went to the shops through the forest, Lucy and Polly went with him, when the pub closed at two and Mr Novák went mushrooming after lunch, the cats went with him, when he went into the cellar to broach a cask, Lucy and Polly also went with him, when he went to bed, the cats slept with him, and as he sliced and chopped vegetables and meat and got on with the cooking in the kitchen, the cats would sit on the window sill and watch Mr Novák lovingly, and Mr Novák knew, and every now and again, knife in hand and wearing his white apron, he went over to the window, bent to the cats' level and exchanged head-butts with them, like clinking liqueur glasses when he toasted his customers in the evening. And the cats, Lucy and Polly, like Mr Novák's children, began wandering among the customers and, just like Vráťa a Míla, they liked to sit on a customer's lap, curled round on their knees and beneath their protective hand, until such time as the customer rose, and the cats, having wearied of being stroked by humans, would curl up in winter behind the enamel stove and sleep a sweet sleep, and sigh and stretch and expose their brindled gingery tummies, and it was if the entire pub was their mother, they would pat the air with their front paws, trample the air from which they would suck sweet, non-existent milk in the form of cigarette smoke and the chatter that rose and fell into the silence of the inn, silence betokening the flight of an angel passing through, sometimes what rose was shouting and swearing and cursing, other times confused blather and singing, but Lucy and Polly knew that none of it was meant against them, but that it was all part of the music of the inn that was their home. So Lucy and Polly would amble past the chairlegs, miaow, and a customer would open the door for them and they would go outside into the wonderful air of the forest, they would sit on the low wall round the terrace or hop up on one of the red chairs and gaze into the sun or the rain so that anyone coming to the inn... so they could welcome them by rubbing against their trouser leg, or just by giving them a look-over, fondly weighing the new arrival up, and almost every one would stroke them, or say something to them, Lucy and Polly became the livestock of the Keeper's Lodge, and by turns they would come inside as the fancy took them, or go back out for a run or a rumble in the oakwood. But Mr Novák also had days when every plus became a minus, suddenly his ears would be pinned back like those of a horse about to snap, he wouldn't bring the beer to the tables, and if he did, then with some snide comment, he wouldn't serve food, but if he did it was cold, on days like that he wouldn't sit among his patrons, but lean against the bar counter and stare at them grimly, then suddenly he'd start addressing people by their surnames, though he was on first-name terms with all of them, and one time when he was going through such a phase, we'd gathered on the concrete road in front of the restaurant and there on the inside was a sign: *Closed. Cleaning in progress*, though only the day before, when Mr Novák had been in a good mood, it had been all first names as he sat among us, and now he'd shut up shop and his face glowed and grinned horribly over the sign, smirking grotesquely like a white mask with Bry-

Říká se, že ten, kdo má si
rád víc než vlastní manželku, s
Mirko Šafka, mluvčna
ech, kteří s

lcreemed hair, only to vanish behind the drape. As we stood outside the inn, more customers kept arriving, and so we swore and shouted and called out and cursed, why hadn't he told us the day before... Or there was another time when we'd turned up, pleased to see one another arriving down all the various rides and tracks, sure of being greeted by a fired-up stove because the inn was all lit up like a lighthouse, like a chandelier, but as each of us tried the door-handle, one after another, we discovered it was closed, and when we tapped on the door, no one heard us, we looked in through the taproom window, the one used to pass beers out into the garden on summer days, and we saw that the tables had been pushed together, with white cloths on them, and Mr Novák, in another world, was laying out spoons and forks round the plates, and the plates were linked together with sprigs of asparagus fern, and when we called out: "Come on, Láďa, let us in, we'll stick by the stove, quiet as mice," we called him by his first name because the night before he'd called us by ours, Mr Novák, lost in his other world and as if under a spell, took a step back and looked, from the door and in sheer delight, at all these preparations for the wedding on the coming day, which had been booked by some outsider from far away, the stove grinned with its red-hot coals, and outside it was cold. And Mr Novák condescended to respond and spoke into the drizzle in an alien voice:

"Can I help you? Only the outside's open today, can't you see?" he said, exasperated, so we stood outside in the drizzling rain, or sat out in it on garden seats and abandoned chairs, drinking beer, we could never get over the swings in the psychological weather of our publican's mood, he, with great flair, went on setting out wine glass after wine glass, shot glass after shot glass, to go with the wines and liqueurs and aperitifs in the order they would be drunk from the next day... and we put up our empty glasses, gesticulating, shouting, but Mr Novák, miles away, kept stepping back to savour from every angle the table so lavishly spread for the morrow's wedding feast. And when he did deign to notice us, he pulled our pints with evident distaste and resentment and revulsion, and when none other than Mr Hubka, the engineer, begged him to let him have another one to hold in reserve, Mr Novák came to the serving window, released the catch and slammed it down so hard that Mr Hubka barely got his hands away in time, otherwise he'd have lost his fingers. But I too was shaking with rage, I too, like the other sad and disappointed customers, swore that I'd never come back to this inn, that I was here for the last time, I too was thinking of all the things I'd do to Mr Novák, but as I looked inside the brightly lit restaurant, I had to concede, as anyone else would, that when Mr Novák was in a good mood, he was the most likeable man and publican in the world, that our Mr Novák had arranged the tables for the wedding breakfast with tremendous good taste, and when I saw Lucy and Polly sitting on a chair and turning their little heads in whatever direction Mr Novák went next, and every now and again Mr Novák couldn't stop himself – if perhaps to show us that the cats meant more to him than we, his outdoor customers, did – from bending down to let Lucy and Polly take turns at kissing his forehead, and then he was back to fetching bunches of flowers or pots of cyclamen, or twisting ever more festoons of asparagus fern for the even fancier cloth that went over all the tables together. And when Mr Novák had satisfied himself for the last time, he bent down and picked Lucy and Polly up, and they seemed to have been waiting for just that, they floated up into his embrace, then with the beloved cats on one arm and his other hand on the light switch, all the customers abandoned any sense of dignity, we on the outside held our glasses up in the drizzling rain, pointing and tapping on the window for him to have pity, for Mr Novák to be so kind as to recall those glorious days past, those times when a pig was slaughtered, those walks together on days off as far as Elegant Antonia and the giant spruce, but Mr Novák, having feasted his eyes on the proffered empty glasses and imploring faces, switched the light off. We'd put every last scrap of earnest, canine devotion into our eyes,

every ounce of humility and entreaty, but Mr Novák
had spurned us, just as on any of those other days when
he went bonkers, when he was overcome with self-pity
and sadness and grouchiness, when his patrons became
so obnoxious to him that not only did he not want to
see them, but he actually wanted to humiliate them, and
to that end he would always choose a day when no one
would, or could, have expected it even in their wildest
dreams. Yet I was fond of Mr Novák, because my own
nature was not dissimilar, also apt to vacillate between
polar opposites, one day I'd embrace the whole of mankind, another I'd be thinking up the most ghastly
genocide for the lot. But I also liked Mr Novák because
of his love for Lucy and Polly, and now that he'd put
out the lights and left us outside in the drizzling rain
and was savouring the notion of us contemplating the
most horrible way of doing away with him, having first
tortured him in ways as yet undreamed-of by any Ko-
rean executioner, I knew that Mr Novák was in his little
room, lying on his back, listening out, with Lucy and
Polly lying on his chest and he'd be stroking them and
showing them his love. Like me, Mr Novák was an odd
character. So it came to pass that those dark days grew
in number, and all the more did we appreciate it when
Mr Novák lit up and smiled at us, by which moment
we would forget to a man all the things he had done to
us, because we were glad to be able to meet up at the

inn, given that from six o'clock onwards the sole pre-occupation of any true man of Kersko and its forests is to spend a pleasant evening over a pint in the pub, and all the banter and chit-chat, the arguments and imbecilities are a brilliant way to unwind from our daily tribulations, so our serenity is fully restored and as we cycle home at night we're on a par with a newborn child, though that only on the assumption that mine host has been good to us. Then the day came when Mr Novák said what we'd long known, that he was moving in two days' time, he wished to invite us to his last day at the inn, he would put on a feast and we would part friends. And it came to pass that that evening, after we'd tempered our food intake at home and were looking forward to the last supper, when we entered the pub one by one, Mr Novák was his alien self, there was no fire in the stove, the chairs were up-ended on the tables by the window, and Mr Novák and his good lady were packing their belongings into boxes, Mr Novák served his last beer, already a bit flat, beer with no head on it, like the specimen you take in a beer bottle to Mikolášek, the miracle doctor, for him to guess not only what's wrong with you, but also what infusion will put it right. And again there was that sorry sight of everyone sitting in their coats, perplexed and disappointed and feeling cheated, and they stared towards the door to see each new arrival's face burning bright with joy and anticipation, then as each one entered, how they were taken aback, then stunned and lamed, but always with that glowing physiognomy that couldn't be dimmed. In the end everyone sat down and Mr Novák brought us our headless beers without a word... and when Mr Franc said out loud that the beer had no head on it, the rest turned towards him in horror at his presumption... and Mr Novák went into the kitchen, brought a whisk, the kind you use to whisk flour into a sauce to thicken it, whisked the beer into a froth and set the whisk down on an ashtray, the bubbles of froth popped quietly and silence descended, and we were all so debilitated by the ignominy that no one felt able to rise and leave, because the greatest dishonour and insult to a true beer-drinker is lacklustre, flat beer... And Lucy and Polly had no idea, any more than us, what they were in for, they padded around among the boxes and crates and helped pack the kitchen utensils that were Mr Novák's own, his butchery knives, a full set of them, with which, on his good days, he would lovingly carve meats and draw up the menu, which on any of those happy days had at least six dishes to chose from, whereas on lean days Mr Novák had no salami, nor would he offer so much as bread and dripping. And it came to pass that Mr Novák stood legs astride and arms akimbo and was about to tell us something terrible, something that he had always held against us and that he would take with him to any other pub in future, since it wasn't loathing for us and our names, but a grudge against all patrons as such. He raised one finger and we goggled, some rose in terror, but all eyes converged on Mr Novák's finger, like bicycle spokes on the hub, but he curled it back into his palm and gave a wave of his hand as if it were pointless to say anything by way of a farewell, with that hand he was damning us just as when Christ, in paintings of the Last Judgement, damns those who have lapsed from faith, those who he is consigning to eternal damnation... And Vráťa opened the door and came running in, artless and childlike, nestling up to us and pointing to the half-open door in which a dancing Mílka, the daughter, appeared, now bespectacled and obese, but dancing with a veil, raising only her arms, because she couldn't lift herself off the ground, hop, yet she danced with so much feeling in her eyes, with such absorption, that she only added to the general confusion and tension, she danced between the tables as if to bid a farewell of which she as yet knew nothing, because the moment she got in from school, she just danced and kept dancing, right through the weekend and on all school-free days, and so she danced us her dance – more an ungainly, if emotive shuffle, with eyes ablaze and cheeks flushed – for the last time, then she danced off out into the darkness, and little Vráťa banged the door behind her so hard that all the glass panes fell out. The tinkling glass helped us pull ourselves together, and one by one we left the farewell feast to take the shortest way home, humiliated, wretched, hungry, to wipe up whatever relics of dinner with a piece of bread or make do with some bread and dripping, since, in anticipation of our last supper at the pub, we'd declined the roast at home.

Next day, as he prepared to move, as he fetched the last boxes and crates and put them on the lorry, Mr Novák brought from his little room a basket containing six kittens, Lucy and Polly expected the basket to be loaded along with them, but Mr Novák locked the inn, climbed into the lorry and Lucy and Polly sat on the low wall round the terrace, the kittens crawled out and snuggled clumsily under Lucy, then the lorry receded and the cats were left alone, staring after the departing lorry and not doubting that it was for but a short while, that their master had gone away on holiday, that sooner or slightly later he'd be back. But Mr Novák didn't come back, it started to rain and the cats dragged the kittens off through a hole in the side of the pub into the dark and dirty, low, underfloor space beneath, and Lucy and Polly sat at the edge of the road and stared in the direction from which their master should be coming back. But he didn't come, some people did come and left, then more came, they opened the door, Lucy and Polly ran inside the pub and lay down by the stove, but the strangers chased them out and shouted at them, stamping their feet, the cats wanted to get close again, after all, previously everybody loved them and they were accustomed to nothing but being stroked, but these people stamped their feet at them, so Lucy and Polly crawled into the bushes and poked their little heads out, but not even that was enough and the people kept stamping their feet and chasing them away through the bushes into the forest. Then it was quiet, Lucy and Polly brought little mice for the kittens, but there was no milk, and so they learned to go to the gulley to drink, until one day they rejoiced: a lorry was arriving, just like the one Mr Novák had left in, but two people got out of it, unlocked the pub, carried their own crates and boxes into the kitchen and back rooms, and then these people started bringing buckets of water and scrubbing the floor and washing the dishes and cursing and swearing because Mr Novák had left all the dishes as he'd brought them from the tables, cups full of coffee grounds and a mess all round, as the old custom dictated, so that the publican arriving after the publican who'd left would get the best out of the pub. And we regulars turned up the very next day and rejoiced that from now on the pub would be as it should be, it was two brothers, Luboš and Václav, and they immediately set to, planning a menu with seven main courses and considering the possibility of instituting Pilsner Urquell as the house beer, or at least Kozel Beer from Velké Popovice, the one with the dancing goat logo. And once more we were delighted, and once more we had our goulash or tripe soups, and the new boys were spry and brisk, and they let it be known that they hoped to make enough money to afford a car, and that there'd be no day when they'd be closed, but that the pub would jolly along right through the day, from morning till night, and they showed us how they'd scrubbed the floors and that cleanliness was their watchword... And we were all delighted, but I wasn't, because as soon as Polly and Lucy ran in and sat on our laps or curled up by the enamel stove, the first thing the new management did was to grab hold of them and throw them out of the door, shouting at them that there was no room for them at this inn, because pub hygiene and cats were incompatible... and so it came to pass that Polly and Lucy were no longer allowed inside, they would stand on the low wall round the terrace then, when it started to rain, all their kittens gradually died, when the snow started to fall, Polly and Lucy, by now quite desperate, came running in several times hoping to be permitted at least a little warmth, but the young licensees chased them out with brooms and sticks, or caught them and literally kicked them out through the open door... several times I went to pat them, but they'd lost their trust, and so while the orchestrion blared away inside and the

stove was blazing hot and the inn was nice and warm, Lucy and Polly, as soon as someone approached, would flee the other way, away from any person, and then, after the door closed, they'd sit beside the door and watch the handle, wondering whether it might not be opened one day by their lovely master, Mr Novák. But Mr Novák didn't come, so Lucy and Polly, though two-year-olds, aged and grew wrinkles on their brows like an old St Bernard, they were run down with hunger and during the day, with nowhere else to go, they preferred to curl upon under the floor of the inn, jumping in through the air vent on the street side. They could see any cars arriving, they could see any people arriving and urinating on their air vent at fly height, they stayed curled up and slept, while above their heads feet and boots clomped around and chairs scraped, they heard human footsteps, but they didn't come out, except perhaps at night to snack on cold, sometimes frozen, scraps. But every winter's day, when the frost was cruel and Lucy and Polly curled up in a huddle so as to keep warm under the floor, they never missed their evening excursion, and when the inn was crowded and the music loud and commingled with drunken singing, Lucy and Polly would trot out onto the terrace, then round the side they would hop up to the window and the boxes full of soil and shrivelled and frozen begonias left over from the summer, and there they would sit side by side and gaze into the brightly lit inn, at the fired-up enamel stove, and maybe they were dreaming or thinking back to the times when, curled up round the stove, they used to lie there contented, sprawling, turned over on their backs, warming themselves from all sides. When I saw them there, I would walk up quietly, I could see their curious, rapt eyes which saw inside the inn something called hope, a memory of wondrous times past, I could see that this sight alone sufficed for them to live in hope that the day would come when this lot would all leave and Mr Novák would come back, the man who loved them and whom they loved back... And they would stay looking until the frost began to draw ice flowers on the glass, flowers other than flowers of hope, the beautiful flowers of winter, and Lucy and Polly, no longer able to see a thing through the snowy-frosty etchings, jumped silently down and slipped through the urine-soaked, frozen air vent back under the floor and wriggled their way across to the spot from which sprang and reared the flue that served the stove, there they curled up in the dust, entwined, breathing onto each other's paws and necks, then with a sigh they fell asleep to dream of the wondrous times they believed would return one day, because the pub belonged to their master, not these people, and because, since it did belong to Mr Novák, and so too to them, it was their, Polly and Lucy's, right to be able to warm themselves by the stove. Later, on my daily visits to the pub, I would pause with my hand on the door handle and wonder, should I go in or not? But because I'm incoherent by nature, I did go in and exchanged a cordial "Good evening" with Václav and Luboš, the new licensees, who might well have kept a clean kitchen, who might well have had a menu with six main courses, who may well have installed a massive orchestrion that drove most patrons crazy because they had to shout to make themselves heard, so in the end they didn't even try, except in the gaps, which were only very short... yet there, next to the enamelled cast-iron stove, the dustpan and coal shovel sat warming themselves, though it should have been Lucy and Polly... the two cats, who for now would sit, ears pricked, in a window-box for annuals, with one little paw raised at the ready, as if they were on the look-out for a mouse, they would stare into the nice warm pub like two little old ladies who'd sneaked up to the inn's windows to watch the firemen's ball, nothing escaped them, they watched keenly all the things they themselves had done in times past, they had danced and drunk griotte and beer and been either happy or unhappy, but they had been in *their* pub, the pub that belonged to them with all their joys and woes. And the frost intensified and the ice flowers changed into a polyester curtain that drew a misty veil across Polly and Lucy's precious world...

14 THE FEAST

YOU'VE NEVER SEEN, nor could you ever have seen, something we saw with our very own eyes. We were cutting a field of forage maize and suddenly Janeček says: "There's a wild boar here, fabulous specimen, pop back and get my rifle!" So I ran and got his Lancaster shotgun. And after we'd been driving the tractor round in circles for a week, all that was left in the middle of the field was an island of maize, and that's where the wild boar was. So we clattered cautiously into the corn and suddenly such a hefty boar came running out that we were positively startled. You've never seen the like, and you never will; Janeček, a gamekeeper with a limp, shouldered his Lancaster and fired, but the boar kept running, limping like gamekeeper Janeček, so both were slowish, and we ran after them because we knew of no greater delicacy than pig meat, wild boar meat even better. And so we ran on, having to wait for limping Janeček to catch up, and we hobbled across the fields bordering the woods all the way to the main road. So the wild pig only slowed down for us by – well, you've never seen the like – as it ran into the road,

luckily there was a Trabant coming along and with one wheel it gave the boar such a clip on the head that the car ended up in the ditch and the boar just lay where it fell. But as we ran up, well, you know what tough stuff a wild boar's made off, it got up and dashed into the ditch and off out of our parish straight into Psárce wood, which belong to Přerov, and as luck would have it, a woman was passing on a bike, so we kicked her off it and requisitioned it, but Janeček couldn't ride a bike, even a lady's bike, so we sat him on the saddle and pushed, the faster to chase the injured boar, which, after being hit twice, had to stop somewhere. But the woman ran along with us screaming: "Thieves, they've stolen my bike, thieeeeeves!" So we ran on, sweating, each of us holding one end of the handle bars, and now we were pushing Janeček along the main road, on the bike, which stiffened our resolve, and so, all hot and bothered, we saw the wild boar run into the village, but at once we were in the village as well, and it being midday and the desperate boar on its last legs and dragging one of them behind it, the red of its blood led us onward – you've never seen the like, nor will you – straight into the village school. And there Janeček hopped off the bike and limped after the limping boar into class four, and in class four the teacher was taking a biology class and just happened to be going through how the domestic pig was domesticated from the wild pig. She had barely finished and was pointing her pointer at a picture of a pig on a chart when the classroom door burst open and in ran the limping boar, he flew between the desks all the way to the teacher's desk and the blood just poured from it, and shortly after the limping Janeček, our gamekeeper and bailiff, ran in, he who would give his life for the hunt, and the teacher was petrified and the kids were cowed into silence and Janeček limped up to the platform with his rifle and took aim and the boar rose to the attack and as it made to lunge, Janeček shot that wild pig in its wide-open maw and the wild pig flew past him, Janeček leapt aside and hobbled over to the window, but before he could get off another shot, and before the boar could rise again to the attack, it suddenly toppled over and let out a death rattle and stretched out its legs and blood poured from its mouth and ran all over the schoolroom floor. We congratulated Janeček and thanked him, saying that we'd take the pig back to our place to gut it and use the 'hunter's perk', meaning the lights and liver, to make a whole laundry-tubful of paprikash. The teacher pulled herself together and went across to the prone figure of the boar with her pointer and said: "Children, you have just been treated to an extraordinary sight, so look now, this is what hunters call its maw, these its tusks, see?" And so we had to wait while she told the kids everything she knew about boars, and what she didn't they got from Janeček. Then we tied a borrowed rope round the boar's legs and hauled it into the daylight outside the school, and Janeček begged me for mercy's sake to find a photographer, because he would like to have himself photographed with one foot on the boar's head and the Lancaster in his hand. So I got hold of the chemist, who also hunted, and he quickly pulled down his shutter and came running to the school with his camera. But meanwhile the chairman of the local hunting club had turned up, he was sniffing round the wild boar and going cross-eyed with envy, because we hadn't seen such a superb specimen hereabouts in a very long time. And as Janeček adopted a triumphant pose, his heel on the pig's ear, we two, despite our overalls, lay down opposite one another to form a group with the pig, and the chairman of the club walked round and round in torment at the image, while the chemist, to make quite sure, took two photos of us. By then the club secretary had shown up, with his rifle, just to be on the safe side, but the boar was already dead, and so he chatted for a while and praised the masterful shot straight into the pig's maw, then he had a quiet word with the club chairman and they were obviously on the ball, because they waited until we took up the rope again and were about to drag the pig to the road so I could pop and get the tractor and load the beast onto the flatbed. When suddenly the club chairman says: "Look here, you leave the animal exactly where it is, he's not yours..." And Janeček said: "So who shot it, eh? Not you, I think." And the secretary said: "No, but it fell in our parish, and where a beast falls, that's the parish it belongs to..." And he laughed, rubbing his hands, and the chairman laughed, but Janeček's dander was up and we closed ranks over the boar's bristles and blood and we looked at Janeček, who shouted menacingly: "It's my boar, I shot him, I only came this far to find him and finish him off..." But the secretary and chairman of the local hunting club laughed: "Yes, but under the game laws...," but they didn't finish because the woman came trotting up from the main road, pointed at us and screamed: "Cycle thieves, they stole my bike here..." And Janeček said: "Take it, we were only chasing this, you understand?" And he poked his rifle in the boar's ear, and the woman grabbed her bike and wailed: "They're crazy, they knocked me off my bicycle, this'll be the death of me...," and Janeček said: "Get away, missus, I'll give you a rabbit to make it up to you, I'm Janeček from Velenka, but...! I'm *not* giving up the boar! He's mine!" And we looked up and our tractor had arrived, and jumping off it and straight towards the wild boar and kneeling down beside it was none other than the chairman of our own hunting club, Hamáček in person. And he looked up and congratulated the marksman and said: "What a feast it's going to be!" And the chairman of the local club said: "Yes, it is, but here, because this boar breathed it's last on our patch... shot on yours, breathed its last on ours, so he's ours..." But we looked at Janeček the shooter and at our chairman, and he said: "The boar's ours...," and we dragged the boar towards the tractor, and having bent down to load it, we were already lifting it when the members of the local hunting club sprang into action and dragged it back down onto the roadway... and again we lifted it and again the locals dragged it back down... at which point Janeček grabbed his rifle and loaded it and bellowed: "If you don't give us the boar, we'll attack!" And their chairman and secretary and the chemist shouted: "And if you load the boar up, then we'll be the ones attacking!" And Janeček yelled: "Get your hands off it, or I'll get nasty!" And he raised his rifle. And the secretary raised his rifle and shouted: "If you so much as move this boar, I'll shoot!" And more people arrived at the double, and more members of the hunting club, and even ordinary folk, because our two villages had never seen eye to eye, suffice it for a field of sugar beet of ours to border one of this village's and when the squadrons of women weeding got within a hoe's length of each other they'd start hacking at each and anyone's heads with their hoes until an ambulance had to be sent for, which was as nothing compared to the idea of losing from their own turf a wild boar that the entire village

had got their sights on. And who knows how it would all have ended, we'd already started brawling, I'd already had my shirt ripped off and my neighbour one sleeve and Janeček was just taking aim when all the school windows opened, one after the other, with a neat little clicking noise of all the catches, the windows filled with children, and the teacher called out: "What you see here, children, is a lesson in civics, what you see here is how international events should *not* be resolved, what you see here is what a divided Korea means, what a divided Germany means, what a divided Berlin means. Comrades!" the teacher cried, "Be reasonable, this brave marksman saved us in our very own classroom, he felled that huge, fearsome beast, so shake hands now, hold a joint feast and you can all eat the pig together, on neutral ground, perhaps in Starý Vestec, at the Start tavern..." And there was a brief silence, broken by the recorded sound of the school bell coming from a loud-speaker, and there was a hush, the barrels of almost crossed rifles glinted like the trademark on Meissen porcelain, I had old Cuc by the throat, I'd had it in for him a long time, and he had my torn-off sleeve in one paw. The chairmen stepped forward and ours said: "I reckon there might be something to what the teacher says..." And the local chairman nodded and said: "Agreed, load up and take the boar to the Start, and we can decide when to hold the joint feast..." The teacher and the kids came back to life, no longer stock-still like posed for a studio photo, and the teacher called out: "Children, we have just witnessed an extraordinary event, here you have seen a graphic example of how international conflicts *should* be resolved, as Comenius..." And the children's faces withdrew and the windows closed and then, after all eight of us together had loaded the boar onto the trailer with ease, the children started pouring out of the school and they were shouting and the colours of their caps and T-shirts were radiant, the kids screamed and punched each other and thumped each other in the back and hit each other with their schoolbags, joyful at being out in the fresh air, going home from school, but we thought their gaiety and shouting were meant for us, that they were paying homage to us, and Janeček, leaning on his rifle, bowed to them in acknowledgement, but the kids went charging past screaming, and the colourful throng kept clattering along, towards the pond which bore the children's screaming and shouting across its surface to every corner, down every street of the village and up to a high heaven...

The hunt feast was no less incident-free than the actual downing of the wild boar. Because our hunstmen had a more refined taste than the Přerov men, our chairman decided that the goulash would be made of the offal, and that the legs and loin would be cooked in a gamey rosehip sauce, and that an extra ten kilos of pork would be purchased and mixed with the rest of the boar so that each hunter could receive a small salami. However, the Přerov men wanted the legs and loin roasted like ordinary pork with dumplings and sauerkraut. So once again, the chairmen and secretaries faced each other and shouted at each other, threatening to settle the matter of the feast by the gun, but the headmaster said there'd been enough troubles locally already, that we were still living in Přemyslid border country, where, back in the tenth century, discord had led to first the Slavníks being wiped out, then the Vršovec family, who had helped the Přemyslids wipe out the Slavníks, and finally the last Vršovec had lain in wait for the Přemyslids and murdered the last king of the Přemyslid dynasty, we though would find a middle way, the loin would be done in the gamey rosehip sauce, and the rear legs would be done as classic pork, so that, given that there'd already been bloodshed on the part of the boar, there need be no major shoot-out before the animal was eaten. That evening, the huntsmen turned up in Starý Vestec, both groups, on the pretext of simultaneously going out stalking, having with them their rifles, hunting daggers and Bowie knives at their hip. The chairmen, before sitting down to the feast, both checked the toilets and back yard for lines of retreat in the event of any possible or actual need to flee. Then we all sat down, not mingling, but with each hunting club having its own long table, we'd spent the entire afternoon bringing in conifer branches to decorate the chandeliers and walls like at a final meet and hunt ball. And there was music, Mr Kučera from Vykáň on the accordion with a drummer whose accompanying flams and diddles made up for the base line that Kučera wasn't very good at. The singing though! That was really something, so beautiful that we all sung along, using the breaks to eat that glorious hunters' goulash, served to the brim in deep plates, and the beer, beer from Braník, and invigorating liqueurs and shots of rum. But behind each hunter was his gun, hanging on a peg, and if any of them went to the toilet, he took his gun with him, because they were all mindful of what befell the Slavníks and then the Vršovec clan, they all remembered from school how, at a banquet, the Přemyslids had told their Vršovec guests: "Set ye aside your sabres, set aside your swords, so you may feast at your ease, for you are guests in our hall...," and as the guests did as bidden, in the middle of a boar roast, the Přemyslids fell upon them so disarmed and hacked them to death to a man, bar the last man, who later took his revenge. It was good that we had our artist, Mr Jaruška, with us, the one who used to have an antiques shop in Prague and did wood carvings, though for years he'd been living among us in the Kersko woods, also he used to make all kinds of comical things at Shrovetide, by hand and out of plasticine, and at the rate of one a minute a man's cock would fall from his hand, or a woman's muff, at the Sokol carnival he created a sort of naked woman, fixed her to his shoes and danced with her, moving with such precision that the figurine seemed alive. He'd brought on her his trailer with him, in part to entertain us again, in part to show these Přerovites who we were and who we had among us, because nowhere in the entire district could they boast of anything of the kind, let alone in some piffling village. And indeed, the moment he started dancing on the table with his naked dummy we all roared with glee, but the Přerovites were deathly pale and crazed with envy and averted their gaze or stayed in the toilet with their rifles until Jaruška's dance was over... but by then the roast boar was arriving and we ate it with its wonderfully gamey rosehip sauce and Pálfy dumplings on the side and next to the dumplings a spoonful of wild cranberries, but when the Přerovites saw it, they pretended to puke and heave and their chairman was deliberately sick over himself to convey his antipathy to the dish that we had dictated... and now Jaruška was dancing on the table again and we raised our glasses to the figurine's breasts, and Jaruška wound up and set off a mechanism and red wine flowed from her breasts and we drank a toast to the great marksman Janeček, and now the Přerovites were licking their chops and maundering happily over the sauer-kraut and roast pork with Pálfy dumplings on the side. And so Mr Jaruška provided the entertainment and the music played and Mr Kopřiva from Vykáň sang whatever we told him to, and because he favoured our side, the chairman of the Přerov hunting club kept deliberately thinking up awkward songs, but Kopřiva always played them for him, and the chairman began losing his appetite and just drank reinvigorating rum out of a mug. And Mr Jaruška danced and the stream of breast wine dried up, but Mr Jaruška wound up another mechanismus, and by now we were just drinking and the clock struck ten, and the figurine stood legs apart and white wine began to flow from her belly button and genitals, Burgundy or Moravian, and we held out our goblets and glasses, and we drank straight off, so niftily, that we spattered our hunting jackets and hunting coats so little as you'd barely even notice. And the chairman of the Přerovites got so agitated that he rose and plumped himself down next to Mr Jaruška, and as he stared gloomily and bleary-eyed at the table, what did he see? Next to Jaruška's tobacco pouch lay a child's whistle, the kind of little whistle we used to make as kids, 'Whistle, daughter, whistle; Whistle, daughter dear', and the hunt chairman smiled at the whistle and the whistle smiled at him, and he couldn't resist and he picked it up in his fingers and blew on it twice, but suddenly he stopped still and the whole room fell silent, and our table roared with laughter because soot had come flying out of the whistle and the chairman's face was covered in it, black all over, and his hands as well, and he grabbed his gun from the wall and yelled that Jaruška would have to pay for this ignominy with his blood... and our people also grabbed their guns and the other hunters from Přerov grabbed their rifles and shotguns, and alone Mr Jaruška stayed on the table, his arms round the naked dummy, whose belly button and genitals kept dispensing Burgundy and South-Moravian wine, and there were no hands and no cup and no mouth that might be offered up to the stream of wine, so Mr Jaruška said quietly: "Now did I ask you to blow it? So, you should have left well alone..." And silence reigned, and everyone knew and shared the view that the chairman should indeed have left the whistle alone, since no one had told him to play it. So he hung his gun on its peg and Mr Kopřiva started playing again and his base line was beautifully made up for by drums and cymbals, but the party was still in two halves, still there were two tables, and heads were drawn inwards and bent over the centre of each table, everyone was laughing, but only at the jokes told by someone at their own table, and each table knew they had truth on their side, and each table had its own in-jokes and its own laughter. And for a change, Mr Jaruška – he'd had enough of dancing with the naked dummy, whose breasts had run with red wine and her crotch with white Burgundy – laid out two flugelhorns and a euphonium on the side table and the hunters shared them out, two even scrapping over the same instrument, and our lot tuned up and sat on the stage and at once the thunder of a new kind of music filled the room, our bodies tingled with joy as we stood there, holding each other at the hips in the manner of true huntsmen, and we sang and were merry, savouring the musical talents of our hunters, while the Přerovites turned even paler and stared at the ground, stunned, and two of them began to throw up and they knew they could never again get the better of us, unless the way the Přemyslids did it with the Slavníks and then with the Vršovec clan, slaughtering the lot at a banquet, on the sword side and ultimately on the distaff side too. Such was their rancour against us, so far had we outdone them in so many respects, and yet we had no inkling of the oil and paraffin we were pouring onto the flames of our glee. Well, they're never going to recover from this defeat, they'll never forgive us, I gloated as I watched the poor wretched hunters of Přerov, those Přerovites... And suddenly the chairman brightened, their chairman, and he smiled a quiet inner smile and slavered over some bright idea he'd had, he let us play five or so numbers more, conferred with his crew and then played his trump card – that we should let his band play, and we knew they were all hotshots, there was no denying that, and their brass band used to be the best, and that they'd play something more intimate for us, *O sole mio*, something our boorish cauliflower brains weren't up to... and Mr Jaruška took the horns from our reluctant players and handed them over, one brass instrument after the other, to the Přerovites, they took up position, stood astride on the stage and the conifer-frond-bedecked room indeed began to ring to *O sole mio*, even the chef trotted in and stood there abstracted, in his apron, and finally we sensed that at least in this regard and by this device the Přerovites could match us, and that there would be a truce, a grand truce, because *O sole mio*, we could manage it as well, but their delivery... but all of a sudden, as they were blowing away with such feeling, a black cloud burst in a shower all round them, and the more they blew more and more delicate soot from their instruments, the less they meant to be outsmarted, so they trumpeted on, but then the first flugelhorn player started to splutter, he dashed down from the stage, the other players behind him, all black with soot, and we roared with laughter fit to split our sides, but for the Přerovites it was the insult to end all insults, a desecration of the host, it was a terrible thing that we'd failed to give a timely pause for thought, timely consideration to this thing that Mr Jaruška had

contrived with the whistle, and now with the brass instruments. He had sown the same contention between us as between the Vršovec and Přemyslid clans, as before that between Prague and Libice... and now the hunters from Přerov grabbed their guns from the wall and the waiter and the chef fled into the kitchen, and now we too grabbed our guns and so we stood facing each other, implacable and with rifles at the ready and safety catches off, and one false move was enough for it all to have ended with a grand exchange of good old Bohemian gunfire, when the door opened quietly and someone's hand reached in for the light switch and the lights went out... and now someone came in and suddenly we saw a brightly lit chest covered in decorations, the apparition left us startled and the medals marched to the middle of the room and they were still all lit up and glinting like a prophecy and its signs, a hand writing on the wall, *mene tekel*... and suddenly the medals withdrew towards the wall and the lights went back on and I saw the figure turn and there stood the police commandant, debonair, and still shining his torch upwards on the medals 'for merit' bestowed upon him by the state, and he was smiling and said: "Do sit down, my chickabiddies, and let the feast go on, with me!" He'd turned up, as ever, at just the right moment... and he sat down and signalled to the kitchen to bring him the food he'd had set aside for himself, and not only for himself, but for his entire squad, his own selection from both courses, and he went and sat with the Přerovites, thus intimating that the victors would be they, and their chairman, black from the soot, cried out at once: "Commandant, you've saved us, I don't know what would have become of us if your medals hadn't appeared, you've restored order and peace... but you!" And he pointed at Jaruška, "you, call yourself an artist, you'll pay for this one day, and how! Because you're the intellectual begetter of our ignominy, our humiliation..." And before anyone knew it, the commandant, wreathed in smiles, smug and self-assured, picked up the whistle, which was still lying there, and blew it, and enough soot whooshed out of the whistle to soil not only the commandant's face, but also his uniform, and above all it covered the medals that embellished his chest... "See that?" the chairman of the Přerovites shouted, "look at me, not that we matter, but now you've gone and sullied the commandant here!" But the commandant had someone fetch the mirror from the wall in the lobby, he tweaked his slicked and perfumed quiff and all blackened as he was, he said: "Serve me right, my fault for having a blow!" And with relish he set about the gamey rosehip sauce and asked if they'd bring him the roast boar with sauerkraut next, the classic version, since he thought of the former as just a starter... And there was more music and Mr Kopřiva from Vykáň sang and the drum kit supplemented the base line, and given that the commandant was sitting there, we pushed the tables together and within an hour we'd all changed places and were all mixed together and we all sang our favourite songs at the top of our voices, and we sang with the commandant who, black as the ace of spades, had pointed the way to our reconciliation, exhibiting a rare command of diplomacy, so we started calling him *Governor of Kersko*. Like I said, you've never seen, nor could you have seen, the things I saw, we saw, the things that came to pass that time when a boar, a wild boar, got shot by us folk from Velenka inside the school at Přerov... When news of the glorious feast reached the teacher, the one who happened to be in the classroom when the boar ran in and our gamekeeper Janeček felled the beast right by the desk so that for the benefit of the children she was able point with her pointer and describe all the parts of a wild pig and their names, she was sorry that she couldn't have fetched the children so that she and they might have watched the feast, if for only a short while and through the window, whereat she would have pointed with her pointer and demonstrated and explained what the 'Bohemian question' was, a question of nearly a thousand years' standing in our neck of the woods...

15 IONIC MAN

I WAS SITTING by an open window, deeply engrossed and without not a single reason to be doing anything, thinking of anything, I just sat there looking out of the window, totally stunned and numbed by non-being. And two black horses turned off the main road and then a dray and on the box stood, legs astride, a man in a huge felt hat, holding the reins theatrically, and when he eased up, the horses got the bit between their teeth and charged off down the forest avenue and I was fearful that the black team wasn't just off for the ride, but was heading for me, and how right I was, they flew through my open gate and rammed the shaft through my window with such fury that I had to step back, but one mighty yank reined the horses in and they stopped where they were, though with their heads and shaft in my front room. And the driver hopped off sideways, patted the horses' rumps, which the black geldings took as an invitation to start munching on my begonias, and then in through the door came Ionic Man, as he was called, I knew him by sight from the pub, where he'd once been with one of his horses, gave him a drink from a pint glass and left. I'd sometimes see his white cowboy hat as he staggered through the village by twilight, I'd seen his hat in the vegetable fields, where he went to screw together the sections of the long pipe for watering the vegetables, he was always sunburnt and in summertime he'd only ever be in the bottom half of his boiler suit as his white hat sailed like a little dinghy through the cauliflowers and ripening cabbages and fields of kohl-rabi. So I said: "To what do I owe the pleasure of your visit?" He sat down and took his white hat off and his curls fell out across his sun-tanned brow, and he told me he'd found a beautiful doorstep at the tip and he'd brought it for me as a gift. "Me," he said, "I like writers because, whenever I write a letter, I can never get it finished, I get so freaked out writing it that I keep drinking shots of peppermint liqueur, one after another, till having failed to finish it I chuck it away." I offered him a glass and placed a bottle in front of him, and Ionic Man drank, not the way you drink alcohol, but the way you drink mineral water, to quench a thirst, and he said: "I've got this felt hat, see, so I get so hot that I drink non-stop – beer, peppermint liqueur, anything liquid – because I get all hot and sticky and being hot and sticky makes me thirsty." I says: "That's all very well, Mr Ionic, do help yourself, but what am I supposed to do with that doorstep?" Having stroked the nostrils of his horses, which had set about my two caps and were munching away at them with the same zest as Ionic Man drinking spirits, he said: "What to do with the doorstep? For a writer, mountin' a doorstep is a bit like a steppin' into another place, an' I reckon, when I read the crime an' casualties pages of the paper, I always imagine the dead person's you, so you'll have this doorstep here as a sign, a sign of foreboding..." He got up to go, put his hat back on, and as he left he was staggering so much that he almost had the door off its hinges. Then he appeared on his dray and with a few mighty heaves on a crowbar he dropped the doorstep onto the ground, it was a step from some church, the like of which I hadn't seen in ages, and if I had, then only in cathedrals and minsters. He jumped back down and again with his silvery crowbar he rolled the step away into the greenery underneath the birch trees, and I turned back to look at myself in the mirror and try to see what Ionic Man had come to tell me about the crime and calamities pages, and yes, there it was, I could see the shadow of death mirrored in my eyes. Ionic Man came back inside and he was sweating, and so as not to waste precious time, he picked up the bottle and drank straight from it, his Adam's apple leaping up and down with every gulp as he sucked in the hard liquor with great gusto and a great thirst. Then he looked at me, patted the back of my hand and said: "If anything happens to you, d'you want to be buried in our village, at

Semice, or in Hradišťko?" I told him I was nowhere near dying just yet. Ionic Man said: "Dyin' natural-like, I know that, but from what I read in the papers, it's all unnatural deaths, an' I reckon that if anything does happen to you, you'd be better off wi' us, in the cemetery at Semice, what I mean is, I think a writer should know what's to become of him if he's suddenly not there one day." "That's true," I rose and went to fetch a loaf of bread and, catching myself in the mirror, I saw I'd gone pale and grey. Then I started slicing the bread, feeding it to the horses turn and turn about, because they'd eaten three books off the table by the window and a towel. Ionic Man sadly bewailed the absence of beer and I went out and fetched a bagful of bottles, cool beer from the cellar, and Ionic Man picked up one bottle and dashed the cap off against the edge of the table, took a swig of foaming beer and began to make his case with considerable enthusiasm: "Listen," he said, "have yourself buried at Semice, for one thing the cemetery is the other side of the forest, so you'd have pine needles an' the smell of pine right on top of your grave, but the main thing is there's a football pitch in the forest, an' knowin' how fond you are of football...!" I said quietly: "So I am." "See then, I knew it, there's no other cemetery like it, the ref's whistle will easily carry all the way to your grave, an' every kick of the ball an' the players' shoutin' an' the crowd mouthin' off...," and he looked me guilelessly in the eye and took off his hat and raked his hair with his hard fingers, and his locks rattled as that living comb ran through them. I said: "It was very kind of you to bring me the doorstep, but I think we'd better hold back on the funeral, okay?" He put his hat back on and at that same instant got thirsty and dashed the cap off another beer against the edge of the table. "No," he said, having drunk his fill, "the step will remain here to tweak your conscience, "because I also do orations at funerals an' I'd like it a lot, if you died, or got killed somewhere, or murdered, if I could do yours... but I can tell you all that later, for now there's our cemetery by the football pitch... Have you ever been inside a charnel house?" I remarked that the horses had eaten all the bread, so I gave each one a handkerchief and they polished them off slowly and with relish. "No, I haven't been inside a charnel house," I said. "So when there's a match on," said Ionic man, "we can meet up there, 'cos the ref uses the charnel house as his changing room, the pitch is only the other side of the wall, an' again, if anything happened, there's often fightin' at our pitch, we love beatin' the ref up, specially if he doesn't award a penalty that wasn't there, but we've got such sensitive fans that they're capable of chasin' the ref out into the fields just for not givin' a ball as over the line, or a corner, or givin' one when there wasn't one... So do you know now where you'll be buried one day? Wouldn't it be just great for you? Though one time we nearly killed the ref for mistakenly failin' to give a hand-ball that wasn't. An' we chased him off the pitch an' up a pine tree that leans over the cemetery, an' we shouted at him to come down, an' he shouted: 'I'm scared you're gonna hit me,' so we spent three minutes shoutin' at him to come down an' him sayin' he wouldn't, so I popped an' got a two-handed saw an' we chopped the tree down, includin' the canopy where the ref was hangin' on like a woodpecker... but he fell into the cemetery an' before we could run round the wall he'd made off into the fields, an' there he got worked over among the cauliflowers, nice story, eh? I bet you're lookin' forward to summat happenin' to you and gettin' buried in our village now, aren't you?" Completely perplexed, I picked up a basket and offered the horses by the window some socks, and the geldings, as if they hadn't eaten since the night before, gorged on the socks and I glimmered with hope that Ionic Man would finally go home, I said: "Okay, in the event of my lot being to get into the crime and casualties pages, in that case I do wish to be buried in the cemetery behind the football pitch...," and I tipped back on my chair to check on myself in the mirror and said with a quaver in my voice: "But I don't look like someone about to die!" Ionic Man opened another bottle and said: "The crime an' casualties pages are not only full of people who had no thought of dyin', but people who didn't even look like it, and suddenly bang and they're gone! A tile flying off a roof, a broken axle on their car, explosion, murder, and they've had it, but I'll tell you this: you're bloody lucky I've brought you that doorstep, 'cos I, if you did make it onto those pages, I mean we firemen, we'd bury you like you was one of us! I mean, the hearse would set off from the New Inn, past the fire station, which will be open, a big red fire engine will be parked halfway out, nose first, there'll be two firemen standin' on it in all their finery, there'll be a fire pump outside the council office, where the cortège will pause, with two more firemen kneelin' next to it, axes raised in homage... then the cortège will make another stop outside the Old Inn, the one where you an' I both go, an' there'll be black flags flyin' from the dormer window an' the spare fire pump, an' two firemen will be kneelin' beside that one too, an' then, slowly, we firemen will take you to the cemetery behind the football pitch, I'll give the oration, please God I'll be fit, an' in my uniform I'll bid you goodbye..." The horses had eaten the last sock, one with holes in, holes like all the other socks waiting to be darned. I said: "Will they eat towels?" Ionic Man said: "They like towels best of all, last year, over by the common, before I popped off an' got back with some beer, they'd polished off a whole line of washing, pegs an' all, then there was

the time we were doin' downhill racin' on our bikes,
down the steps of the sports hall, an' I won, but I fell
head first on the stones during the second heat, cuts
everywhere, they plastered my head with about thirty
sheets of loo paper, but I was supposed to be doin' an
oration the next day, a lovely oration I'd got, but I
couldn't get up on my feet, I spoke anyway, I trimmed
the loo paper away so I could see my notes – I have to
have my orations written down – but the oration was
done! Though there was a wind blowin' and it kept
rustlin' the sheets of loo paper stuck to my cuts and
sores..." said Ionic Man, and having looked at me, he
suddenly started to cry, crying so much that the stream
of tears dripped down in a steady trickle, he wiped his
eyes and having looked at me again, again he started
sobbing uncontrollably, and the tears cascaded into his
hat like a fountain and they got pumped back into his
lacrimal sacs and so the tears he had shed a moment
before started over again. I was taken aback and tilted
my chair back and, having had a good look in the mirror, eye to eye with myself, I let out a howl and brought
the chair's front legs back on the floor with a bang...
"My God," I says, "why on earth are you crying like
that," I says, "what's come over you to make you cry
like that...?" He nodded his head and his curly hair
bounced and he said: "Yes, yes, I'm cryin' over you, 'cos
I've brought you that doorstep as a present..." He rose,

set his white hat on his head, a felt Stetson, pulled it down over his forehead with his fingers, knocked back the rest of the spirits, when the sun came out from behind the clouds, glaring bright, and its blazing light glittered on the terrets and chains and filigree of their harnesses and the sun's rays passed through the corners of the horses' eyes and cast blue-green shards, and the horses were standing to attention and I could just see them hauling a hearse with each steed having the tiny gejzir of a black funeral plume spouting from its head. Ionic Man staggered out, his white hat went out into the sunlight, and he placed his arms on the window frame, so he was standing there between his horses and their shaft, on which he lay his black hands, and he smiled at me through his tears and I got a fright, because only then did I notice that Ionic Man had no teeth, just a few sparse, hollow black bits of bony material, just one sneeze and the sorry remnants of his dentition would come flying into my room like so many dry petals of jasmine shaken with every gust from the bushes alongside the road like a snowstorm in summer. Then Ionic Man hopped up onto the box, disentangled the reins from the handbrake, stood astride and started jerking the reins and with the reins the bridle, and the horses, with frenzied eyes, fell back on their hind legs, beating the gravel path with their shoes, the chains jangled against the shaft and the team reversed through the gate, as tight a fit as a piston in a cylinder, then the dray turned and Ionic Man slackened the reins, the horses got the bit between their teeth and galloped off, flying down the main road, they slipped off into the trees and I watched as the white felt hat sailed through the branches and between the tree trunks, watched that white hat sailing away, and my eyes lit long on the stone step, a step that once led up to some church, some basilica, a step so well worn that I sat by the window deeply engrossed, staring at the step, and I could see little shoes and boots lifting off it and people's feet marching up it and down it, people's ankles and insteps and shins, cut off by the edge of the step, with which several past centuries had entered my garden...

Ever after, I did my best to give the white felt hat a wide berth... But there was no preventing the remarkable encounters when, out of the blue, the white hat would come sailing by, out of the blue I saw Ionic Man ambling zigzag down the road, coming the other way a cyclist, a fat woman pounding the pedals so hard she risked snapping them off, just like, if she had a mind to, she might have lifted the handlebars with her mighty arms and sailed off up into the air, and coming towards her defenceless Ionic Man dodged to the right, then to the left, and finally the cyclist ran him down, leaving a gouge in his belly from her right brake lever, but she rode on as if nothing had happened, while Ionic Man lay in the road, his white felt hat lying there next to him, and he sat up and first tenderly dusted off his hat with his elbow, then he put it on and said: "It's nothing, it's nothing, though I were just thinkin' o' you an' your funeral, I have to keep thinkin' about your funeral 'cos I follow the crime an' casualties pages every day, all stories about you, though under different names..." And I drove home in consternation, looking in the mirror and wondering where from my portrait Ionic Man had got the certain knowledge that I was a casualty in the making. Another time Ionic Man came to invite me to a pig-killing, and took me straight there with him, he put a rope round the pig's bottom jaw and as he led it out to the place of execution, he jerked the rope and the pig moaned and squeaked with pain, but Ionic Man laughed and said: "Hear that? He's also scared...," then came the murder followed by the insipid smell of the disgusting innards and then soups and goulashes and alcohol, and by the middle of the proceedings Ionic Man was so drunk that he fell into a tub filled with diced lard, knocked the stove-pipe out of the wall and shunted the stove, and his wife screamed, at me as well, and grabbing a broom handle she laid about first him, then me, but I lacked the fibre to part company with the white hat, which terrified me, but drew me ever to it. Whenever I entered the inn, there in the corner behind the massive stove, there sat, in the smoke, the white felt hat, Ionic Man so tanned that he merged into the half-light of the nook, and when he rose, the white hat rose and the white newspaper, and Ionic Man read out to me the whole crime and calamities page, which he'd read himself ten times already. Once, I was returning late from the inn, where Ionic Man hadn't been, and so I was pedalling happily past the cemetery wall, the white hat was floating above the wall, moving slowly the length of the wall with its dense mat of houseleek, the white hat shaded out now and again by black cross-es. I hopped off my bike and heard Ionic Man's voice, his solemn voice... "Dear friends, how sad it is when we must surrender to the earth that which sprang from the earth! Yeah, the days I have weighed in the palms of my hands!... No, better if I say 'vanity of vanities; all is vanity', we're here today to bury a man who has left his mark on Czech literature in letters of gold, but weep ye not, for this is a man who has gone before us, and if there is no resurrection, we weep in vain..." And I was visited with sadness and sorrow and I shivered, and that shiver proceeded from somewhere in the nails of my toes, a shivering and shaking that ended at the tips of the nails of my fingers, and I walked on as the white hat walked on the length of the wall, while Ionic Man's voice declaimed again and anew his funeral oration over my open grave, and I walked along, still living, past the cemetery wall. And so I gained the cemetery gate which you could see through and one half of which now gusted open, leaving just the gateway with its spiked finials and cast-iron openwork. And before me stood Ionic Man and his white hat shone in the dark and as an extra his little dog was padding about next to his feet, and the little dog's ear was bandaged with a white rag and Ionic Man's nose was bandaged with a white rag, the white fabric, the white calico, enhancing the mournfulness of the graveyard, where the hazy lights of the lamps on the graves cast a sombre glow on the shiny ribbons of withered wreathes. "Glad to see you!" Ionic Man cried, "I'm glad you're here," his white hat tottered as did his nose, which seemed bound round with a white tie, "I were just rehearsin' my funeral oration, which, even though I've broken my nose, I could deliver tomorrow, do you want to hear it?" I says: "No way, Mr Ionic, I don't, I heard it across the wall, a minute back, but for God's sake, what happened to your nose?" He brushed that aside and sat down on a gravestone, the little dog hopped onto his lap and he began to stroke it, and the white calico bound round the dog's head, the white rag, merged with the calico of Ionic Man's nose. "We were playing a game," said Ionic Man, "an' Muffy bit me on the nose without warning then dived under the bed, so what was I supposed to do? I dived after him an' bit him on the ear in exchange, an' now we're both ailin', eh, Muffy, aren't we?" he said, caressing the little dog, but then he stood up and got carried away with what he said next: "You see, I haven't been able to sleep for days, so I come to the cemetery instead, to get closer to everything, an' so as to think everything through on the spot... what I'd like best for your funeral is to convene a county-wide trainin' exercise for all seventy fire brigades at once. One brigade, that's nowhere near enough for you, you deserve seventy brigades at your funeral. There are so many pipes and elbow joins for the water-distribution system in the fields of the cooperative farm – for waterin' early vegetables – that if they were all joined together for the day, the procession could leave the New Inn with your coffin and come all the way through the village to the cemetery, an' if the fire brigades set up their hoses within a formation of crossed fire ladders, the cortège could pass through an undiluted paradise of crossed water jets gushin' from the extended ladders, at the top of each ladder there'd be a fireman with his own hose nozzle an' down below there'd be six firemen with axes, which they would raise in a final salute, but the high point would be at the cemetery, but I haven't quite got that worked out yet, but you're a man with imagination, so how about this, what if, to round off your funeral, we had fire pumps in every corner, an' what d'you think, might it work, suppose we held your coffin up over the grave an' trained the hoses on it from underneath an' had them lift you

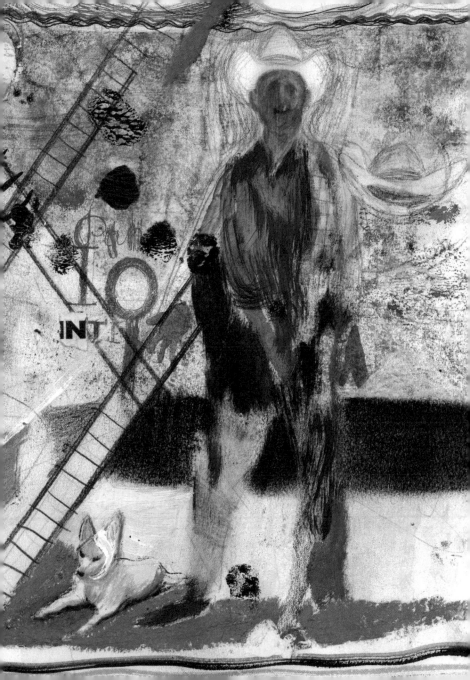

up as high as each hose could make it, what do you think, would the jets hold you up, I'm thinkin' ping-pong ball, like when one's cast up and held up high by that vertical jet of water in the château grounds at Lysá, what d'you reckon, would those jets, ten of 'em, hold your coffin up? And then, at a signal from the chief fire officer of all the chief fire officers of all the brigades, your coffin would float slowly down as the through-flow of the fire hoses slowed, what d'you think, wouldn't it be wonderful, sort of bless the region with your coffin an' at the same time carry out a region-wide exercise for seventy fire brigades?" Ionic Man stood there pointing, and I saw it all in the dark and half-light, I saw it all clearly and suddenly I knew that Ionic Man should have been a writer, that Ionic Man was a writer, except that Ionic Man didn't write, though he did *see* things perfectly well, but that only now, here at the cemetery was *I* seeing that I should have thought the same thoughts as Ionic Man, I should have thought like that and from that moment on I would think in terms of the crime and casualties pages, like monks... oh dear, that doorstep Ionic Man had brought me, yes, it would have been none other than a step from the destroyed and defunct monastery in Sadská, any house of Augustinians would bring one step from Rome with them, and this will have been the step mounted by scribacious monks, who wrote and gilded beautiful codexes in response to the crime and calamities pages, those memento mori... Chirpily and gleefully I said: "Mr Ionic, give me your hand, you've opened my eyes, my inner eyes, that white hat of yours has taught me to see, only now can I see things I haven't been seeing, but that you *have* seen..." And Ionic Man stood there and he had a radiant glow – how could I have missed it before? – his hat, it wasn't the kind that cowboys wear, but a halo in the form of a hat, a circlet floating over a man whose powers were akin to those of the Holy Spirit... the very essence of being.

A few days later I set out to say thank you to Ionic Man once again, but they told me he'd died the day before, all of a sudden he'd died, out of the blue, suddenly, within three hours, he was dead. I asked: "And where's his hat, that white felt hat, the hat he used to sleep with, where's the hat?" They told me: "Oh he lost it, well not lost, but having finished loading a truck with cauliflowers, he briefly hung his hat on the lamp-hook of the truck at the end of the train, and it would be the end one, wouldn't it? And the train started to move and his hat departed on the lamp-hook of the end truck and when Ionic Man went back to his horses, the train was gone, and with it his hat. And so without his hat Ionic Man lost his strength, and after he got home he took to his bed, and in three hours, all of a sudden, he was dead. Where *did* that end truck take Ionic Man's halo?

16 HAIR LIKE PIVARNÍK'S

I SAW HER ONLY ONCE, but having seen her, I took to her, and she took to me, and so we took to each other and we rode our bikes one behind the other in the night-time, and it was not just nice, but glorious, because where does it come from inside you, seeing things that aren't there? And I saw that her bike had a glass frame, and the frame was pumped full of neon light, a kind of blue, luminescent core, as if the bike were constructed out of Geissler tubes. And I know this, I know full well how everything starts to metamorphose before my eyes as if by magic, so I tell myself, watch it, lad, go easy, you're already paying one lot of alimony, but I know myself, the more I avoid a thing, the more I'm likely to bite the dust chasing it. And when all's said and done, that's how it should be, who wouldn't want to go for a ride at night with a strange girl who I'd bewitched at zero cost, merely by having pageboy hair, just like the Slovak footballer Ján Pivarník's. So I rode along with this brunette with chocolate calves, and I had this nice vision of whatever I looked at spouting tiny little sparks, everything fizzing, so that tiny little

lights spouted even from her pedals like fake diamonds. Into the quiet of the night she said: "You know, I'm really glad it's all over, that uncle of mine would have driven anyone crazy, see, he had a decent enough farm, but he sold up and bought a miserable little house, and he lived there with his sheep, he gave the money left over to my dad, who squandered the lot, see, uncle used to sleep with his sheep, and after ten years he smelled like the sheep and he even stopped talking, he just bleated when I took him some cake and a box of chocs for Christmas, see? And it was awful, it was snowing and uncle had a hole in his roof and a fire on the floor and the sheep were bent over round his head, and uncle had a long beard, even his whiskers reeked of manure, and wherever he went the sheep went too, well, I've never seen such love before, see, and when he went to bed, he lay down in the hay, the main room *and* the kitchen were up to the window ledge in manure, and the sheep nestled round him and the ram lay at his head like a fur coat, and uncle breathed sweetly and the sheep followed suit, and I backed off from my uncle in disgust, shuddering and screwing my face up, because he stank horribly of manure, see?" "Sure," says I, "just what I needed to hear," says I quietly to myself, meaning this twaddle about her uncle, but I looked about me and saw that I was actually seeing something in our woods for the first time, and that was that I was pedalling along behind this girl, whose pedals were spouting tiny lights, and through the girl I was seeing our entire forest range as from a helicopter, that it resembled the trunk of a skeleton, we were riding up its spine and the side avenues were exactly like ribs and ribbing, and as I looked about me I saw that the shadows of our bikes were purple with Marian blue edging, that the six sodium lamps, which were set four hundred metres apart, these lights created a kind of long bridge with six piers and a green river of dark leaves running beneath them. Wow, that's quite something, it had never struck me before, except when the lads and I'd got hammered, but honest, I'd never have seen it, not even if I were on a high, I watched as we rode under one of those sodium lamps and what did I see? – I saw me toss my own shadow behind me, like when a decent footballer does a scissor kick over his head as he aims for the goal, or when Mr Pivarník kicks the ball away, and I looked behind me and what did I see? Nothing short of a purple rudder growing out of my back along the surface of the road, as if I was a purple sailing barge... And as I revelled in my vision, the girl prattled on and on... "...see, and this uncle used to graze his sheep at the edge of Kersko Forest, and one of his rams ran across the road, but a bus ran over it and my uncle collapsed on the spot, and the bus driver tried stopping cars in case there was a doctor in one, so he wouldn't be to blame not only for running a ram down, but also for injuring a man, and in one car there was a lady doctor, but the young rams and ewes stood all round uncle, so first they had to shoo the rams away, and when the doctor knelt down with her listening thingy, the ewes surrounded her, but the doctor got up in disgust and there was no one willing to unbutton uncle's coat until a plumber got his metal shears and cut it open, and a layer of shirts, see, that's because uncle, when it got warmer in spring, he would take off a whole layer of shirts, like a tortoise's shell, and put a new one on, and when it got cooler in the autumn, he'd put on one shirt after another and by the spring he had seven on, so the plumber sliced through the shirts with his metal shears and they curled away like old lino, or sheet metal, and only then did the doctor put her listening thing on uncle's chest and discovered no more than what the sheep had known at once, and that's why they were shaking, that uncle was dead, of a stroke, because his favourite young ram had got run over, see? Then the cops arrived with their tape measure and drew a chalk circle round the ram in the roadway and uncle in the ditch, and then a hearse arrived and the men tossed uncle into a coffin with disgust, and when they put the lid down, they trapped uncle's beard in it, his whiskers were sticking out like a tussock of flowering cactus poking out of a rock garden, and you know, when the hearse moved off, the sheep ran after the coffin until they collapsed exhausted in the ditch, and did you know that we put the dead ram inside the gate and that before nightfall someone stole it?" "Really?" says I, "Did they?" says I, but I was looking at her white dress, which threatened to split at the seams the way she was pounding at the pedals, like some kind of corset, it was, this beautiful girl's dress, a girl who'd taken up with me all because of my beautiful, long and well-kept hair, exactly as worn by the blond footballer Pivarník, and me, as soon as I clapped eyes on the girl, my eyes melted then and there, and I know the signs, I know how once a year and all of a sudden my eyes go beautifully blue and doe-like, then I rise in my own estimation since I know I'm about to learn things about which I haven't a clue, yet suddenly I know things I didn't, I look up and down the forest road, I can see the odd chalet with its lights still on, and suddenly I can see inside the chalets, things there probably aren't quite as I see them, but I feel that they are, I see people getting ready for bed, I see that for these weekenders it's not enough to get on each other's nerves at work, on the communal staircase or in the home, but that they have to pack their jealousies and bring them with them out here, to our cemetery in the forest, I could see how these outsiders so loathe each other's guts that they're on the go and up and down all day long, blasted by their

hatred into a far corner of their plot, only when a cloud-
burst or night arrives do they withdraw into their
shared chalet, their family tomb, where they deceive
one another with sweet talk while actually checking
them out to see how much longer they're going to live.
I saw these incomers laying themselves down in common coffins, a common pit, like freaks tidied off into
crates after the last show, I can see sleepers tossing
about in bed and getting the sheet in knots as they
worry whether or not they've forgotten to put away
their name-tagged picks and forks, spades and mat-
tocks, whether or not they've forgotten to raise their
ladder skywards and prop it against a pine tree and bind
it with a chain through the rungs round the tree, and
whether or not they've forgotten to padlock the chain…
and so I rode on with ever more beautiful ideas, ever
prettier images, streaming lightly from my eyes and
brain, and I knew that what the girl, going on and on
at the top of her voice about her uncle, it had suddenly
dawned that what she was saying she wasn't saying just
to me, but to the entire forest, and not even just that,
but to the entire world, so sure was she that her uncle
was the oddball to end all oddballs. And she rode nice
and slowly and I, like a faithful hound with my eyes
sunk into her like her saddle, she rode as if riding
through tar or honey or gum arabic, just sauntering
along, and then she turned off into a side avenue and

the way brightened through a birch grove, and this very birch grove is the one like when you're reading Chekhov, all television stories are also shot here in this little wood, and the little meadow beyond the trees was bright, with a mist floating over it, and down at the whole thing gawped the moon, but a moon so stupid that it was as magnificent as some moron, a breeze gusting from New Leas rustled the reeds and I'd never noticed that rustling before, but now, on that leisurely ride, I heard it all and I was proud of myself and wished for nothing more than to be pedalling behind that girl on a bike, spurting thousands of little lights from the buckles of her black shoes adorned with fake diamonds. And I envied the bike its exquisite load, and the girl kept looking back and when she looked at my hair, her bike began to zigzag, she had to make a quick grab for her handlebars to counter an imminent fall, but all of this was due to me shampooing my hair every other day, spending ages with a comb in front of the mirror and constantly checking with my right hand that my hair had the proper hippie look, of that I'm sure, but if she wants to have a good time, so be it, I mused, because I could see myself and my tea-washed toupee riding through the dark woods, if she wants a good romp, okay, she's the right age and figure for it. And suddenly I looked and there in front of us was a white gate, and the girl hopped off her bike, unlocked the gate and

I was into the yard after her, she propped her bike against the fence and I put mine against hers, but the frames slipped with an almighty racket into the sand and the handlebars got hooked together and in that I saw a promising sign. She'd unlocked the gate, now locked it again, and next to the white fence with white laths stood a white-painted bench and the moon was reflected on the seat and the girl sat down on the moon, the bench was gloss-painted, and I sat next to her and she swapped her shoes for something lighter, handing me some white sandal things as well, and I took them, so light they were that they almost flew up and away like the wings of a bird, and they were like crêpe paper to the touch, but they fitted me like a glove, and as I looked round the plot I knew for definite that something was going to happen here, because the whole yard was marble sand and as meticulously raked as my own fair hair, like corduroy, and as the girl walked about the yard in those shoes, the sand crunched, and only now, by the full light of the moon, did I see this creation, saw that her body was like a spindle with threads unwinding from it that I rewound optically straight round my genitals, and what turned me on most was that as she walked, her thighs heaved fabulously and described such a beautiful curve that I knew that this girl had fallen from the fifth floor of Ottoman heaven. And I saw that the walls of the chalet had been whitewashed the day before, as it seemed, and I saw that the windows had been cleaned with glass cleaner that very morning and the curtains washed the day before and rehung that day, not that that was really the case, but everything was so neat and tidy that I, a young and messy old thing, couldn't fail to notice until it hurt. After that I wasn't in the least surprised by the white Octavia estate parked under an oak tree, its seats covered in white sheepskin, spare shoes on the floor, and the whole Octavia gleaming as if it had just driven out of a beauty parlour. And I told myself 'Get a grip, lad, here we go,' because she'd unlocked the front door and having gone inside, she stopped and suddenly turned and pressed herself against me, and I could feel her thigh touching the key in my pocket, and her hands went straight for my hair and I knew it made her feel good, my straw-coloured hair, and I held her by the waist, but she still had all ten fingers in my curls, so I had all my ten about her body, twenty fingers in all, and ten of them couldn't get enough of my coiffure and my ten couldn't get at her skin, and I thought this was the one thing on her mind, but then she went on with her family saga and full of her own mystique, she burbled tenderly on: "… see, darling, uncle's funeral was just as sad as the rest of his life, he didn't have a single friend left in the village, because for these bumpkins uncle was a lost cause, him letting his animals get too close, see, darling, in the country he put sheep above people, that's a sin, see? So it was just me who buried uncle and even then I was on tenterhooks in case the sheep smashed the gates down, because all the way to the grave I could hear them bleating in the knowledge that uncle was in the cemetery, so the sexton quickly shovelled soil over the grave, because, dear, if the sheep did break through the gates, they'd have jumped in and trampled the coffin, see? – when a farmer doth die, his animals cry, so I sold the sheep on the hoof to some butchers, they got planks and trestles and rigged up a place of execution right there in the yard, and it was sad, one sheep after another, and they laid them on their backs in among the planks and cut their throats, and you know, dear, I understood why the sheep is a symbol of longsuffering and Christian humility, and you'd never believe, dear, how handsome those butchers were, beautiful as bulls, yet ox-eyed, like you were looking at statues of Greek demigods, see, if the sins of the world were wiped clean at abbatoirs, they'd be like the priests, the last ewe, dear, she jumped up on her own, all they did was lay her down, and trotting after her came a little lamb, which also jumped up and was still suckling... so first they snicked the ewe, then they watched lovingly for a moment at the suckling lamb, and then like this, one quick swish of the knife, and a trickle of blood started, mingling with the milk, but the butchers were so handsome,

dear, with black forelocks, that if they'd been even a teeny bit handsomer, they'd be like part of the family, dear, almost as beautiful as your golden hair…," the girl kept gushing at me, thinking it might make her feel better if she could transfer these images of the sheep onto me, but I was holding her with all ten fingers under the arms, and when I lifted her up, she ran all her ten fingers into my hair and I carried her over to the sofa under the window into the moonlight, so I had to look out into the yard, where one half of a white-painted shed door had opened, and the gloss paint shone back so like a floodlight that I put the girl down and stood up and looked, and out of the door came the white figure of a man in a long, white, knitted sweater, the kind of sweater, it was, last seen on St Wenceslas, a sweater knitted of thin wire, and the young man was walking barefoot across the marble sand and straight towards our bikes and he stood legs apart and kept staring at them until he threw up both arms and almost shook the stars, so angry was the man that both bikes collapsed with a clatter into the sand and I saw my pedal get tangled in the net skirt guard of her rear wheel, a net that makes a peacock's tail… and the young man, this alarmed me because the door wasn't locked, came across to the front door, I heard him put an ear quietly to the door, I heard him quietly, lightly finger the door handle, try it, open it, but then close it again and it went quiet, and the girl held me in all her ten fingers and dug her little nails into my skin, and I could hear the handwriting of her fearful heart as she inscribed the fear into my head… then the quiet footsteps receded, then the back of the man crossed the yard, suddenly the young man was withered and aged, his back like the body of a cello or tiny double base, heading straight for the shed, suddenly I felt sorry for him, because that long, knee-length sweater made him into a saint, and also, the moment he entered the shed, the door half seemed to shut itself behind him, and again I was dazzled by the white gloss until it hurt my eyes, and then all went quiet again, only the Moon moaned on like a moron, like a monotonous idiot. I says to the girl: "Who in heaven's name's that wandering around in the yard?" She said, and she still had all ten fingers in my hair, as if holding on to some priceless vase or something, she said: "Don't worry, dear, it's my ex, that's all, see, but I can't love him any more, on the other hand he can't live without me, so I let him sleep here in the shed when he comes for the weekend, and he's come…" I said: "But what manner of man is he, for God's sake?" And she said: "Well, my dear, I don't mind that he's a hangman's assistant, the reason I broke up with him was his name, you should remember, dear, that's how fussy I am, hangman's assistant fine, but the fact that his name's Tělíčko, like 'bodikin', goodness no... ugh, Tělíčko!" She did that spitting thing like when you've got a hair or something on your tongue, right in my eyes, but she was still holding my head in all ten fingers as if she was carrying a rugby ball across the line. I stiffened my resolve and said: "Look here," I said, "and who are you, my little beauty?" She said: "I've got a degree in aesthetics, you know, that beautiful science of beauty, but I've only recently found a job that suits me, a job I enjoy..." And I said: "And what do you enjoy, darling?" She sat up, did up the button on the fabulous sweatshirt given me by my ex, the one I was paying alimony to, and having done that, she bent down and handed me one of the endless array of little crêpe paper shoes and sandals, and then she told me: "I wash and dress corpses ready for the coffin..." And before I could compose myself she placed her lips against my chattering teeth, and at that moment I clearly registered that this girl had beautiful eyes, like two butchers, eyes almost as beautiful as my blond, drained spaghetti-like hair, hair like the footballer Pivarník's.

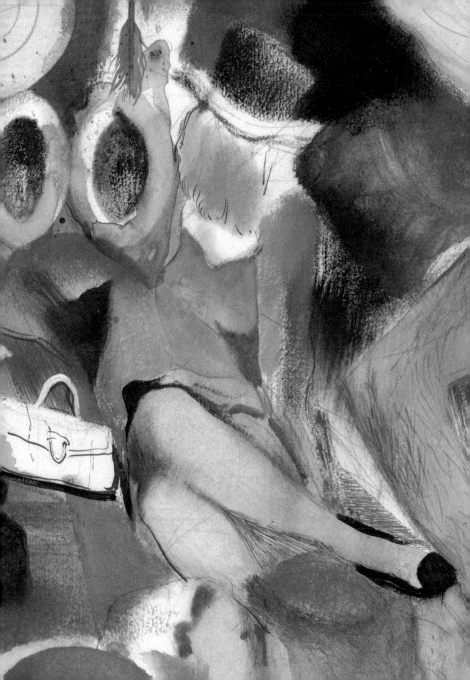

17 THE MAID OF HONOUR

"MY DEAR," I TELL MYSELF, "you no longer need to butt in on people's conversations and have someone hang on your shoulder reeling off all their troubles, I don't want," I say, "anyone to blow on your cuts and bruises to make them better or you to find in their eyes some universal validity for your snap judgements." I say: "You no longer need to look for the common denominator of your nearest and dearest, instead, my boy, pretend you're dumb, pretend your hearing's gone, instead, beset by any torrent of talk, lend an ear to the interior monologue of your lost youth, instead lend an ear to the secret of sameness, and the solitude which you are entering won't frighten you, and instead, by staying silent, transport yourself beyond the curtain of human conversation and be brought face to face with a mirror of silence. Thus, my dear, will you pass through the din into a vacant silence in which you will be, a second time, in mystical union with all things, as you were first time around in your mother's womb, swathed in central heating and conjoined by your umbilical cord to the beginning of infinity...

And from the front platform of a tram there was a bleached blonde watching me for a long time with enormous interest, and having attuned my eyes I saw that, yes, it was the dream-girl of my youth, whose heart I sought to break and in return she promised to afford me the most beautiful proof of love. And I reached out and she stepped forward through the swaying tramcar, and as our hands met again after so many years, I let out a snort of excitement and a frightful bogey shot from my nose, a great long thing, like little kids get. And my dream-girl immediately extinguished the flame of her delight and her green eyes froze with revulsion, in my agitation I sought, but failed to find, the pocket in which I usually keep my handkerchief, and so I stood there in the middle of the car, riven by embarrassment and ignominy, passengers who up to then had been envious now schadenfried me, and the soulmate of my youth struggled towards the step, grabbed the brass handle, extended one shoe and her heels clacked down one by one and off she ran across the pavement, sling-shooting with her enraged eyes and spouting abuse from her mouth so as to cauterise the predicament I'd contrived to put her in. And I had no alternative but to go for a pint.

Things were quite lively at the White Lion. A wedding party, much the worse for wear, was staggering into cabs, the bride came back for her bouquet and as she tried to find the way back out, she cast about for the door handle in the wall, the groom, a dreamboat in the Berber mould, had his tuxedo lapel covered in sauerkraut, these remnants of the wedding feast twinkling on his jacket like a recruit's rosette, and as he led his new other half off, by drunken misjudgement they ended up in the kitchen. The waiters having taken the newlyweds outside, one bespectacled guest rose from the floor next to the toilet, the 00 sign on the door floating above him like a double halo, and started clapping and shouting: "Encoooore! Bravoooo!" And the taxis left and the waiters closed their eyes and heaved a theatrical sigh of relief.

However, the maid of honour, drunk, came back inside and started knocking back the party's leftover Gambrinus, that golden pilsner brew, which trickled past her pink lips onto her pink bosom, inside her pink bodice, over her pink dress, which clung to her beer-sodden pink lap. Having downed the last dregs from the wedding feast, she didn't dare lean forward, because the beer inside her reached all the way up to mouth level. And I just toyed with a beer mat, too scared to think of that unpleasantness in the tram. So instead I watched the hairy male arm encircling and squeezing the leg of a plump female at the next table. A pale man in an indeterminate uniform rose beneath the chandelier and staggered off to the toilet, and the

door's double zero having settled back in place, there was a bang of the bakelite seat followed by a long, mournful mooing sound, the kind tritons would blow on sea-shells to summon errant nymphs. The maid of honour's fish-eyes roved about until they alighted on the hairy male arm.

"Got a license for that? Bet you haven't!" she shouted.

And all eyes turned to the male hand, which may indeed not have had a license for such public intimacy, since it ceased to fondle the precious flesh.

And the pale guy came back from the toilet, drops of clean water twinkling in his hair. The maid of honour stared long at this watery halo and cried out, delighted as it dawned:

"'Ad a good puke, did yer?"

And the man in the indeterminate uniform nodded, sank onto a chair and worked his jaws. And I went on toying with the beer-mat, still staring at the cardboard circle going round and round in my fingers and a pink shadow fell over me, then the maid of honour's pink hands rested on the tablecloth and her pink frame drooped over me and I froze in fear lest her pink throat start gushing beer over me as from a pink fountain, as from a pink jug. But instead the maid of honour spewed out words that shook me even more.

"Old man," she cried, "you bought yourself a rosary yet?"

And I went on toying with the halo, the maid of honour watched me and she can't have been more than eighteen, her chubby pink arms, pink neck and all her exposed flesh shone with golden beer, she was like a little pink piglet, which, to give it nice crunchy crackling, has been gone over with a pastry brushed soaked in beer. And I put on my best human eyes, that look of an apologetic little dog who's just caused a car crash, and with those eyes I begged the maid of honour to retract that with which she had just soaked me. By this point, the two middle-aged lovebirds had paid and were standing in the doorway, waiting to see how I would come to terms with the next home-truth. But the pink maid of honour raised a finger at me and cried:

"Old man, writers and pigs are only memorable after death!"

The drunk patron in spectacles rose from by the toilet and clapped and shouted:

"Hurraaah! Encooore! Bravooo!"

Then a woman came running in and before we knew it she'd felled the man in specs with a single punch, his glasses flew up and away, then clinked against a brass bracket and the woman grabbed the patron and dragged him lightly towards the door as if she was trailing her jacket, and as she dragged him along, she couldn't stop herself pushing his bleeding face against the wall, leaving a long streak along it. Then she jammed her straw hat on her head and barged out onto the pavement with the drunk patron, who was enjoying every minute of it and shouting: "Bravooo! Encooore!" And the middle-aged lovers left in a hurry, as if they'd just seen what the future held for them. And the pink maid of honour danced off out of the White Lion and I drank one Gambrinus after another, such sweet beer that it is, and thought back to that blonde girl of thirty years before, sitting in a rowing boat with a red parasol, and I'd walked into the river in my suit and asked if I might take her out for a row. And she'd said yes, and I, waist-deep in the water, swung one leg straight into the boat and then got rowing and I was dripping wet, and far beyond the city I jumped into the water and pulled the boat up onto the sand, then I offered her a hand to help her out of the boat, so we lay there on the hot sand and she begged me to dry my clothes, there wasn't anyone around anyway, and once I stripped off, she calmed down and lay down next to me and closed her eyes; I plucked up the courage and silently undressed her too, but once she was naked, I couldn't go any further, so beautiful was that white body among the osiers beyond the city that I did no more than gaze on it. After that we only ever met with our clothes on, never again was I so carried away by her beauty that I walked into the river with my clothes on forgetting to strip off. So for thirty years I remained that young man, until last year, when I was walking down Lazarská Street and this woman ran into me and: "I say, granddad, where's the court around here?" I said: "Sorry?" And again: "Where's the court around here, grandad?" Since when I've been an old man, leading up to last year when a student offered me her seat in the tram: "Do sit down, pop."

Now I'm sitting in the White Lion, drinking pink Gambrinus, the whole pub is pink, pink curtains, even the table-cloths are turning pink, I'm sitting in pink solitude and lapsing into pink doldrums and nihilities, the two floating zeros on the lavatory door are my pink emblem, 'Little pink life of mine,' I muse, 'your once prosperous business is going bust, you must settle with all your creditors, making sure you owe nothing to the elements from whom you've taken everything for the book, little pink life, I'm slipping into bankruptcy and it's beginning to dawn that with true contrition and penitence a new account can be opened at the bank of infinity and eternity, those two zeros, those two cavernous gullets of yawning nullity, the two zeros incised heraldically in the doors of all gentlemen's toilets...' I'm in the White Lion and finishing off my last beer, on the wall the waiters have fixed a yellow board at which they're throwing sharp-pointed darts trimmed with gaudy flights, darts of the sharpness and weight of a pair of compasses bent back straight, each player starts with three hundred points and the first to reach zero wins. I've also played and, playing, have won, I was the first to have nothing left.

I paid and went out into the fresh air. From now on, dear heart, I say, you only need to open the paper and every obituary is your own death notice, every fatal accident in the crime and casualties pages is yours, every ambulance hurtling along, siren screaming from its roof, is heading your way. So for you, my dear, I tell myself, everything is somewhere else, returning to the beginnings is your way forward, dreams of beautiful girls are the interior monologue of ageing flesh, my dear, I say, through conversation you have sought the hypertexts and subtexts of all conversations, but now, instead of humour, you find an awkward silence broken by an angel's song. You may, my dear, consider it a mercy that this night's end will be marked by the daystar, though you well know that lights-out and reveille are blown on the same trumpet. So, my dear, your sole inheritor is a certain grave from which the sight of the night sky hauls you by the hair, a sky in which from eternity to eternity invisible hands holding two invisible knitting needles knit a dark-blue sweater adorned with visible stars... Meditating thus, I reached Palmovka. The main road rolled its paving stones out into a chequered carpet, the mauve lights of traffic islands cooed amorously and the breeze blowing off the river gave the tramlines a good polishing and the tram

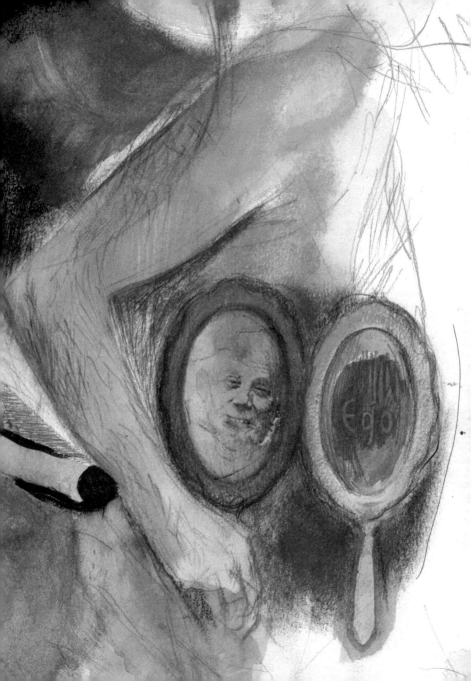

wires glinted like saliva trailing from the mouth of a love-crazed swain. Then in the distance a pink figure flitted beneath the lights, I caught the smell of pale beer. And there below, above the railway line, a red light glowed and a bell jingled, and the lamp floated slowly down and I, full of bitterness, asked myself, 'Am I really a granddad, an old boy, old man?' And as with my youth restored I raced the descending level-crossing barriers, having to bend low to run under them, so, head down, I ran onto the tracks like a true athlete breasting the tape. And at that very instant a pink mist fell across my eyes and I fell, toppled by the shock of the impact, and fireflies came swarming from my head. When the pink mist dispersed, the pink maid of honour was sitting next to me on the tracks, like me she had hurt her head, against mine. The furious lady crossing keeper ran up and dragged us off the tracks. Just then a steam engine trundled past, splattering my face with a mixture of water and oil and scalding my trousers with hot steam. The crossing keeper raised the large and the small barriers and the red light rattled happily away on the erect pole.

"Pea-brain!" the railwaywoman hollered, "where were you going in such a hurry, come on!"

"To the other side," says I.

"And where were you rushing to, you scarecrow, where?" "I was hurrying after him," said the pink one, and she crawled across to me on all fours, pulled out a little round mirror and held it up for me to see the blood dripping from the gash on my forehead. As the level crossing lady left, she couldn't resist calling back out of the darkness: "You'd be better off investing in a rosary, old man!"

I was infuriated and would have given her a tongue-lashing.

But the maid of honour calmed me down: "Leave her be, Venoušek, you don't have much time. You must try and be nice to people, or they won't come to your funeral."

And she took her tiny round mirror and looked at her own forehead, which was trickling with blood, and by the light of the street lamps I read, on the back of the mirror: "Savour the flavour of EGO chocolate." Then the pink maid of honour wiped my forehead, breathed into my face and I turned away and weighed up how it was that I, the only drunk I can put up with, how it was that only now I grasped why my wife would turn away whenever I breathed beer-sodden sentences at her at night, and that if I really loved her as much as my own EGO, I'd better drink wine instead, or stop drinking altogether. And I took the little promotional mirror and my own vile breath bounced back off it at me and I felt thoroughly disgusted. And at once I kissed the maid of honour's pink cheeks in gratitude for the discovery, but she snuggled up close and a current of affection ran through her entire body, our foreheads were all tacky with drying blood and she mouthed hotly: "Jerry, my dearest love, let me taste your saliva, go on..."

And suddenly her breath was sweet and she whispered how nice I smelled, and I whispered back how nice she smelled, and so we became each other's pink nosegay and we kissed and tasted each other's saliva and breath and the more we kissed, the nicer our breaths smelled and the more we created the glorious sensation of swimming in a 3000-gallon barrel of export lager, bathing in a tank of beer with the balmy smell of hops and malt.

"Marylou," says I, "you're beautiful."

"I know," says she with all the authority of an expert.

"And what else do you know, Evie?" I babbled.

"Everything, Georgie-boy," she exhaled.

We stopped outside a building about three streets from where I lived, a gaslamp guttered, spewing vitriol onto the pavement. The black, cast-iron, Art Nouveau balcony embellishing the entire tenement was like the paper trimming round a coffin. The maid of honour handed me a key.

"Open it quietly, Frank," she said, "daddy's such a light sleeper, see?"

"I do see, my Marylou," says I, but my hands were shaking.

"Wait, Freddy," she decided, taking the key from me, she braced her knee against the door, opening it and letting out a whiff of the hallway, which bulged out at us like a flag soggy with beer. The yellow light of the gaslamp alighted on the first step. I held up the little mirror and cast an unblinking eye of reflected light on the greenish wall.

"Jack," she said tenderly, "you can keep this mirror to remember me by, it quite suits you, do you know that?"

"I do," said I.

"You don't know anything," she whispered, "this mirror was the last thing my mum looked at before she died, see?"

"I do see," I nodded.

She closed the door, but before she trapped the reflection from the little mirror on the wall in it, I had an apparition of Charles Baudelaire at the same spot: having missed his footing on a kerbstone, he was raising a hand to grab his halo, which, as he stumbled, was heading down into the mud. And the draught from the hallway was wafted by a pinion of imbecility.

18 ADAGIO LAMENTOSO

In Memoriam Franz Kafka

I gaze at your lovely figure and and there is no need
to call upon the imagination in order to trace a return
to the beginnings, your morning attire is of a fine,
oyster-coloured linen and you are a voucher for a peat
spa, your blue eye stares at me with a lacteal tinkle,
with a stiff forefinger you part the yellow branches of
a weeping willow and you are fully aware that you can
expect from me all the very worst.

At the finish emotive flashes of lightning and a gold-
en one-0-eight open the way to a sewer, a sorry weekend
in the life I'm now starting to live.

The clothes I dream of are woven from the laughter
of Siberian cellulose, eight hundred girls' green hands
are the foundation of a sweet confession, contours
of laughter solidify in a mask of politeness and the
mini-crisps of your tiny porcelain ears are perfectly
concealed in the eavesdropping thickets of your fine
peroxide-infused hair.

The hands of timed things and events wind counter
to the flow of clock hands back to zero hour, though a

single day spent with a girl you love on a Norwegian glacier is the stock exchange of love of all good people. The friendship of a woman is pain for two, yesterday the foxes moved away and rewarded a brass band by clapping.

How I'd like to summon up the strength to rip off your face, with a single yank, how I'd like to lay bear all your thoughts with a single thwack, with a single brutal yank, like whipping off a bra, like whipping off undies!

Along a belt of pathways I return to the beginning of going, the revealing magnificence of animal experience wants thirsty cities to have lidos filled with children. Your forget-me-not eye, damaged by a fragment of Modra majolica, now understands my cool gaze, it is right that you watch the knife of my imagination carving its way back to the sources of things.

The last brook is sucked into a stream down to its last drop, the last river into the sea and the ocean evaporates up into the azure sky down to its last little bright cloud.

I can see you watching with me that rising fall, I can see that not one stage in this striptease has escaped you. I'm apparently pursuing the memory of your white silk, gold-embroidered dress, the sleeve furnished at the wrist with little slits for my desire, two hollow folds of cream-yellow cashmire, but I watch all the more closely as a pure spring and divine Ago go forward to meet the Spring, and you

smile at me seeing me scoop up whole handfuls of creative clay, and I, sniffing the earth, am also sniffing you.

Thus enriched with a bowl of curly cuttings, I sip the hope of an hourglass and for a healthy diet I prefer sorrow, a bit of copper wire found near a petrol station links me to eternity, the cage-rearing of lake trout is my disrupted honeymoon.

Now I'm sitting on the bottom of a little inn at Krč, the window panes are the walls of a great aquarium, you are floating in slow motion up by the ceiling, like a bee that has fallen into the honeycomb of my brain, fluttering curtains are an incessant process of hope and my destiny's dues are stored in a freezer.

The last flame of evening in the colour of orange tulips licks at the last beams and rafters, but I prefer to read in the papers about lions gnawing an upright piano for twelve minutes and how the lion cubs captivated some sports journalists, how via the swing-doors of coffin lids people are sucked through static architraves of clay into the earth, but the aura of humanity is best honoured by a striking picture and the future of mankind is a bookshop.

Meanwhile inside my brain I can hear the rustling of your sweet limbs, your skin is embellished with delicate crevices, you are buoyed up by contours of cigarette smoke, you rise upwards like bubbles in soda water, trees and flowers describe circles, an apple falls from an apple tree with an apple already in its core, the last ruins of evening slide silently into the soft dust, though for now I enjoy the extremes and eccentricities of the textual songs of newspaper poetry. And for now this is your youthful bodice and this is your skirt drawn into delicate bulges at the waist and this is your ivory-coloured silk robe and it is in Empire style and this is a girls confirmation outfit kept as a memento and this is your back dappled with beer mats and this is your unloosed hair and musical staves stream from your head. I see you floating naked now beneath the dark-brown beams, I see your arms moving in rhythm lit fiercely by the spatter from a yellow chandelier, I see hot springs spurt from your beating feet, droplets rise from all the pores of your body, you're immersed in a phosphorescent bath and streams of seltzer gush from your flickering ankles, fizzing fins, carbonated pinions, the little wings of flying fish, the flights attached to the ankles of the handsome young god Mercury.

The full moon glints in the first print of Armstrong's sole, but I'm more deeply affected by the item in the evening paper about the sixty-eight-year-old picker of medicinal herbs who dozed off in a flower-filled meadow and was sucked in by a harvester and whose corpse tumbled out with her herbs and the hay beyond recognition. The stellar minibus stands in the same place all the time, but this is your little dress for cycling in and this costume of dark cheviot has a velvet rosette in the middle, but for now I envy the air for the way you slip through it as toilet soap slips through the hand, I'm envious that your face is anointed with fresh tears of royal jelly, I envy your glass-paper coating and how men's gazes are easily struck on you like mercurial matchsticks, I'm envious of the squadrons of sperm and little angels who are your constant retinue, I envy myself for envying, because human desire can surmount all, desire explosive as a child's unhappiness. Your trunk is atilt and from your mouth a broken necklace of breath-freshening pastilles comes fizzing, you sparkle about the saloon like a huge lime-wood spill.

Life is a process of removing impurity, mercy and fortuity *and* necessity are the chubby triplets of a miracle, but girls' football boots are words of Maytime, little boots but one size smaller than a spaceship. Shards of shattered dolls have wounded my soul, a caterpillar crawling in close proximity to my eye is bigger than an express train in the far distance.

A peasant in the mountains of Moravia, having failed to get a job some years back, took it out on a statue of Jesus with his belt.

I see my life being sucked into my mother's womb, I see how, by an umbilical cord, I am being wound right back into the belly of our progenitrix Eve. I see that soiled underpants are an imprint of the infinite and intestines churned up by noble dread lead to a higher vision. I see my seed being sucked upstream like a mountain trout back to my first wet dream, I see me injaculated into the sperm duct of our progenitor Adam through the reproductive system of all my ancestors. By my sense of touch I experience resection of the rib that I've been missing right down to the present.

My every pore is in a state of high alert and the visible world is stored in a fine sheet, beyond the table-cloth of this landscape lies a life-giving void and I can never reach the cusps of the crossed swords of contradictions, I can never untie the tips of the four corners of the earth.

It's lovely to hear that jangling of panes of glass and see you thrusting through to the far side of things. Now you're flying quite low over a meadow like a swallow before a storm, Siberian irises in bloom scrawl purple flashes across your breast, you've just paused and hang transfixed in the air like a mermaid over the counter of old chemists' shops, now you've sailed into the scent of an olive tree in bloom, knowing how much we like to pick flowering sprigs of olive and interline our shirts and bodices with them in our chests of drawers, all the smells of an alluvial forest are postcards from you, a sand dune beyond the translucent heat is the colour of

your grainy thighs and hips, a meadow of flowering ox-eye daisies emits the inaudible sound of your unblinking eyelashes.

So we strode that time hand in hand in silence through the reed-green of early evening, from an army barracks a plaintive bugle sounded a plaintive lights out, the lining of the evening was made of purple washable silk, from an army barracks a bugle sounded a plaintive lights out, shadows lay themselves down in brown-green folds.

Evening Prague vendors cried: Two ministers fall from plane! Border guard's vigilance saves church pictures worth several million crowns! Lenin gets party card number one signed by Leonid Brezhnev himself! Corpse of unknown man found in the woods at Krč! I see that grotesquely melancholy beauty enduring in a pedestrian subway beneath Wenceslas Square, a joyous vacuity wraps events in a plastic mac, I'm standing before the demolition site of a sunny day and see how repetition brings jocund devastation, and signs and shouts invigorate me.

Bank then the Vltava embankment gleamed with black velvet ribbons, from the barracks a plaintive bugle sounded a plaintive lights out, your vulva was locked tight with tacking stitches and clips made from golden ribbons and velvet buttons, a vulva locked like a taffeta blouse.

Once, in the pouring rain, we saw two snails making love on a big rock, they merged into one whole sticky body like two slices of buttered bread. Now I stride through the depth of night without lights, steering solely by a sector of starless sky, ever on into the fuzzy wedge of converging pine tops, and the deeper I stride into the depths of the forest, the more precisely I know that I'm heading for your parted legs and that soon my dream of entering your inner parts as a haywain enters a Baroque gateway is to be fulfilled. But a bend has straightened the forest track and pushed the root and wellhead from which your legs sprang back to a respectable distance.

So tied to the circle of a water-mill, I wade into situations in which I haven't been before, a cathedral's statues crumble into the letters of posters, but an apple with letters pasted all over it can be used to recompose the Bible, the Empire frontage of the furthermost station in remotest Galicia can be restored to a Greek tympanon.

From a barracks a plaintive bugle has sounded a plaintive lights out, an aqueous green daybreak, the window onto the river is open, a loose bodiless bustier swings on a hanger.

I'm walking through damp sand thinking of your complexion thinking of your back, thinking of the tall and tender sleeve of your neck, thinking of your

peasant hips corset-constrained and decorated with two strangulation stripes, in front a tie woven from tufts of fluff struggling up, thinking of a bit of broken Sèvres porcelain. I've clambered down to a forest brook and again and again I dash the stream's water on my face, quietly savouring the distilled juices of gorgeous village maidens long buried in the local graveyards, juices filtered through heather, sand and fern and, with the gradient, purified into the aromatic mirrors of quiet springs and fast-flowing streams, I wet my face in that holy water and baptise myself with the sign of the cross, with the vertical of your vulva, the horizontal of your lips.

An *Evening Prague* vendor called:

Is anyone missing a family member?

A partisan, Czesko, writes to say that I am the well in which a child has drowned. From a barracks a bugle has plaintively sounded lights out, although sober, I show signs of being drunk. Water has rejuvenised itself and my eyes put on the finery of wall-bars.

When a farmer doth die, his animals cry. Thereafter nought but burning, burning, burning laughter. I'm dead tired, but happy. And amen.

June 1976

19 AN APPRENTICE'S GUIDE
TO THE GIFT OF THE GAB

I AM A SUN-WORSHIPPER in garden restaurants, a drinker of the moon reflected on wet pavements, I walk upright and in a straight line, whereas my wife at home, though sober, keeps doing things wrong and tottering, a whimsical version of Heraclitus' *panta rhei* flows down my throat and every public house in the world is a group of stags entangled by the antlers of conversation, the great inscription *Memento mori* that emanates from things and the destinies of men, now there's a reason to have a drink *sub specie aeternitatis*, the Olšany cemeteries, Pankrác Prison and St Bartholomew's Street police HQ likewise, hence my being a dogmatist of allergy in a fluid state, the theory of the oak and the reeds is my driving force, I am a human cry of fright undermined by a snowflake, I'm in a constant rush so as to be able actively to spend two or three hours a day in inactive daydreaming because I know that human life is short and flows along like cards being shuffled, that it might be better if I'd been put in the wash, tossed about inside a handkerchief, laundered, my face sometimes seems to say that I've had a promising whiff of a million, though I know full well that in the end I'll win the smirking square root of bugger-all, that the whole shebang started with a drop of semen and will end in the crackle of flames, from such glorious beginnings such glorious ends, behind the pretty face you're making love to may be lurking the merry Angel of Death, I water my flowers when it's raining, in flaming July I drag December's sledge behind me, so as to stay cool on hot summer days I drink away the money set aside for the coal to keep me warm in winter, I'm constantly edgy as to why people don't get edgy that life is so short, with so little time for doing silly things and getting drunk while there's still plenty of time, I experience a morning hangover as a sample, not with no commercial value, but as the absolute value of a poetic trauma with a tinge of discord that demands to be savoured like a sainted bilious attack, I am a spreading tree full of watchful, laughing eyes that are forever in a state of grace and the coupled wheelsets of chance and mischance, oh, the joy of young twigs on an old trunk, oh, the sheer delight of the gaiety of barely born leaves on young twigs, my climate is the changeable weather of April, a spattered table-cloth is my banner, in whose wavy shadow I experience not only the merriment of euphoria, but the slippery slope and resurrection, that dull pain in the back of my neck, that terrible tremor in my hand, with my own teeth I extract from my paws the smithereens and detritus of last night's shenanigans, each morning I'm amazed not to have died yet, I'm still in abeyance but may yet kick the bucket before I've had my fill of folly, I see myself not as a rosary, but as a snapped link in a chain of laughter, the most delicate bladdernut determines the strength of my profligate imagination, there's something castrated about me, something that is and at the same time retrocedes into the past only to be catapulted arcwise into a future that keeps jerking further away from my lips and eyes, making me squint with the double refraction of Iceland spar, today is yesterday and the day before yesterday is the day after tomorrow, I am then a maker of rash generalisations, a taster and sampler of adulterated space, to me forgetfulness and dementia and the twittering of children are the start of potential discoveries, through playfulness and play I convert the vale of tears into laughter, I invoke reality and it does not always give me a sign, I am a shy roebuck in a glade of impertinent expectation, I'm a solid bell of imbecility cracked by a thunderflash of cognition, in me objectivity takes on a measure of extreme subjectivity, which I consider an increment of Nature and the social sciences, I'm an anti-genius, a poacher in the game enclosures of language, I'm a keeper of the game of humorous inspiration, a sworn guardian of fields of anonymous anecdotes,

podo. aji.
o sen že celá dodávka filmů
výrobce se po vyvolání ukázala
filmy stejné šarže, prodávané
adné. I šetřilo se dál. Skutečnou
st, že vagón

3 KNIHY PRO V

an assassin of good ideas, a water-bailiff overseeing
dubious hatcheries of spontaneity, an eternal amateur
and dilettante of moronity and pornography, a hero
of thoughtful imprudence, an impulsive Augustinian
of premature parallels who would fain eat a slice of
bread buttered with infinity, who would drink from a
pint pot of the cream of eternity, now, now and at no
other time, so never, I consider misconstruction of the
words of Christ to be the very charm of the writings of
the Apostles, Brussels lace soaked in the saliva of an
epileptic, drift ice on the banks of a stream in winter
is my adornment which can do one an injury, I am de-
pression and dejection and feeling down, preparations
to dash headfirst into a wall are a constantly deferred
experiment to see whether it is possible to live differently from how I've lived hitherto, I'm a nervous
wreck who enjoys fantastic good health, an insomniac
who only falls fast asleep in the tram and gets taken
all the way to the terminus, I am a great presence of
small anticipations and anticipated great pratfalls and
bloopers, glinting on a grotesque horizon I see other
horizons of tiny provocations and miniature scandals,
hence I'm a clown, animator, narrator and home tutor,
just as much as I'm a great putter-down of myself, an
informer against myself, a writer of threatening letters,
unsigned, I think of worthless reports as a possible pre-
amble to my constitution, which I keep altering, which

I can never finalise, in the design of a lightly sketched shadow I discern a gigantic edifice, though it is actually a baby's grave long since collapsed, I'm a gent pregnant with youth, but already ageing, my mimicry and language are the mercurial grammar of an inner lingo, some hot meatloaf and a glass of cool lager have the power, in half an hour, to transubstantiate matter into a good mood, what a cheap metamorphosis and the first earthly miracle is born, a hand on a friendly shoulder is the handle that opens the door to that blissful state in which every belovèd object is the centre point of a paradise, the heart of nature is an accessible state of *bodhi*, in which it is possible to love in spirit the refractory and obstinate vagina, enfolded moreover in the most beautiful curves of flesh, *verbum caro factum est*, cannibalism dryshod with no priest or school-leaving exams, cows' sad eyes rolling quizzically above the sides of lorries, they're my eyes, an underage heifer on the way to face the butchers and their gleaming knives, that's me, a blue tit, wings dislocated, pumped out into a bucket of cold water at the frosty end of the day, that's me, a flame to which faithful wasps return only to burn to death along with the rest in their burning nest, that gives me a pretty accurate idea of a burning honeycomb ready and waiting for me alone, so I'm a corresponding member of the Academy of Rambling-on, a student at the Department of Euphoria, my god is Dionysos, a drunken, sensuous young man, jocundity given human form, my church father is the ironic Socrates, who patiently engages with anybody so as to lead them by the tongue and through language to the very threshold of nescience, my first-born son is Jaroslav Hašek, the inventor of the cock-and-bull story and a fertile genius and scribe who added human flesh to the firmament of prose and left writing to others, with unblinking lashes I gaze into the blue pupils of this Holy Trinity without attaining the acme of vacuity, intoxication without alcohol, education without knowledge, *inter urinas et faeces nascimur*, and our mothers as it were bore us straddling crematorium furnaces, or through the grass of overgrown graves, I am a bull drained of its blood through laughter, whose brain is being spooned out by someone like ice-cream.

Waiter, do you have any more of that splendid goulash?

P. S. As I analyse this text, which was meant as the postscript to the present book, a text that I wrote in the course of five hours in irregular breaks between chopping wood and cutting the grass, a text that has the slackened vertical pulse of an axe and the melody of the horizontal sweep of an Austrian scythe, I must draw a distinction between the sentences that surfaced as the sum of internal experience and sentences that

I have acquired through reading. I must identify the sentences with provenance that have so fascinated me ever since I first read them that I'm sorry not to have thought of them myself. 'I see myself not as a rosary, but as a snapped link in a chain' is an inversion of Nietzsche's 'I am not a link of a chain, but the chain itself'. 'Every beloved object is the centre point of a paradise' is straight from Novalis. '*Verbum caro factum est*' is St John: 'The word was made flesh'. 'Dionysos, jocundity given human form' is Herder. '*Inter urinas et faeces nascimur*' is probably St Augustine: 'we are born between urine and faeces'. And yet we're so wonderful. 'Our mothers bear us straddling open graves' is from a Spanish schoolman whose name I've forgotten. And yet we're magnificent and hence we're here. That's all.

The present collection of short stories by Bohumil Hrabal dates from the 1970s. From the end of the 1960s, the short story, which had previously predominated in his work, had begun to give way to longer texts (*Obsluhoval jsem anglického krále* [I Waited on the King of England], *Příliš hlučná samota* [Too Loud a Solitude]), often with a strong autobiographical slant (*Postřižiny* [Cutting it short], *Městečko, kde se zastavil čas* [The Little Town Where Time Stood Still], the trilogy *Svatby v domě* [In-house Weddings]). Thus, given that in the 1990s Hrabal confined himself to reflexive literary journalism, this volume is actually his last collection of short stories.

History is like a see-saw. Nothing complicated, just a plank with a bit of tree trunk in the middle for a pivot. Whoever's heavier will tilt the plank in his direction. In this duel of weights a small nation doesn't have much of a chance, unless it were to shift the pivot towards the wrong end, then it wouldn't need so much strength to win. Something a bit like that occurred in the second half of the 1960s in Czechoslovakia. The plank rose slightly towards the right side until the tanks roared in and the plank snapped. Czechoslovak history began to shift back in the wrong direction and just a handful of individuals tried to carry on upwards along the axis of the remaining splinters. The rest followed the direction of the main plank, in a process known technically as 'normalisation'.

Bohumil Hrabal was one of the discoveries of the golden 1960s, and after the plank snapped, hard times ensued. In 1970 Mladá fronta published two of Hrabal's books – *Poupata* (Buds, 35,000 copies) and *Domácí úkoly* (Homework, 26,000 copies). Both did come out in the stated print-runs, but both were then banned. The spanking new books were trucked to a state recycling centre and destroyed (except for the small numbers salvaged by Hrabal's wife Eliška, who was, by a whim of fate, employed at that very centre). Thus did Bohumil Hrabal become (in his own words) a writer to be disposed of. Then came the long five years when no book of his was permitted to appear. Then in October 1975 *Postřižiny* was allowed to come out, followed in November 1978 by *Slavnosti sněženek* (The Snowdrop Festival); the latter makes up the bulk of the present edition.

The author dated his original typescript 'January February 1975' and it was about then that he submitted it to the publisher Československý spisovatel. The typescript was returned to him with the requirement that three stories ('Zdivočelá kráva' [A Feral Cow], 'Variace na krásnou slečnu' [Variations on a Beautiful girl] and 'Vlasy jako Pivarník' [Hair like Pivarník's]) be omitted and the rest reworked. Hrabal was quite quick to produce a new manuscript, but that too went through a series of editorial interventions: 'Měsíčná noc' (A Moonlit Night), 'Beatrice' and 'Rukověť pábitelského učně' (An Apprentice's Guide to the Gift of the Gab) were left out, while 'Jumbo', 'Nejkrásnější oči' (The Most Beautiful Eyes), 'Dětský den' (Children's Day), 'Školení' (Training Course) and 'Hostina' (The Banquet) were greatly altered and mostly renamed. It was almost three years before the book appeared.

Between childhood and retirement age Bohumil Hrabal lived in quite an odd mix of homes: his grandparents' house in Brno-Židenice, the service flat at the local brewery in Polná, the brewery at Nymburk, where his parents eventually acquired a house of their own and thereafter led the typical lifestyle of the financially secure middle class, then he left (some might say fled from) his parents and went to Prague and a number of often bizarre sub-lets, leading finally to working-class Libeň and bare, non-residential premises that he furnished himself and where he finally felt happy. Life goes on, however, and the 43-year-old bachelor got married in December 1956. And although his accommodation on Na hrázi Street saw some gradual improvements, his wife never stopped dreaming of a proper flat with central heating and a flush toilet. The couple joined a housing cooperative and in June 1973 moved into a tower block in Kobylisy. It has to be said that Hrabal never felt happy in the tower block, and whenever he could, he would escape to his chalet at Kersko, where, among others, his brother Slávek lived quite close. The famous writer soon became a kind of icon for the chalet colony and he himself drew widely on the lives of his neighbours for many of his stories.

Cottages or chalets as second homes were quite a phenomenon of Czechoslovakia under normalisation. Anyone who could would escape for the weekend from the towns and cities to the countryside, where they would work hard on doing up their second dwelling. This was almost a reflex reaction to multi-occupancy living, where people were crammed in cheek by jowl with no escape distance, which we are genetically encoded to need and without which we are apt to suffer stress and other psychological problems. The perpetuity of normalisation added another argument: in a situation with endless prohibitions of anything under the sun one looked for a space for self-realisation. And that is what gradually turned the tiny community of Kersko, not far from Nymburk, into the 'sylvan township' so brilliantly portrayed by Jiří Menzel in the opening sequence of his film version of *The Snowdrop Festival*. Bohumil Hrabal's stories have ensured Kersko's immortality.

In the present edition we have sought to preserve the author's original intention. As against the original *Snowdrop Festival* collection, we have omitted 'The Most Beautiful Eyes' and 'Children's Day', which in both form and content seem rather out of line with the rest. The text of 'Variations on a Beautiful Girl' appears in its later version as 'Adagio lamentoso', and we have added the 1972 story 'The Maid of Honour', which is entirely in harmony with the other texts in the collection. The texts are based on Vol. 8 of *Sebrané spisy Bohumila Hrabala* (The Collected Works of B. H.; Prague: Pražská imaginace, 1993), where further details can be found on the collection's evolution. Let it be noted in conclusion that the collection, as *Slavnosti sněženek*, has re-appeared in the Czech Republic several times already and continues to do so with various editorial changes.

Václav Kadlec   February 2014
Pražská imaginace

Translating Hrabal, one is frequently constrained by two things in particular. One is his habit of using words unknown to anyone (including lexicographers) but himself. Here one can but make one's 'best guess', but without resorting to invented words in the translation. This problem is, then, unlikely to be detectable. The other is Hrabal's creative method, relying heavily on 'cutting and pasting', which he himself mentions time and again in *Kličky na kapesníku* (translated as *Pirouettes on a Postage Stamp*, Prague: Karolinum, 2008) as one of his key creative devices. Believing oneself bound to adhere to sameness or slight difference between cut-and-pasted chunks of text is what makes the task maddening – one is forever chasing back and forth between the different points in the text of both the original and one's translation just to check. Thank goodness for the various 'search' functions one can resort to these days on a laptop or PC.

One often has the feeling that many things did not matter much to Hrabal. Although an obvious polymath

343

with considerable knowledge of cats, dogs, football, optics, butchery, cinema, philosophy, motor-cycle racing..., and very widely read, he does sometimes get or appear to get things wrong. By design, to tease, or just because he has forgotten, cannot be bothered to check, or because it doesn't matter anyway? Take Emerson Fittipaldi: one can understand why, in the ramblings of the particular oddball being reported (Leli, in the eponymous story), we find ourselves reading about Messrs Fittipaldi and Emerson, that is, *two* riders. That Hrabal himself knew that Emerson Fittipaldi is *one* person only transpires from another story not included in the present collection. But he also 'forgot' that Fittipaldi had two *t*'s in his name and Emerson one *m*, which would scarcely have shown in the diction of the character being reported; Hrabal is generally abysmal at foreign names, personal or geographical, though I have rectified them all in the translation. In another story omitted from this collection, Leni in the film *Three Faces West* is described, again by others, not by the narrating Hrabal himself, as played by Helen MacKellar, whereas in fact she was played by Sigrid Gurie, though Helen MacKellar is also in the film. Does it matter? Perhaps not, but it does irk this particular translator. And when Hrabal decides to cite something in English, he, like possibly every Czech writer at least since Karel

Matěj Čapek-Chod (1860–1927), and doubtless before him, gets it wrong: the famous tune played by Helmuth Zacharias was called *Fascination*, not 'The Fascination', as reiterated umpteen times in the original of one of the stories herein. Where Hrabal got the definite article from is a mystery, not least because the first reference to the song is of its title's actually being read from a gramophone label; I have elected, I believe fairly, to drop the article. In *Pirouettes on a Postage Stamp*, conceived as a fully edited translation, it was appropriate to use footnotes; in the present collection I believe it would not be. I offer the following sparing remarks as a partial substitute.

The more enquiring reader can easily, if lacking the immediate knowledge, discover what the wartime (Nazi German) Protectorate (of Bohemia and Moravia) was, and he does not need fully to understand the details of the civil administration of post-war Czechoslovakia with its hierarchy of 'national committees', but he may be largely in the dark about the earliest history of the area in Central Bohemia where Kersko lies (see map). In somewhat hyperbolic terms, the up-and-down hostility between neighbouring villages is portrayed with all the whimsy of an arch 'rambler' who knows his history as reaching back to the tenth century and the power struggle arising out of the dynastic rivalries between the

Slavníks and Přemyslids, two powerful houses in this very area. Members of the powerful Vršovec family, on the Přemyslid side, did, as described herein, slaughter most of the Slavníks in the church at nearby Libice.

The reader can probably infer easily that a Czech hunt is carried on rather differently from how it would be run in Britain, whether before or after the ban on hunting with hounds introduced in 2005, and is in fact more like stalking (though that is not the word used by Hrabal). I believe it is also easily read between the lines that there is a ritual element to the domestic slaughter of a pig and that the whole proceeding is an entirely 'normal' custom among quite ordinary Czech folk. It can equally be so read that other customs, whether to do with food (fining salamis like fining wines, to give them that extra edge; beer ordered from and served at the table in a pub, not stood for at the bar) or with the Christian calendar (carolling and some pagan frolicking between the sexes at Easter; the mass domestic production and consumption of a range of sweetmeats at Christmas) are precisely that: customs that the reader may not instantly recognise, but should be able to take on board and accept as genuine local colour. More subtly, the reader accustomed to death personified as the 'grim reaper', portrayed as male, may initially be puzzled by references to Death as female. Among various metaphorical expressions for death, in Czech *she* likewise carries a scythe (and is skeletal), but *her* gender is simply motivated by the word for death, *smrt*, which is grammatically feminine (Czech and the other Slavonic languages have, like German or Latin, three genders).

The Czechs are sometimes portrayed as rather materialistic in their outlook (if not noticeably more than many other nations), so, amongst other things, money matters. That does not transpire particularly in this book, though a crude form of materialism is perhaps what channels into monomania, whether this is to do with apple-growing, rabbit-breeding or the hoarding of utterly useless bargains. Money does figure in a reference to a 'hard-currency shop', which may be lost on some readers: the Czechoslovakia of the day had, in essence, two currencies: the Czechoslovak crown (*koruna československá*) as standard, but non-convertible, and the Tuzex crown, which was obtained by exchanging any (strictly legally, but frequently illicitly acquired) foreign, convertible currencies and then used in the special Tuzex shops filled with sundry 'Western', thus highly desirable goods (there are a few other scattered hints in the book that 'West is best', common throughout Communist central and eastern Europe). Hence the dream of one character's purchasing through Tuzex a Simca, that late lamented (?) French car. The observant reader will no doubt notice that not once does the everyday Czechoslovak car, the Škoda, get a mention, though we find plenty of East German Trabants, relatively easily obtainable at the time, but often rudely dismissed as a two-stroke wheelbarrow with a cardboard body and the butt of countless jokes; and the local policeman (incidentally, a splendid caricature) drives around, as they did, in a Volga, a fairly lumbering saloon from the unloved Soviet Union. Both cars mentioned (ignoring the Opel owned by a resident of West Germany) have, then, inherently negative connotations.

For the rest, I believe that these stories have a deep core of general humanity and as such they call for no further comment and can be read for the sheer pleasure of it.

The Czech, or uniquely Hrabalesque, version of what I have finally called *rambling* (the underlying verb *pábit* is not actually Hrabal's invention, though most Czechs associate it uniquely with him) varies in fact from almost hectoring at one end of the scale to burbling at the other. I quite liked the notion of 'burbling' for at least one of its dictionary definitions as 'talking excitedly and rather incoherently' (*Chambers's Twentieth Century Dictionary*, rev. edn., 1966), and because, in its Czech manifestation, it is apt to exploit asyndeton to a degree far in excess of the neutral norm, and Czech already uses it rather more than English, inside and outside literature; this rate of asyndeton is just one of the features that add to the sense of 'incoherence'. Yet it remains – in Hrabal's Czech – sustainable, 'natural', while in English it would definitely be 'too much of a good thing'. Consequently, I have not reproduced it here at every occurrence; the two grammars are sufficiently different overall for the slightly incoherent in one language to verge on the incomprehensible in the other. I finally selected 'rambling' as the core notion, since to describe some of the narrations, whether in the *Ich* or *er* mode, as 'burbling' would seem a little harsh. What I was *not* predisposed to do was to sustain the link with previous translations of *pábení* as 'palavering' and of *pábitelé* as 'palaverers'. However, readers familiar with other translations from Hrabal containing these expressions should know that this is what my 'rambling on' is.

Besides the striking rate of asyndeton, the language of these stories is rich in almost every other structural or artistic device – synonym pairs, oxymoron (heightening the depth of a thing; black teeth compared to white jasmine petals), anacoluthon, rhyme, alliteration and a general, but not universal rhythmicality. I would not wish to catalogue all the cases and how they were resolved in translation. Suffice it to say that where a feature was not soluble *in situ*, so to speak, I freely resorted to the hallowed (by such as Jiří Levý, a leading Czech theorist of translation) device of 'compensation', that is, allowing, for instance, alliteration or a casual rhyme at a point where there was none in the original in order to compensate for my failure to alliterate or rhyme in English where the Czech text *is* alliterative or rhyming. Possibly the trickiest to translate or compensate for are many of the anacolutha, since strict adherence to and/or compensation for them could easily create an unnatural, even unreadable text in English, and Hrabal's texts are nothing if not readable, even where you have to wait several pages for the next full stop. The random, quasi-accidental nature of anacoluthon makes it difficult to 'fake', hence its incidence in the translation is markedly lower than in the original, as that of the semi-colon or full stop is somewhat higher. In other respects, I can only hope that I have been faithful to this increasingly appreciated writer, who, maddening though he can be, is always a pleasure to work on.

David Short   February 2014

CONTENTS

RAMBLING ON: AN APPRENTICE'S GUIDE
TO THE GIFT OF THE GAB
SHORT STORIES
BOHUMIL HRABAL

English translation by David Short
Afterword by Václav Kadlec
Illustrations by Jiří Grus
Layout by Zdeněk Ziegler

Published by Charles University
in Prague, Karolinum Press
Ovocný trh 3–5, 116 36 Praha 1
http://cupress.cuni.cz
Prague 2014
Vice-rector-editor
Prof. PhDr. Ivan Jakubec, CSc.
Edited by Martin Janeček
Typeset by DTP Karolinum Press
Printed by PBtisk, Příbram
First English edition

ISBN 978-80-246-2316-0